THE COWBOY SAYS YES

Zack's gaze never left hers and in the stillness of the barn, with nothing and no one around—no audience or camera or enough lights to fill Broadway—Hadley leaned in. She couldn't fix their lack of a family. And she might not be able to carve off more than a day or two for the next stretch of months.

But they had now.

This moment.

And she was done waiting.

Leaning in, she pressed her lips to his. He held still for the briefest heartbeat before opening to her, an easing of the tight reins he kept on himself and his emotions. And in the easing, she found her advantage. The hard press of lips they'd shared earlier on the lunch shoot was nowhere in evidence. Instead, she felt the gentle merging of tongues—almost tentative as the kiss advanced—and the blended breath between them.

How easy it was to fall into him. To take a moment of ease, together, at the end of day. Partnership. Commitment. Camaraderie.

Her Zack.

HarperCollins books may be purchased for educational, business, or sales promotional use. For information, please email the Special Markets Department at SPsales@harpercollins.com.

THE COWBOY SAYS YES

Rustlers Creek

ADDISON FOX

AVONBOOKS

An Imprint of HarperCollinsPublishers

THE COWBOY SAYS YES. Copyright © 2022 by Frances Karkosak. All rights reserved. Printed in the United States of America. No part of this book may be used or reproduced in any manner whatsoever without written permission except in the case of brief quotations embodied in critical articles and reviews. For information, address HarperCollins Publishers, 195 Broadway, New York, NY 10007.

First Avon Books mass market printing: April 2022

Print Edition ISBN: 978-0-06-313519-2
Digital Edition ISBN: 978-0-06-313520-8

Cover design by Amy Halperin
Cover illustration by Larry Rostant
Cover images © Shutterstock

Avon, Avon & logo, and Avon Books & logo are registered trademarks of HarperCollins Publishers in the United States of America and other countries.
HarperCollins is a registered trademark of HarperCollins Publishers in the United States of America and other countries.

FIRST EDITION

Printed in Lithuania

22 23 24 25 26   SB   10 9 8 7 6 5 4 3 2 1

For Amelia, Audrey and Grant.
My favorites.

THE COWBOY
SAYS YES

Chapter 1

Rustlers Creek, Montana wasn't exactly the epicenter of cool, contemporary or classy. Or it hadn't been, until the creative brains at the Cooking Network had descended on Hadley Wayne's small hometown with all the zeal of locusts in August.

Forest and Evans Publishing had followed suit with a deep and urgent desire to publish her Christmas cookbook, which they eagerly followed up on with an Easter decorating guide and a summer party planner.

And then there'd been the inevitable cookware line that QVC hawked as today's special value at least three times over the past year.

It had all come together with the speed of summer lightning descending over the ranch and there were moments Hadley's head still spun with it all.

And then she'd push it aside as another camera

crew set up shop in her eight-hundred-square-foot kitchen while a lighting designer added strategically placed kliegs to halo her in concert with the spring sunlight that streamed in her large bay window.

Two months could pass like that, with barely a thought beyond show schedules, meal planning and cookbook edits. She'd then look up, trying to surface for air, desperate to remember what—and who—she'd put on hold.

She'd had no idea her dreams could be this big. Or grow this huge. And yet . . .

"Hadley. You ready?" Her producer, Beatrix Malone, stood before her, clad in perpetual black and the four-inch heels she raced around the ranch in as if they were the most comfortable pair of cross-trainers she'd ever owned.

Bea's assistant, Aimee (pronounced: ahhh-may) swooped in behind. "The guys need to get this segment wrapped in an hour so we can get set up outside when the cowboys come in for lunch."

Hadley pulled herself back from the sour direction of her thoughts, Zack usually at the top of that list, and focused on the day's work. "I don't like how the apple turnovers looked yesterday. We need to reshoot the last shot when they come out of the oven."

Aimee started to argue before Bea held up a hand. "We'll get it after lunch. I'll make a note of it with the director. How much time do you need on the turnovers?"

"I've already prepped them. I'll put them in

when we get back inside after lunch. We can get them dressed and ready in under an hour."

"Done." Bea was already off, presumably to talk to the director as well as whoever was on the endless lists she carried on the tablet that rarely left her hand, leaving Hadley to the pre-prep before shooting began. Her own assistants had already prepped the pork shoulder and chopped the onions she'd need for the next segment and it was only a matter of finishing up in makeup and changing her clothes.

The camera didn't favor navy blue T-shirts and yoga pants.

Although she'd set specific ground rules early on, namely that the cameras never came upstairs to her bedroom, that edict didn't extend to makeup, hair or wardrobe. After the show had taken off, she'd gotten Zack's reluctant agreement to alter one of the ranch's six bedrooms into a haven for the hair and makeup crew. The en suite bathroom had been transformed, with lighting more blinding than a winter squall all while racks of clothing stood sentinel in the bedroom.

It had been a fair trade and kept her eagle-eyed makeup team from seeing the inside of her own bedroom. One that now stood down the hall from the master she'd shared with Zack. The oversized room she'd once loved waking up in, done up in subtle tones of cream and peacock blue, had become a mocking reminder of all they no longer shared.

Not that anyone else needed to know that.

Aside from the gossip she had no interest in being the subject of, there was no way the Cowgirl Gourmet could let the world know she and her husband no longer shared the same bedroom, the same meals and, as soon as the cameras stopped rolling, the same air.

Even if today's segment had them sharing far more air than either of them was comfortable with any longer.

"Time to make that porcelain skin even more flawless." Chantal, her makeup guru, took her arm and gently pulled her toward a large chair set up in front of all those lights.

Did she go anywhere any longer without lights? They were everywhere in her home. They accompanied her on the photo shoots she was now regularly a part of. And they were, even now, covering her bathroom mirrors. Yet for as bright as they were, they weren't able to uncover any of the dark places where her marriage had gone so wrong.

God, why was it so overwhelming today?

She'd barely spoken to Zack since their last fight ten days ago. It was the last time the crew had set up outside, filming him in the predawn hours as he did his work around the ranch. Oh, he'd done his contractual duty, smiling for the cameras and giving them the whole "cowboy show," detailing for her viewers how the calves would be paired up with their mamas as Zack and his team moved them to new pasture.

And then he'd stomped into the house and, after

being satisfied no one was lurking, had picked a fight with her as big as the Montana sky lightening outside their kitchen window.

When would this season finally be over?

Why did she have to go to LA to do promo?

And why in the hell had she roped his mother into the decorating of the Trading Post Hadley was building in downtown Rustlers Creek?

The slam at his mother had been her final straw—likely the barb Zack knew would hit deepest—and she'd succumbed. The words had flown with all the icy venom both of them seemed bogged down with lately. Including the final shot she'd landed, that if he gave a damn about his mother he could fucking well call her himself instead of hiding behind a wide-open field laden with cow shit.

"Yo, Hadley." Chantal waved a hand. "You here with me?"

"I'm sorry. A lot on my mind."

Chantal nodded, her dark brown eyes sharp even if her words were casual. "Big day today. The shoots outside always get everyone all worked up."

"The cowboys try not to be, but they get nervous."

"Hmmm."

Hadley was grateful for the diversion. "You still have your eye on Garland?"

"The tall, skinny one?"

Hadley held back the smile at Chantal's sudden casualness, as if she didn't know exactly who Garland Cook was. "That's the one. He's been looking at you."

"Probably because I'm the only Black woman he's ever seen."

"Not true."

Chantal cocked a hand on her hip, stepping back to survey the layer of foundation she'd applied. "You mean there are actually other Black people in this state?"

"Yes. A few."

"I don't believe you."

"And I do believe you're changing the subject. He likes you. He'd like to go out with you."

"I'm not a circus side show."

Hadley laid a hand on Chantal's arm. "No, you're a beautiful young woman who has the zing for a very good man."

Chantal rolled her eyes, but Hadley didn't miss the small smile tilting the edges. "I'll think about it."

"Good. Because I've got no doubt Gar's thinking about you and doing some zinging of his own."

Chantal started in on Hadley's eyes, smiling wide. "The zing. I like that."

Hadley liked it, too. Could even still remember what it had felt like, that excitement quivering low in the belly every time Zack came into view.

She still had it, truth be told. But layered overtop was the oil slick of anger and frustration that their marriage had become a facade. That the dreams they'd once shared together had split somewhere, each of them taking different paths.

And that the one thing they'd always dreamed of together—a family—was never going to be.

ZACK WAYNE EYED the moving herd of cattle from the back of his horse and wondered where the morning had gone. Or the month of September, for that matter. Or the last fucking three years.

They'd all vanished like smoke, just like his marriage.

"Zack!" His foreman, Carter Jessup, waved him down from where he'd been riding behind the south end of the moving herd.

Zack turned his mount, Gator, in Carter's direction and slowly worked his way toward the other man, all while keeping a close eye for any stragglers. They hadn't worked this hard to lose one of the calves now.

"You ready to head in?" Carter asked.

"Yeah."

"Camera crew's all set up and waiting on us for lunch. Rumor has it we're having pulled pork sandwiches today which means there is a god in heaven and he loves me very, very much."

"Whoop-de-do."

Carter's gaze narrowed, the man seeing far more than Zack was comfortable with. "I thought you liked camera days. It's good for business."

"I didn't say otherwise."

Carter shot him one more narrow-eyed gaze, his blue eyes as bright as the sky, before dropping it. "Calves look good. There's one I want the doc to look at. Little guy seems a bit wheezy in his breathing. But we'll get 'em all settled and counted this afternoon and then weigh 'em tomorrow."

"Good." Zack nodded, well aware of what they had on tap this week but always pleased when his foreman was in sync. "And you don't think Gray needs to come out sooner to look at the calf?"

"Nah." Carter gathered his reins in his hand, seeming to consider the guidance of their large animal vet, Gray McClain. "He's still eating, just hanging a bit close to his mama. Since Doc McClain already confirmed he'd be out early tomorrow to keep a close eye on each of them as they come off the scales, I think we'll be alright."

"Good."

"You sure you're okay?"

"I'm fine." Zack shook off the distracted sour mood and tried to focus on the things that had gone right. It wasn't a sure fix, but it was a hell of a lot better than wallowing in all that sucked ass in his life right now. "It's been a good day so far. The herd looks healthy and strong and the heifers don't look worse for wear." Zack assessed the land that spread out before the two of them. "We'll be well set for winter."

"You going to get a bit of free time in? Maybe go to LA with Hadley in a few weeks?"

The question was casual and Zack didn't sense anything behind it besides congenial conversation, but it was jarring all the same. Was there anyone on the ranch who didn't know about production schedules and travel commitments and national fucking book launches?

"I'm not sure. Dad's been a bit ornery lately and I don't know if it's a good idea to leave him alone."

"And here I thought he was his calm, level-headed self."

Zack laughed at that, his first real laugh in days, even as his father's current mood was one of the contributors to the excessively suck-assed mood around the ranch. "Is he terrorizing the bunkhouse again?"

"Every day for a week. Garland's 'yes, sir'd' your father so many times it's a wonder he hasn't gone insane." Carter shook his head, suddenly contrite. "I'm sorry I don't have better news."

"Nothing to be sorry about, especially since it sounds like I'm the one who should be apologizing."

Carter waved a hand, his tone kinder than Zack's family deserved as he dismissed the apology. "No need for that."

If Zack's own sham of a marriage wasn't problem enough, his mother had unceremoniously kicked his father out two months ago. Said she was sick of playing housekeeper and was damned if he was going to tell her she couldn't have a job. The fight, as he'd been led to believe, had been one for the ages and it had left his normally frustrating father—a challenge on the very best of days—damn near impossible to live with.

The reality of age—and his increasing inability to work the land—coupled with whatever the hell this was with his parents had put the old man's balls in a sling.

And hell if Zack wasn't the one stuck with the consequences.

His sisters had been zero help, all four of them

taking his mother's side. And his brother had been gone for so long it was hard to remember a time when Jackson had been around with any regularity.

Even Zack had seen his way to his mother's point a time or two, but there was no discussing it with the old man. When he got the rare opportunity to get a word in edgewise in between all the ranting and railing, he'd learned it was easier to just listen and keep his mouth shut.

Especially because he'd caught a few of his own sentiments toward Hadley in the old man's rants about his mother and it didn't sit particularly well. He *was* proud of his wife and all she'd accomplished. And while he was frustrated at times with the circus that seemed to come with that success, it was never directed at her.

Then why does it feel like it's all the two of you fight about?

The commotion out near the edge of the pasture was easy to see and Zack shifted his attention that direction and off his uncomfortable thoughts. He was curious, as always, to see how much time, effort and sheer *stuff* was required to shoot a TV show.

And don't get him started on the people.

Endless reams of people who had no business on a Montana cattle ranch and, as the show seasons had gone by, had shown less and less care for their surroundings. There were days where he felt like a cross between a side-show circus freak and the king of the universe the way they framed shots of him on his horse or baling hay out of the back of one of the ranch's oversized trucks.

They'd glamorized it all, making it seem effortless, somehow. Which had been amusing at first but had quickly begun to chafe.

He worked damn hard. And to have it dismissed as if the fucking ranch fairies showed up every night and did his work had grown tiresome.

Add on the crisscrossing tracks that lay all over the damn place to move the cameras that captured him up on that horse or to get images of his hands working the land and it was a wonder they hadn't had any injuries yet.

He'd draw the line there, and Hadley knew it.

Not that it would matter for much longer. She had some postproduction to shoot and wrap up and then she'd be on her way to LA in October. And once that was done, on to her book tour. He'd be lucky if he'd see her for more than a month.

And since he'd already successfully avoided her for the better part of two they'd steamroll right on into the holidays by the time she got back.

Fuck it all, where had it gone so sideways?

He loved his wife. Had since the first time he laid eyes on her, across the counter at a bakery in town.

And in the last two years he'd slowly come to hate her.

HADLEY FUSSED OVER the food set up on the open flatbed of one of the ranch trucks. The Wayne and Sons Ranch logo was visible on the side and the truck had been shined to within an inch of its life, the black paint gleaming in the late September sunshine. It was warm, even if the nights had grown decidedly colder since Labor Day.

The food designer had already set up, fixing the pulled pork Hadley had prepared that morning for the stand-alone shots, but Hadley had stepped in to finagle a few things for actual serving. Zack hated this part, even as he'd smile and coo at her— and her food—for the cameras.

It hadn't been that way at first. Sure, he'd seemed amused by it all, but he'd been a good sport. But over time, she could see that the steady presence of so many extra people and the fussing and bother of it all raked his nerves.

Which was his own damn problem, she thought, stabbing a fork into the jar of pickled onions she'd prepared the night before, since his business certainly wasn't hurting from all this. Wayne and Sons had already been a large enterprise, its legacy of putting food on American tables for well over a century standing them in good stead. But since the show and the resulting attention, his business had gone through the roof. Hell, the damn truck she had all this food set out on bore a Wayne and Sons medallion right next to the Ford logo in show-rooms all over the country.

And was selling, too.

Which meant that this whole "shit show" as Zack had come to call it all, wasn't just about her any longer. The Cowgirl Gourmet might have won the hearts of American home cooks, but her hot cowboy husband was doing damn fine on his own.

Hadn't Chantal just shown her last week the

Facebook fan page devoted to images of Zack without his shirt?

It had galled her at first, the idea that the masses had objectified her husband. And then she'd looked at the photos and had to admit it was hard to blame them. She knew intimately how wonderful those broad shoulders felt, and the way all that corded muscle in his back would flex beneath her fingers as he made love to her. Heart emojis and questionable captions aside, she had the reality of those photos and knew nothing about them was airbrushed or exaggerated.

Except the comments that made swoony references to her and Zack's grand romance.

Maybe they'd had that once. Maybe they'd known how to make each other laugh and enjoy their time out of bed as much as they had in it. But those days were gone.

She was the Cowgirl Gourmet. And he was the hot cowboy who shared her roof and little else.

"Cowboys coming in!" Bea shouted to the assembled crew, her voice echoing from the interior of a bullhorn.

Hadley set down her utensils and focused on her prearranged placement in the shot. The hands would ride in on their horses, Zack most likely in the rear. Not because any producer could make him do that, but because he always put his team in front of him, sweeping behind with a watchful eye.

Three sets of cameras would capture the ride in, from a drone flying overhead, a panoramic camera moving on tracks at ground level and a handheld which would capture her reactions. It never failed to amaze her how much went into the production of each show, but the outside shots were the most elaborate.

And the hardest to shoot.

Zack had little time for do-overs and the producers knew it. That need for precision had been his ultimatum from the start. Wayne and Sons was a working ranch and, as such, he had as deliberate a production timeline as the studio.

The work didn't wait. He'd spent his life waking up at 4:00 a.m. for that very reason and a TV show on his property or his wife's livelihood wasn't going to change that.

And on some level, she didn't want it to. She respected what he'd inherited, building the business to even greater heights since taking over from his father. She was as committed to her own business, and regardless of all that they no longer said to one another, she prized his commitment to the work. To the land. To his family.

Garland rode through the opening in the fence and Hadley searched the crew—assembled in a wide arc around the equipment so as to remain off camera—and saw Chantal had noticed the same. Unbidden, a small smile edged the corners of Hadley's lips. She remembered those days. That awareness of another person and the anxious questions of what they might think of you, too.

It was even headier when the person you noticed had noticed you back.

It was magic, really.

Carter followed after a few of the hands and, as Hadley knew he would, Zack came in last.

The cameras captured it all before the drone flew away toward an empty plot on the north side of the ranch. Once it was out of range, the light but persistent whine of engine noise gone, the boom mics could capture the conversation.

Or sexy banter, as Bea was fond of saying.

Whatever impossible barriers might stand between her and Zack, they still excelled at that. They always had, she mused, some of that remembered magic adding a zip to her pulse.

Even as she now knew sexy banter wasn't enough. Sex wasn't enough. Even love, apparently, wasn't enough.

Shaking off the maudlin, Hadley watched as Bea directed things from the sidelines, marching up and down, shifting people into position as the show director, Ted, kept things moving with the camera crew. He'd already shot her a thumbs-up when he saw she was in position and focused instead on the hands tying up their mounts.

The studio kept an animal trainer on set and she and her crew set to feeding and cooling the animals out of camera range, leaving Zack and his hungry cowboys to lunch.

It was an extensive, expensive operation and it was funny how it had changed nearly everything about her life. Once upon a time, she'd done this several times a week, driving lunch out to the ranch hands and waiting while they cooled down and watered their own horses before coming to get their lunch.

Now someone else handled it all, to keep production moving.

Because for reasons that still eluded her on some days, the world was fascinated with her and her ranch life and her big strapping husband.

And only Hadley knew the truth.

Those cameras showed the world a sweet, idyllic place that didn't know sorrow or anger or the grief of impossible dreams.

She might live in Montana, but for those who saw her world through the other side of the camera, all they knew was the homespun magic only Hollywood could create.

Chapter 2

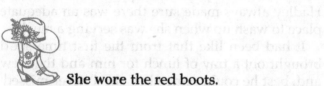

She wore the red boots.

Fuck, shit and damn, the woman had the audacity to wear them.

That lone thought—uttered in any number of combinations with every swear word he knew, as well as a few he made up on the spot—ran through Zack's mind.

Along with the delightfully X-rated video that lasered dead center through his head, imagining Hadley in nothing but those boots.

They were his favorite pair. They were hers, too, but for entirely different reasons. Namely because she likely had no idea how mind-numbingly gorgeous she looked wearing them and nothing else.

Currently, she'd paired them with jeans that fit over her ass like his hands used to and a button-down chambray shirt respectfully unbuttoned to just shy of her cleavage. She shot a family-friendly show, after all, a fact he was happy about after realizing his wife had become a reluctant sex symbol online. A fact that bemused her even as Zack had no problem understanding why.

Dealing with it, however, was a whole other matter.

He cleaned up at a small station they had set near the edge of the fence line. Although he'd been known to unwrap his lunch and eat anywhere on the ranch his day's work happened to take him, Hadley always made sure there was an adequate place to wash up when she was serving a meal.

It had been like that from the first time she'd brought out a tray of lunch for him and the crew and, best he could remember, she'd never missed. That sense of orderliness followed her to all other aspects of her life. The ranch kitchen was spotless and not only because a TV crew was paid to keep it that way. While it seemed the production team never left, the show only shot about four and a half months out of the year on the property. The rest of the time, Hadley's kitchen was even more spotless than when a professional cleaning team went through.

"This is good, ma'am." Garland nodded his head as he heaped potato salad onto the plate Hadley had fixed for him, loaded up with two pulled pork sandwiches. Rail-thin Gar would likely have a third, Zack knew, before they headed back out for the afternoon, a fact that never ceased to amaze him.

And then his amazement vanished as he came face-to-face with his wife.

"Hey there, cowboy." Hadley smiled, big and wide—her Hollywood smile—before planting an equally big kiss on his cheek.

He knew his duty and snuck a tight arm around her waist, pulling her close for a smacking kiss of his own. He put a little heat and even a little more anger in it, something goading him about that overly effusive smile.

The fake one that he'd never seen before some-one had shoved a damn camera in her face.

The heat he'd amped into the kiss boomeranged right back at him, sizzling in his blood straight through to his nerve endings. The urge to linger was strong—to see how crazy he could drive both of them—before he pulled back.

Fucking family-friendly and all that.

But he was inordinately pleased to see the small furrow between her brow and the equal rise of heat in her green gaze.

"This looks amazing, darlin'." Zack focused on the trays of food set out on the back of one of his pickups, moving into the banter they were known for.

"Nothing like a hearty meal for my hardwork-ing cowboy and his crew."

They continued back and forth, the camera crew so close Zack could practically swat them with the serving spoon, as he fixed his sandwich. She pulled the lever on an oversized cooler of something called Dusty Punch—whatever the hell that was—and handed off a glass of the concoction that looked like something between cherry-red Kool-Aid and the cough syrup he'd taken as a kid.

He shot a side-eye to his assembled hands, seated at a few picnic tables that had been set out for the show segment. Every one of them had a matched glass and no one seemed to be complaining.

Not that anyone would.

They'd suck down three glasses with a smile, even if it tasted like rat poison. Such was the Hollywood mania and brush with fame that had come to paint their small corner of Montana. Hell, Carter was even getting fan mail now. A letter this past winter and its accompanying photos—a rather sexy shot of a woman in minimal lingerie—had made quite an impression. Even if Zack was the only one Carter had shown it to as he blushed to the roots of his hair, the blush fading on down through the open neck of his shirt collar. The ever-patient—and unfailingly gentlemanly Carter—had then enclosed the photos back in an envelope with a thank-you note.

And no return address.

So yeah. They'd drink the punch and eat the food and scrub their work-worn hands at the cleanup station for all of America to watch. And then they'd all ride back out to the ranch, doing their work and raving about Hadley's cooking.

And he'd be left with nothing more than memories of those fucking boots.

HADLEY TIDIED UP the set, shooting glances at Zack where he sat with his team. She'd fixed a plate for herself but the camera crew wanted one more shot with her at the truck, describing how to make various leftover dishes with the pulled pork.

Then they'd get her sitting at the table beside her husband and the outside shots would be done. All that was left was the reshoot on the apple turnovers and she'd be done for the day, too. For the week, actually. The crew had strict vacation hours worked into their own contracts and they were all on some R & R for the next four days.

She was both thrilled and annoyed, as it meant she had four days of solitude and quiet. There was a time she'd have relished that, spending her free time with Zack and heading out to help him with whatever needed doing. Now she'd spend it inside. Alone.

Because despite their sweet banter for the cameras and the steady string of *darlin*s he tossed out effortlessly, after they wrapped up she wouldn't speak to him for days.

All she'd have was that kiss to tide her over.

And damn him, it was a good one.

His lips were warm and he had that scent she'd always associated with him. Earth and animal and sweat. It should have been a turnoff, but from the very first it spoke to something inside of her. Pulled at her. She even caught faint traces of it after he showered, the scent of soap only enhancing that lingering, telltale fragrance.

She made her life cooking any and all types of food, from meat to veggies, soups to desserts. Nothing—and she could honestly say, *nothing*—had ever smelled as good to her as Zachary Charles Wayne.

And that included her most favorite food in the entire world, pound cake.

"And that's a wrap." Bea bustled into her line of sight and Hadley abruptly shut off the sense memories of how her husband smelled. "Crew's getting set up over by the picnic table and we'll get you taking a bite of your sandwich."

"Okay."

Bea's gaze narrowed and she moved in closer. "Are you sure everything's good today?"

"Yeah, why?" Panic buzzed beneath her skin. "Did something come off wrong?"

"No, not at all. I mean with you. You seem—" Bea broke off as if weighing her words. Which was odd since Bea never appeared to weigh anything. "Sad or something."

"I'm fine. Really. Just a lot on my mind."

Bea's dark gaze lightened instantly. "Oh, right. The book. It's going to fly off the shelves. You should see the comments on your social media about it."

"I need to go take a look at them."

"I can have Aimee pull some for you. There were more than six thousand on yesterday's Instagram post about the finish out work at the Trading Post and several people also mentioned their excitement about the book and seeing you on book tour." Bea tossed out that quick fact all while snagging her own plate of pulled pork, signing off on an expense the production lead brought her, and then steamrolling on in the direction of the lighting crew to discuss the shot.

It was fascinating to watch and often left Hadley wondering if Bea slept.

Ever.

Six thousand comments. There weren't even that many people in Rustlers Creek. A third of that number, actually.

Ignoring the shot of amazement that the food she cooked or the books she'd written or the store she was opening up downtown in time for the holidays garnered that sort of attention, she picked up her own plate and walked to the picnic bench. Most everyone had finished—all but Gar who'd already heaped more on his plate—but the crew would only do closeups of her and Zack anyway.

"Hi, everyone. How's the day going? You started out early."

"Moving the herd always takes time," Carter said, taking a sip of the punch she'd prepared to go with lunch. "This food at the end of it has been a treat."

"End of it?" Zack shot his foreman a dark glare. "There's an afternoon of work still to be done."

"Keep your boots on." Carter shook his head. "Hadley knows what I meant."

"Sure I do." She smiled at Carter, hoping to

diffuse the moment, suddenly sharp with spikes. "And hopefully everyone's well fortified for round two."

Zack's shoulder was pressed against hers and she felt the slightest release in the tense set of his big frame. He got so touchy when anyone suggested the work could slide—especially because of the show—and to be fair to Carter, that wasn't what the man had said at all.

But it was one more of those ridiculous moments that seemed to fill the air between them. Anger and disgust the lead-in instead of the simple ability to listen to one another.

Determined to keep the discussion light, she turned to Zack. The brown eyes she loved were hidden behind sunglasses and he wouldn't take them off until the director shouted "action."

"Did you enjoy the pork?"

"It's good."

"I made extra and wrapped up a portion for your dad. I haven't seen him today."

"He's sulking in the bunkhouse."

"Why?" The shot of alarm was swift and immediate. "What's wrong? Is he feeling bad? Is it his heart again?"

"He's fine. Just being a first-class son of a bitch today."

Although their discussions were limited these days—and every one had the ability to go off in a direction she didn't plan—talk of Charlie Wayne was particularly sensitive.

And wildly incendiary.

"What has him upset?"

"What doesn't have him upset? He's pissed at Mom but he won't admit it, so instead he picks a fight with every other damn person he comes into contact with."

Sort of like you.

The words hovered, tempting in their simplicity, but Hadley held them back. The fact she had Zack talking was more important than a well-placed barb.

Wasn't it?

"He's also pissed he's not allowed out on a horse for the roundup."

And in that moment, Hadley was more glad than she could say that she'd held her tongue. She might have a heap of animosity toward her husband, but she wasn't blind. And it had been all too easy to see that her father-in-law hated the increasing limitations age had put on what he saw as his place in the world.

Even if they'd all tried to convince him that retirement held its own place. Its own joys. Charlie was having none of it. And ever since Hadley had offered her mother-in-law, Carlene, a role at the Trading Post, that piss-poor slide into retirement had taken a decidedly sour turn.

"It's weigh-in tomorrow. Can he come for that?"

"We'll see."

She'd known Zack long enough to know a "we'll see" meant no and she nearly asked why when the director, Ted, walked up to the table. Hadley stared down at the sandwich she'd forgotten and tried to get herself back into that place—the one where she flirted with her husband instead of imagining how to deal with aging parents and a dead-battery marriage.

"This is the last shot. You two ready?"

Zack smiled at Ted, whipping his sunglasses off in the process. "I was born ready."

Ted smiled back, even as Hadley didn't miss the sharp awareness that hazed the man's gaze. And then it winked out, leaving her to wonder if the crew saw more of what was going on than she gave them credit for.

Than she gave anyone credit for.

"Let's do this," her cowboy growled, low enough so only she heard.

Zack leaned into her, snagging a bite of potato salad off her plate within moments of Ted calling "action!"

"Thieving my lunch, cowboy?" The words tumbled out, soft and easy, even as she fought the sinking sensation she was lying to the world.

"Consider it payback."

"For what?"

"Rustling up pork on a cattle ranch." He pointed at her sandwich. "You're just lucky it tastes so good."

She cocked her head. "I thought you were the lucky one?"

"Every day, darlin'. Every day."

Before she could say another word, his arm wrapped around her shoulders, pulling her close. It was a split second of time—barely a heartbeat or two—as he stared down at her while she stared up, but everything shimmered to a haze around her.

Around them.

It had been like this once. Just the two of them, wrapped in a cocoon of their own making.

And when he pressed his lips to hers, the taste of vinegar from the potato salad still lightly there, as tart as the words that now framed their lives, she wondered when they'd begun pretending.

ZACK STARED AT the email and wanted to curse the world. So fucking convenient.

Not.

He rarely traveled, content to leave the business of his business to the crack sales team Wayne and Sons employed. But Bryce Donnelly, his expert head of sales, had requested his presence at a major retailer summit in Los Angeles in a few weeks and Zack could hardly say no.

Bryce asked for about one thing a year and it was usually an extension on his travel allowance because he'd made more deals than they'd originally estimated for in his expense budget. So the fact that he wanted Zack there meant it was important. More than important.

The national chain had their annual store managers meeting and they wanted to introduce a line of Wayne and Sons beef to their gourmet fresh food sections nationwide. They were also incredibly eager to feature Hadley's new holiday cookbook at their stores, kicking off her book launch with a major promotion exclusive to them. In the

email, Bryce had already given him the heads-up
that Hadley and her agent would be receiving the
same request.

Expansion of his business and support for his
wife's.

How the hell did you say no to that?

Oh right, asshole. You don't.

He shifted in his chair and caught a whiff of
himself and stood, letting out another string of
curses. He'd come in here to wrap up his day and
get a bit of paperwork out of the way before heading in. The paperwork sucked, but it was a handy
excuse to himself to basically prove he wasn't hiding out.

And it gave the crew time to get packed up and
get gone.

Only now it was past eight and instead of giving the crew time to leave, his procrastination-that-
wasn't-hiding-out had ensured he was sitting on a
bit of information that had to be discussed.

Especially if she had the same news.

Only now he had to discuss it while smelling
like a pigsty. And he was probably insulting the
pigs.

Slapping his hand against his thigh he stood
and left his office, housed in the back of the stables.
The horses had all been seen to, tended and bedded down for the night. A few whickered at him
as he moved past and he stopped when he reached
Gator's door.

Gator's dark chestnut coat gleamed in the
dimmed overhead lights. He was a magnificent

animal but here, now, standing in the quiet, Zack also knew him as a friend.

"When did my life become a clichéd country-and-western song?"

Zack barely realized he wanted to speak before the words came out. Silly at first—as the question lit up the quiet barn he recognized the desperate need to say them.

He had more to be grateful for in his life than he could have ever imagined. A successful business. Land that had passed down to him through generations and which lived in his bones. And people he loved. Why was it so hard to talk to them? And where had this seemingly endless well of anger and resentment and the sheer bile of it all come from?

He wasn't the easiest person to get along with and knew it. He had four sisters and a brother, all younger, which meant he'd been coddled, teased, indulged and, more than he ever should have been, revered. As Charlie Wayne's son—and the only one who'd followed him into the business—that reverence had blown from a different angle as well.

He was the legacy. A weight no matter the situation but one even heavier by dint of his younger brother's determined walk away from the business. And while his father would never have stood in the way of his daughters having a piece of the ranch, none of them wanted it. They took their financial share, as was their due, and wanted very little else. Beyond that, what Zack built, he kept.

It was only Hadley who'd seen him differently.

Hadley who knew how to build him up or tear him down. Mercilessly on either count. And Hadley who was his partner. She could do it all because she was his equal. With her, he'd never felt that his life was a legacy. Rather, he'd just been Zack Wayne. A guy who owned some cows. And who she looked at like he hung the moon.

Or she did once upon a time.

Gator bumped his head beneath Zack's chin, the gesture of affection also one of support. If the horse could actually pull a Mr. Ed on him, he'd likely have said, "Chin up and pull it together, man."

Instead, Gator butted him once more before his nose quivered.

"Yeah, yeah," Zack groused, not sure if the horse's reaction was to his own pungent scent or the sugar in his pocket. "You can tell me I stink but I've got a few cubes for you in my pocket."

He fed the horse the sugar, the light brush of whiskers tickling his palm before Zack gave the horse one last pat. He'd stalled long enough. And as much as he'd like to find the answers to the universe in the support of his horse, life simply wasn't like that.

In minutes he'd crossed the large field between the barn and the ranch house and come in through the back door. His one goal—of avoiding the crew—had been a success and other than a dim light reflecting from the kitchen, the house was silent.

It was so quiet he could almost believe he hadn't

had sixty extra people taking up space on his lawn, his property and inside his home for the past four weeks. Curious to see if everything was back in its place, he passed through the kitchen, the countertops practically gleaming in the light over the stovetop. He didn't see Hadley—and was as relieved as he was disappointed by that fact—before he caught the soft glow from the far end of the hall after he crossed through their dining room.

Something strange tugged him that direction, even though he could take the back stairs and avoid her entirely.

As a practical matter, they needed to discuss the email.

But he wasn't feeling all that practical. And something about those moments outside earlier, when he'd pulled her close at the end of the shot, had crawled under his skin all afternoon.

How could she look so fresh—and *feel* so brand-new—even after all that had happened between them?

And how was it the woman could still leave him feeling as if he'd been skewered straight through after just one look.

It had been like that from the first moment he'd seen her. That sort of breathless awe that tightened his chest because his heart was inexorably expanding beneath his ribcage. It was a ridiculous thought, made even more so by the reality of their marriage, yet he felt it all the same.

And once, she'd felt it, too.

With that thought thrumming through his mind,

he took the last stretch of hallway until he hit the entrance to the small library they kept on the first floor. He'd built the house the first year he made a profit on the business—all on his own—and had some specific rooms in mind for the design. The library had been a throwback to an idea he'd had as a kid. A library meant you were smart. It meant that even if you worked with your hands all day or came in smelling like cow shit, you had something in your home that celebrated learning.

And it had been a wonder the first time he'd brought Hadley to his home, walking her through the house room by room, when she'd stopped at the doorway to the library, her mouth dropping wide open at the wall-to-wall bookcases. She loved cooking, but she'd often said this was her favorite room in the house. Her sanctuary when things got crazy and she just wanted an hour of quiet.

He expected to find her curled up on one of the overstuffed chairs near the window but instead, found her seated on the floor, a large set of architectural drawings laid out before her.

"Hey." She looked up, her gaze refocusing on him and off the small words that littered the drawings.

He nodded at the greeting before his gaze drifted to the notepad beside her, her handwriting covering the page from top to bottom. "What are you doing?"

"Making notes for all the things I want to go over with the architect on the Trading Post. I want to make a few changes to the front area."

He thought they were close to done on the interior work so the plan changes were a surprise. "Aren't you supposed to be moving in product to be open in time for the holidays?"

"We have a few more weeks and your mom brought it up to him when he was in today. He can make changes if we move on them quickly."

"My mother is now directing architectural design?" The words were out before he could pull them back, the deeply rooted resentment at his mother's new "job" layered underneath each and every one.

To Hadley's credit, she held her tongue, her tone even and measured in her response. "She's had some wonderful ideas, Zack. Her eye is sharp and I'm grateful for her help."

He wasn't sure if it was the obvious gratitude or the calm tone or the fact that all the ire and confusion and tension that had ridden his shoulders all day finally had a place to land but in seconds he was lobbing an emotional grenade straight at her.

And wasn't shocked when it imploded dead center of the room, all over her precious plans.

"Grateful? Or coming to realize you're abandoning her with this project when you go on your book tour."

"Did you come in here for a real reason? Or was it just to continue part two of this afternoon's episode of *How to Be An Asshole* by Zachary Wayne?"

"And here we go. God forbid I suggest Princess Hadley might be thinking only of herself."

She'd remained calm up until that point but the princess remark hit a straight bullseye.

"Who do you suggest I worry about, Zack? The imaginary children we don't have? The ranch employees we hide our problems from? I sure as hell can't take care of you since you make yourself scarce around here." She stood at that, her hands finding her slim hips. "Who the hell else should I worry about?"

The question was left, hanging in the room, when his phone went off with a text at the same time the ringer kicked in.

He dug it out of his pocket, Carter's name on the face. His foreman never called in the evening unless there was a problem. "It's Carter."

"Answer it."

He heard no malice beneath the suggestion, only an odd understanding.

"Wayne."

"Need you down at the south pasture. We've got a problem with that calf I mentioned earlier."

"What problem?"

"He's on the ground and he's not responding. His mama's in a bad snit and we need to get the herd moved off around them."

"You call Gray?"

"On his way."

"So am I."

Zack shoved the phone back in his pocket, suddenly aware his wife was still standing there. "I need to go."

"I heard."

"We—"

The anger he'd worked up—the one he'd been

so determined needed a place to land—suddenly seemed empty. Flat.

But it was Hadley's order—and that gentle understanding that still laced her voice—that had him moving. "Go."

Chapter 3

Hadley had finished her notes a half hour ago, the task nearly done before Zack's ill-timed entrance and the brewing fight.

"Is that what we're calling it these days?" she muttered to herself as she slammed the baking pan on the counter, her intention to remove any lingering air bubbles in the brownies a convenient excuse for the anger that still roiled inside. That fight hadn't needed any time to brew at all. Nope. It had full-test strength from the first verbal bomb Zack shot into the room.

She wasn't mad he'd left. The ranch needed tending and a sick calf was a problem. For the animal in question and, in the event there was a bigger situation afoot, for the health of the broader herd.

It was the neat hand grenades that had come before his departure that still had her pissed off.

She wasn't abandoning his mother to the work

of the Trading Post. Carlene wanted it—had asked for more to do—and Hadley wasn't above helping her out. Although she'd been incredibly careful to avoid mentioning any of her troubles with Zack, Carlene hadn't been so quiet on her own troubles with Charlie. And the man's mounting frustration at his role on the ranch—or increasing lack of one—had spilled over to their marriage.

While she had a lot of compassion for her father-in-law, she wasn't above taking sides on the current situation and her loyalties lay firmly with Carlene. They'd all known the daily physical pressures of running the ranch would grow too much for Charlie. And somewhere inside, Hadley thought to herself as she set the brownies in the oven, Charlie did too. But they'd all grown tired of coddling him and his aging ego.

Carlene most of all.

The Trading Post had started out as a great diversion, but as time had gone on, it had become something so much more. Carlene had taken to the planning of the shop with a sharp eye and eager attitude and the time they'd spent together had made the two women even closer. Hadley missed her own mother, but it had been so long since she'd lost her she'd believed herself well able to handle all life tossed her way. She still had her father and her sister, Harper, and was grateful for them.

How amazing it had been, then, to realize all she and Zack's mother shared. And how much she'd missed that gentle guidance of an older female in her life. Carlene had never seen her as the woman who'd "taken her beloved son," and they'd had a good relationship from the start. But these past few months working on the Trading Post together had bonded them in ways Hadley had never expected.

It had bonded them so much she'd nearly spilled all her marital issues to Carlene more than a few times.

Yet something always held her back.

Loyalty to Zack?

Embarrassment that they'd gotten to this point?

Or some lingering sense that no matter how close she and Carlene were, Zack was still Carlene's child.

And so each time those words burned the tip of her tongue, Hadley swallowed them back. And focused her attention on fabric swatches, menu items for the restaurant they were building into the entire Trading Post experience, or the inventory they'd carry for the holiday launch and beyond.

With the brownies in the oven, she headed up to her room to change. The warm afternoon they'd had had quickly turned cold as the sun set and she needed a few layers to head on out to the south pasture. She'd bring the brownies and drive out to see how she could help. Even when things were good between them, Zack had never liked her in and around the heifers when they had their calves, but it was also getting late and every one of them had put in a hard day. An extra pair of hands was invariably always needed at times like this.

After dressing she whipped up the frosting

she'd use for the brownies and put in a call to the ranch office. If they'd managed to get the calf back into one of the various stables they had scattered over the property the call would ring through and she could get an update on what was going on. When it went straight to voicemail, she could only assume they were all still busy down in the south pasture.

Which didn't bode well for the calf's condition.

She made quick work of frosting the brownies and snagged keys off a small pegboard on her way out the door. In a matter of minutes she was bumping over one of the paved roads that made up a grid pattern over the 80,000-acre ranch.

They had lights strategically placed around the property, managed off a sustainable electricity grid Zack had installed as one of his first projects after taking over the ranch. The lights ran on a rotating system to conserve energy, but as Hadley got closer to the south pasture she could see they'd all been turned on. The collection of trucks in the distance was further proof the work to save the calf was not only still going on, but was a full-team effort.

Hadley pulled up and out of the way, her father-in-law visible just as she cut her lights. She hopped out, leaving the brownies on the passenger side, and crossed to him. "Hey, Charlie. How's the calf doing?"

"Hell if I know." Charlie's shoulders were still large, the lines of the man he once was clearly visible beneath the thick layer of leather jacket, even as there was increasing room in the width. "Zack's stomping around in there like he owns the damn place."

Hadley avoided mentioning that Zack did, in fact, formally own the place now. Instead, she moved in next to Charlie and put a warm, reassuring arm around his back. Always a soft touch, the move had her father-in-law wrapping her in a tight side-armed hug. "He's a stubborn cuss." Charlie let out a hard sigh. "And I can hardly argue where he gets it from."

"Probably not."

"It's just that—" He broke off and Hadley just caught the look of remorse and regret in his faded gray eyes before his brows shot down. "I know how to handle a pissed-off heifer protecting her baby."

"I've no doubt that you do."

"All the young cowboys are in there trying to prove themselves."

Since it was obvious the old ones still wanted to as well, Hadley stayed put in his warm hold and used his decades of knowledge to gently diffuse the situation. "What's going on? Carter called Zack about a sick calf but it looks like it's gotten out of hand pretty quick."

The question did the trick and in moments she had a full understanding of the concerns over the sick calf, the work being done to move the rest of the herd away for their own safety, and then the subsequent handling that needed to happen to move the animal for medical attention.

"It's delicate work and fifteen hundred pounds

of pissed-off heifer doesn't make it a damn sight easier."

"No, I suppose it doesn't." Two hundred pounds of pissed-off aging cowboy didn't make things easier either, but she was pleased to see Charlie's initial ire fading.

As further proof, her father-in-law pulled himself out of his sulk. "What are you doing out here?"

"I wanted to see how things were going and bring out some sustenance."

Charlie's eyes lit up. "What'd you bring?"

"Brownies. And you get first pick even though I already know you want the corner piece with extra icing."

She led Charlie over to the passenger side of the truck, pulling out the brownies and suddenly incredibly glad she'd taken the time to make them. They spent a few more minutes in easy conversation, him enjoying his large corner piece as she'd expected and her nibbling on a smaller square of her own. She asked a few more questions about the calf, once again struck by his vast breadth of knowledge.

And then they were wrapping up and she let out a small sigh of relief that Charlie didn't ask after Carlene or the latest progress of the Trading Post.

Even if that same topic had been the last sour note between her and Zack.

Wiping her fingers off on one of the paper towels she brought along with the brownies, she shot Charlie a bright smile. "I'm glad we got to catch up. We haven't had a chance to do that in a while."

"Me too. You're my favorite daughter-in-law."

"I'm your only daughter-in-law."

"Doesn't change how I feel." Charlie leaned in close and pressed a warm kiss to her cheek. He stepped back and patted his stomach. "And with this sweet treat lifting my mood, I think I'm going to leave that angry mama to the young'uns."

Since he headed off with a soft whistle for his vehicle, Hadley took it—along with the compliment about being his favorite—as a success and headed toward the assembled trucks in the distance. Someone had set up portable lights around the perimeter and it was easy to see the situation wasn't improving. The calf was laid out on the ground on his side, the mother hovering around his body and stamping her feet every time one of the hands made a move closer.

Hadley's gaze went unerringly to Zack, impressed as always by the sheer responsibility that rested on his shoulders. Earlier that day she'd watched him ride in after lunch, leaving everyone to come in before him. And now, staring down the pissed-off heifer, he was first. And all of this with a day that had started at 4:00 a.m.

Yet there he was, still at the center of it all, taking full responsibility for his animals and his ranch. Charlie's assessment of the situation was spot-on and Hadley crept closer, her attention fully focused on Zack. Especially as Charlie's description—fifteen hundred pounds of pissed-off cow—rang in her ears like a gong.

What if something happened to him?

She heard Gray's shout from behind that they had two tranq guns ready. The thought that the mother had to be sedated for doing what came naturally was a fleeting sadness that she pushed aside at the reality that her husband sat squarely in the animal's crosshairs.

Whether it was that innate worry or the simple need to get closer, she had no idea. But one moment she was standing beside one of the ranch trucks, hanging on the situation and the next the heifer's wild gaze turned on hers as Hadley took a few steps forward. She barely had time to register the flaring nostrils as the cow took off at a run, straight for her.

ZACK SCREAMED THE order to shoot the tranqs, the words rushing out in a mix of shock and something that felt a lot like a bullet to the chest. Had anyone even heard him? Or had the scream stuck in his throat along with his heart?

The sudden sight of his wife and an enraged animal that weighed nearly a ton bearing down on her had them all moving the same direction, even as Zack felt as if his feet were rooted to the ground in cement.

Gray and Teak aimed true, both hitting the cow with darts from the tranq guns. Carter was already lining up a third while Gar and Bobby Ray had lassos up and at the ready to add their strength to the mix and further restrain the mother if needed.

All of it happened in a blur because Zack was already in motion, passing them by in his desperation to get to Hadley.

He barely noticed the earth shake beneath his feet as the cow dropped to the ground, his only concern for his wife. He had to get to her. The distance seemed endless, yet in what had to be a matter of seconds he had her in his arms, wrapped tight against his chest.

"Damn it." He whispered the words over and over against her hair, his arms shaking as he held her close.

"Zack, I'm sorry. I didn't realize."

"Shhh. You're alright. You're okay." He could already hear the men behind him getting to work, Gray moving toward the calf while Carter and the ranch hands got to work on the heifer. She'd be treated well for her troubles, but it wouldn't erase her distress or her instinct to protect. And they needed to get her moved and secured before any trace of the tranquilizer wore off.

Suddenly aware that he still stood there with Hadley while the rest of his crew moved around doing work, he stepped back. What was she even doing out here? First his father had gotten in the way and left in a huff. No sooner had he removed that worry from the mix of an escalating crisis than his wife had showed up.

"What are you doing here?"

The softness on her face vanished, wariness returning. And despite the fact that it was his own damn words that put the wary there, he was angry, too. Why the hell couldn't she have stayed behind? It was bad enough he had to deal with his father who, while aging out of this sort of crisis, still knew how it needed to be handled. Now he had to worry that his wife was going to be stampeded by a pissed-off cow with protective instincts set off to hell and back.

Fuck it all to that very same hell. And right the fuck back, too.

"Go home."

"I came to help."

The bark of laughter was hard and harsh, just as he intended. "We've put up the rest of the herd, darlin'. There's no other creature besides me to piss off tonight."

"Wow." The fear that had filled her gaze only moments before faded. So had the wariness that had come after. All of it had been replaced with a steady fire. "You don't miss a beat, do you? Tossing insults the same way you toss orders around here. I'm capable, Zack. And since you can't seem to see it, I'll go give Gray the help. I'm sure he'll be happy for an extra set of hands. Especially since, like all of you, he's been up before dawn."

She stomped off toward their large animal vet, her shoulders stiff and her carriage regal. He hated the Princess Hadley routine about as much as he hated her Hollywood smile, but he had no one to blame but himself when it made its appearance.

Because unlike the smile, the princess jabs were his alone. They came out each and every time she got that stiff back and disappointed look in her deep green eyes. He'd started using the term as a proxy for all he didn't know how to say and somehow it had stuck. And it was an ugly reference to make her as angry as he felt inside.

Which meant it was small of him. And unbearably mean.

He might be the world's most stubborn son of a bitch but he wasn't mean—not in heart or spirit. His mother hadn't raised him that way and he didn't tolerate it in others.

Which meant he had no place tolerating it in himself.

He eyed where Hadley stood next to Gray, her hands on her hips as she stared down at him and the calf, her head nodding as she took in the vet's instructions. In seconds, she was on the ground opposite him, ignoring the dirt to kneel beside the calf. She held the animal's head, following whatever instructions she was given as Gray did his exam.

And as he watched, separated by far more between them than thirty yards of dirt, Zack knew he owed her an apology.

Not sometime. Or when he got around to it.

But tonight.

Because it was time to talk.

HADLEY KEPT A hand on the calf's head, stroking his coat and running her hand over his ears in soothing motions. She had no idea if it was helping—the calf's labored breathing hadn't improved all that much since she and Gray had gotten him inside one of the large field barns scattered around the property—but she'd already reasoned it couldn't hurt, either.

They'd come to the barn closest to the south pasture, and now, about two hours later, she could hear the frustrated mother bellowing from where she was being held, protected inside a gated enclosure.

She'd seen it before but the process always fascinated her. Getting the calf loaded on the truck and the heifer on a larger flatbed due to her size and weight. Ensuring they were well situated and protected as best as possible.

And then sitting through the inevitable wait as they hoped the calf would make it through its diagnosis.

Gray had already administered much-needed antibiotics and now it was a waiting game. Medicine ensured the odds the calf would be alright were way better than in Charlie's early days of running the ranch, but it wasn't perfect. They'd lost calves before and accepted it was part of the whole.

Because it was, she'd sent Gray off to one of the small bunks in the back of the barn. He was close enough to call on if they needed him but could get some well-deserved rest. Although she could tell he was exhausted, the telltale sign he was in dire need of sleep was that he didn't even ask after Harper.

She adored Gray but, unless asked directly, Hadley had stopped sharing news of her sister a long time ago. Harper and Gray had shared something

special once . . . until they didn't. And since love,
loyalty and the bonds of sisterhood put her firmly
on Team Harper, it was easier all around when the
subject didn't come up.

"Hey."

Zack stood at the entrance to the stall, his exhaustion as visible as the day's worth of work,
sweat and grime.

She wanted to be angry—still *was* angry,
actually—for the bullshit move out in the field. But
she'd also had time to calm down and now, sitting
there with a struggling animal in her arms and the
evidence that her husband barely had the energy
to stand, she couldn't quite find the mad.

"Hey, yourself."

"Gray gave me an update before he grabbed a
bunk."

She nodded, well aware that raising the issue
that the calf might not make it through the night—
even though truthful—wasn't what he needed or
wanted to hear.

"You don't have to sit here with him." Zack's
voice was shot through with gravel, the words
thick and laced with a tenderness she hadn't heard
in a long time.

"I'm in it now. Besides"—she traced the edge of
the animal's ear—"I want to make sure he's okay."

Zack nodded, wavering slightly on his feet.

"Why don't you go grab one of the bunks, too.
I'll call you if I need you."

He stood there another minute, shifting from
foot to foot as if to keep his balance. Even as Had-

ley wondered how he was able to put two thoughts together she watched the determination and sheer force of will that kept him standing. That and some sort of decision that traveled from the grooves in his forehead to the slash of his eyebrows and down to the grim set of his mouth.

"I owe you an apology."

Although he did owe her an apology—a sizeable one—since he was nearly dead on his feet, she was willing to wait for it.

"And it can't wait until morning," he added, that gravel suddenly threaded with steel.

"Okay."

"I was mean outside. And there's no excuse for it. Not worry for you. Or for my father. Or a shitty day. Or the fight we had before. Or all the crap we've stopped saying to each other."

She'd expected an "I'm sorry," and would have forced the issue tomorrow if one never came, but this was way beyond. Beyond snapping at her after an adrenaline rush of fear. Beyond a long day of physical labor.

This was about them.

And all the anger that lay between them.

"If you won't grab a bunk why don't you at least sit down." She gestured toward the slatted wood wall of the stable where they had the calf bedded down.

He shifted once more and she had the uneasy thought that he might fall down right there, but the sheer force of will that was Zack Wayne had him edging toward the half wall. He eased down, stretching his legs out in front of him as he pressed his back to the wooden slats.

And in that small moment of vulnerability, Hadley saw it. The pain and anger and confusion that she'd felt for what seemed like forever now, written plainly on his face.

"Thank you for the apology. I appreciate it."

The eyes that had briefly closed as he'd laid his head back popped open. "You're welcome."

Since she wasn't above using that vulnerability to press him on the things she didn't understand or agree with, Hadley took her shot. "What was that about your father?"

"I'm worried about him. He doesn't have the physical strength anymore. And he's so stubborn he refuses to see that or help on the things I really need him for."

"You'd want to be relegated to a life of paperwork?"

"Hell no. But that's not what I'm asking of him. I want him to work on the business of the ranch. He's forgotten more than I'll ever know and he can still be useful. Damn useful. But all he wants is to be up on the back of a damn horse. And since I'm not willing to give him that it's all or nothing."

"He's doing it to your mother, too."

Zack's eyes narrowed and before he could get a head of steam going, she added, "You owe me an apology for that one, too. I'm not using your mother or asking her to do anything she doesn't want." Hadley waited a beat. "And you know it."

Zack stood back up then and Hadley thought

she'd rung the bell for a new round when he walked closer, taking a seat beside her. Only instead of starting the next round of arguments, Zack reached for the calf. "Here. He's bigger than he looks and he's got to have put a crimp in your legs."

Since the weight of the calf had done just that, Hadley shifted, giving Zack room to reposition the still-growing body. They'd put down several stall blankets and hay and Zack gently repositioned the calf into the small nest, careful in his movements.

Something raw speared through her. God, how she loved this man. How she'd loved him from the very first moment. And every time she believed she knew why, he did something else—showed her some new facet—that she'd never seen before, reinforcing those feelings all over again.

Why was it so hard?

And how had they lost it?

"Zack—" She broke off, the pain of the past two years leaping up and jamming her words in her throat.

His eyes never left hers, that deep and oh-so-familiar brown her own personal haven.

She wanted him. Wanted to go back to the way they were and the life they had. The way they effortlessly worked together to accomplish whatever stood in their way.

"What?" That lone word hovered between them.

"I know—"

She knew what?

That they didn't see eye to eye any longer? That

they needed to find some time out of their crazy-busy lives to find one another again, but there wasn't a single moment to be found until the following summer? Or that they needed to talk about the reality of having a family.

Or not.

Because the limbo they found themselves in on that front had begun to wreak a certain sort of havoc she could never have imagined.

Zack's gaze never left hers and in the stillness of the barn, with nothing and no one around—no audience or camera or enough lights to fill Broadway—Hadley leaned in. She couldn't fix their lack of a family. And she might not be able to carve off more than a day or two for the next stretch of months.

But they had now.

This moment.

And she was done waiting.

Leaning in, she pressed her lips to his. He held still for the briefest heartbeat before opening to her, an easing of the tight reins he kept on himself and his emotions. And in the easing, she found her advantage. The hard press of lips they'd shared earlier on the lunch shoot was nowhere in evidence. Instead, she felt the gentle merging of tongues—almost tentative as the kiss advanced—and the blended breath between them.

How easy it was to fall into him. To take a moment of ease, together, at the end of day. Partnership. Commitment. Camaraderie.

Her Zack.

It was only as he pulled back, much too soon, that she saw it and felt something dark and panicky unfurl in her chest. Subtle regret, overlaid on all the frustration they both carried with each other.

But it was his words that pulled her up short. "We never talked about the email we both got today. About the publicity event in California."

Emails? California? Events? Why was he bringing up any of that now?

"I think we should do it. Put on a happy face and do what's right. For your business and for mine."

"Okay." Her mind whirled at the change in topic, especially after the quiet peace of settling the calf and the familiar comfort of their kiss.

"We can use the time away to talk. And after we get home we can decide what comes next."

Chapter 4

"Talk about what comes next?"

Her voice held an odd calm, especially in light of the fact that she thought her husband just asked her for a divorce, but Hadley willed herself to listen. To make sure she was hearing what she thought she was.

Because whatever misery she and Zack had been causing each other, had it really become so untenable that divorce was waiting for them at the end of the line?

"We're both so angry all the time." Exhaustion painted his words and filled his face, but that implacable steel that she'd always associated with her husband was still in evidence.

And it was in that implacability that she found her own desire to fight.

"Both of us?" She held the line, keeping that calm, but something sparked underneath. "Because I wasn't the one shooting daggers out my eyes today at the shoot. I wasn't the one picking a fight about your mother. And I wasn't the one delivering edicts in our barn."

"But you are the one picking a fight here and now, when I'm nearly falling over I'm so fucking tired."

"And there's the excuse. There always is one."

"What do you want from me?"

Hadley struggled to her feet, careful not to disturb the calf as she did so. But as soon as she cleared that overgrown body she scrambled for the barn, determined to escape.

"Hads!"

His term of endearment fell on deaf ears as Hadley kept going, even as she heard his footfalls quickly close in behind her. Damn it, what did he keep making her pay for? Every time she thought they had a moment that felt like the two of them, the wind changed, blowing so hard and destructive she couldn't see a way past it.

And despite it all, the thought of going their separate ways filled her with a sadness that felt like death. Worse, in some ways, because they'd both still be breathing after it was over.

"Hadley!" His hand brushed at hers, stopping her. Even in his weariness, he was gentle, his hold only to stop her progression. "Talk to me."

She whirled on him, dragging her hand back from his light grip. "About what, Zack? What is it you want me to say? Would you just tell me for once? Because every fight we have, I come up lacking even though I have no idea what I did."

"Nothing! You haven't done anything. That's half the damn problem. You're Saint Hadley and I'm just the miserable, clueless bastard you married."

Clueless?

What was that supposed—

The questions faded as he wrapped her up tight in his arms, his lips descending on hers. This was nothing like the kiss over the calf. In that she'd felt tentative care and a desire to understand. But here . . .

Here she felt the fire.

The anger.

And the passion that had always flowed so freely between them she'd come to realize she'd taken for granted. She'd always been grateful for it, but she'd also never expected to lose it.

And then there wasn't anything left to think or feel because he was devouring her with his mouth and his hands were holding her tight against his body and all that anger and frustration that brewed between them bubbled up and spilled over.

MADNESS.

That was the only word for what he felt for his wife.

It was one of the last vestiges of thought that rattled around in his mind as Zack kissed her. Held her. Tried to brand her with all these feelings he had no idea what to do with.

Clueless bastard.

The words whispered through his mind once

more and he knew them for truth. He had no idea how the two of them had gotten here, but he knew something was wrong between them. A sort of empty day-to-day that they both drifted through, trying to find what they used to have.

And unable to understand how they'd lost it.

Over and over in his mind, he came back to the things they didn't say. The fights that, no matter how heated, never scalded enough to reveal the big secrets. The one that would finally reveal all the ways they'd failed each other.

And all the things that remained unsaid.

With his hands firm on her shoulders, Zack held her still as he stepped away from her body. "I can't do this. Not tonight."

"Then when? You're the one who laid down the ultimatum."

Since he had, with a rash statement spoken out of bone weariness, he tried to make up some ground. "It's a lousy excuse, but it's the only one I have. I'm tired and I'm not speaking to you in the way I should. I'm not saying the things I should."

She nodded, her eyes wide in her face in the darkened lights of the barn. "I can accept that."

"Come on, I'll drive you back to the house."

"No need. I brought a truck out. I'll get myself back."

"Had—" This time she did turn at the use of her name.

"You're tired, Zack. See to the calf and try to get some sleep."

Then she was gone.

And he was no closer to understanding why there was a mountain of resentment between them.

He only knew there was.

CARLENE MARIE WAYNE, née Butterfield, had always taken considerable pride in her home, her children and her marriage. And in a matter of months, she had cobwebs on her baseboards, her youngest son was hell-bent to fuck his way through the National Football League and her husband was the last man on earth she wanted to see, talk to or spend an ounce of time with.

And don't get her going on her eldest son's bull-headed approach to till death did he part.

She shook her head, frustrated with all the men in her life, as she re-tallied the inventory for the initial delivery to the Trading Post.

The Trading Post, Carlene looked around fondly, months of construction debris and dust barely visible any longer. Her brilliant daughter-in-law's first entry into the local real estate market. Despite her frustratingly circular thoughts, Carlene gave herself the mental break to stop for a moment and look her fill.

It was all coming together.

A sense of style that Hadley embodied on her TV show and in her cookbooks, and that could now be experienced in person.

Carlene knew Hadley had been toying for some time with an actual place that would make the Cowgirl Gourmet lifestyle real and tangible, but the Trading Post was beyond her wildest imaginings. And to think that she got to be a part of it, too. Not just a part, Carlene thought proudly.

Helping to bring it to life.

With a pride that was intimately interwoven with all those troubles she was carrying around like a mental tally board in her head.

Late fall sunlight filtered through the large cavernous windows, brought back to their pre–World War II glory. The entire space had been Rustlers Creek's first mercantile, built in the late eighteen hundreds, even before the town was fully incorporated. It had survived as the town's largest purveyor of goods until the Great Depression, falling on hard times like everyone else.

After the Depression hit hard, the building had lain dormant before moving into its second incarnation as a munitions space during the war. It had served several other purposes in the ensuing seventy years including town meeting hall, overflow for the elementary school and, for a while, even an aerobics gym when Jane Fonda had made that all the rage and the matrons of Rustlers Creek decided they needed a space to "get physical."

Carlene shuddered at the memory along with the vivid purple body suit she used to wear in this very spot.

Even if Charlie had liked that purple gym suit an awful lot . . .

Brushing off images of her husband and better times between them, she moved over toward the seating area for the small café. The counters and cabinets were set up in the same color scheme as Hadley's kitchen, with a coffee bar that could double as a demonstration area when they did cooking classes. Even now, with the scent of sawdust still lingering in the air and blue stickie tape on various surfaces keeping tabs for their punch list, Carlene could see it.

Could see the excited patrons, enthusiastically taking classes or mingling at tables, enjoying the café's food and coffee. Could see the extra boost in tourism that was bound to come from Hadley's latest endeavors. Could even see the way her husband's and son's gazes would light up in fondness at what the name of Wayne was capable of creating.

It was tempting to think Charlie and Zack's bullheadedness up to now was tied to the fact that they'd not built it all themselves, but Charlie preened often enough about Hadley that Carlene wasn't convinced it was all a case of misplaced male pride. She knew her husband, and for all his faults he'd never subscribed to the idea that women were inferior or that his son's wife had somehow embarrassed them by going out and making a name for herself.

And as for Zack . . .

Carlene didn't think it was misplaced pride there, either. What it was, though, she'd been unable to land on.

Of all her children, Zack had always been the hardest to read. He might be her firstborn, but from the day he'd taken his first steps, he'd done his level best to stand on his own two feet without assistance.

The fact he'd married an equally stubborn—and closemouthed—woman had Carlene in knots.

Because despite the bright smiles and chatty small talk about life, Hadley hadn't fooled her for an instant. Shame she couldn't say the same for everyone else around them.

Oh, Carlene mused, she certainly didn't want the rest of town up in their business—everyone managed that quite well already—but she was surprised the troubles between Zack and Hadley seemed hidden to the rest of the family. Charlie had no idea, nor did her eldest daughter, Charlotte, or the triplets for that matter. Jackson was too far away to notice anything, even if he could get his head out of his professional sports ass for more than three minutes at a clip.

An ass she loved to the moon and back, but one that had caused some heartache of late.

No, for some reason she was the only one who'd been able to see the strains and cracks at the edges of her eldest son's marriage.

Strain that, of late, had begun to mirror her own.

"Takes one to know one," she muttered to herself.

Although she was sick to death of her own thoughts, Carlene hadn't found a way past the sinking hole in her stomach that had opened up over Charlie. A hole that continued to grow wider because, after forty-two years of marriage, she hadn't figured a way past things.

The man hated retirement.

A fact she could support if he had to well and truly *be* retired.

But he didn't. His doctor wanted him to slow down and Zack had made that fact a reality. Seventy-two-year-old men didn't belong on the backs of horses for ten hours or more a day, no matter how stubborn or "seasoned" they were.

That didn't mean Charlie's contributions weren't welcome at Wayne and Sons. Zack had made that clear in every word he'd said to his father the day he and Carlene had had "the talk" with Charlie.

Only her stubborn fool husband hadn't heard a damn word past "Dad, we need to make some changes."

Between his connections, his innate understanding of the beef market and his years of experience, Charlie was incredibly well positioned to manage much of the business end of Wayne and Sons. His own father had done it for years and Carlene knew it would be a true help to Zack, especially with all the expansion her son had done over the past five years.

But all Charlie wanted was to be on the back of a horse, riding in the thick of things, herding cattle.

There was a time she could never have imagined her husband *not* being able to do that. Of course, there was a time she hadn't imagined staring at a sixty-five-year-old woman in the mirror every morning, too.

Life's a bitch and Mother Nature's its queen. It had been her grandmother's favorite saying and Carlene had adopted it as her own of late.

What she really resented, though, was Charlie's inability to see all he still did have. They were lucky. They'd spent a lifetime running a successful business. They had six beautiful children. And they both, thankfully, had their health. A few issues along the way, but relatively hale and hearty all the same. Mother Nature had tossed them a few flairs of bitchiness, but they'd survived each and every one.

What Carlene really resented was Charlie's inability to age into this part of their lives *with* her. He was so busy being mad, he'd alienated her. It had been building for a while, but when he started poking around all her time spent at the Trading Post she'd lost it.

"So you're suggesting I should sit around this big house all day on my ass?"

"You know it's a gorgeous ass."

When she only stared him down instead of responding to the sexy tease, he'd bumbled on.

"Now, Carlene, don't misunderstand me." He waved a hand. *"There's plenty to do. See your friends. Have your lunches. Go up to Bozeman for a spa weekend. Whatever you want to do. Enjoy yourself."*

"I am enjoying myself."

Charlie shook his head, staring down at his feet, before giving her the big soulful eyes he'd perfected around their third date. "I just don't see why you want to take all that on. It's Hadley's business and you're working like a stock girl during the Christmas rush."

"*Aside from the fact that there's no job beneath me—*" Carlene had wagged a finger "*—beneath any of us, Charles Wayne, that is not what I'm doing.*"

"*So what are you doing? Ringing up the receipts?*"

It had been the sneer on his face and the bitter resentment beneath the words that had done her in.

"*Just because you sit around this place on your ass moping does not mean I need to do the same.*"

"*I'm not moping.*"

"*Come the hell on, Charlie, you most certainly are. You have been every day since Zack asked you to step back from working the fields.*"

"*I can do my damn job.*"

"*Zack can do the damn job. He doesn't need to add keeping an eye on you to a long day's work.*"

The fight had gone from bad to worse and he'd finally stormed out. Leaving her with an empty chasm between her and her husband that she had no idea how to get around.

Not one fucking clue.

The buzzer from the back entrance went off and she headed toward the stock room, the remembered fight a dark miasma that hovered over her shoulders.

And damn him for that.

They'd been living like this for nearly six months, with the last two of him living in the bunkhouse courtesy of that great explosion. And she deserved better. They both did. They'd worked too long and much too hard for their later years to be filled with such unhappiness.

Such ugliness.

And so many precious hours wasted apart.

Carlene saw the waste of it all but she refused to give in. And it wasn't simply a matter of stubborn pride. Her husband needed to work through this problem on his own. Neither she nor anyone else could fix the passage of time. And she couldn't fix the reality of the risks to an aging body from hard physical labor.

So he'd wallow.

And he'd mope.

But Charlie Wayne needed to be the one to find his way out the other side of this.

"Carlene!" Hadley's face lit up as she trudged in the back door, her forearms laden with canvas bags and five bolts of material filling up her arms. "I'm glad you're here."

Carlene rushed forward to help, taking the material before reaching behind her daughter-in-law to close the back door. The sun was high but the air swirling outside had a decided bite to it and she shivered as the cold washed over her before firmly shutting the door with a hip.

"I didn't think you were coming in today." Carlene carried the fabric into the main area of the store, setting the bolts on the counter. Maybe it was the lingering thoughts that had already been swirling or the fact that her gaze was focused on the counter, but when Hadley spoke Carlene heard the hitch in her voice clear across the room.

"I didn't sleep well and was up designing a new installation for the holiday area."

"Everything okay?"

"Sure. Fine. One of the calves had a bad night and it had us all out in the barn for a while."

"How's the little guy now?"

"Word this morning is that he's going to be fine."

It was a relief to hear they wouldn't lose the calf and Carlene would have moved on, taking Hadley at her word, until something a lot like misery stamped itself in her daughter-in-law's normally bright gaze.

"Are you sure that's all?"

"Oh yeah." Hadley shook her head, those hints of vulnerability fading as her shoulders straightened. "I was too wound up when I came back in to sleep. Just a lot on my mind, I guess."

Carlene *could* guess and nearly did before pulling herself back. She'd made a vow to herself years ago to stay out of her children's personal lives. She had many friends who'd made it their mission to nose in and all-around interfere and it had never sat well with her. You didn't raise strong-minded adults only to step in on each and every little thing. A philosophy that she'd done damn well with, if she did say so herself.

Only now . . .

It had gotten harder and harder to remain silent. If she thought Zack and Hadley had fallen out of love that might have been one thing. A sad thing, to be sure, but also a reality for many good, decent people. Only that hadn't seemed to be it.

Far from it, actually.

What she saw wasn't the absence of love. If anything, that had remained as strong as ever. But the grief and unhappiness layered overtop of it had been a continued surprise.

Sort of like you and Charlie, that small, nagging voice rose up in censure. The problems in her own marriage had been the thing keeping her from interfering in her son and daughter-in-law's life.

Because it was the one thing that was guaranteed to backfire on her.

She couldn't get her own personal life in order. One also steeped in love, commitment and, in her and Charlie's case, more than forty years together.

It was hardly her place to try and talk sense into her son.

HADLEY BUSTLED AROUND the Trading Post, out of sight of her eagle-eyed mother-in-law. She loved Carlene and treasured their relationship, but the embarrassment over the demise of her own marriage wasn't something Hadley was ready to admit.

Even if said demise was approaching far faster than she could have ever imagined.

We can use the time away to talk. And after we get home we can decide what comes next.

Zack's statement had kept her awake for what little was left of the night and had haunted her as she'd gotten dressed and ready for the day. He might have meant the comment as something collaborative—a discussion between two mutually involved adults—but she'd heard the real truth. Had understood it for exactly what it was.

There was an ultimatum beneath those words.

Zack was sick of the way things were between

them and he wanted a change. Or, worse, he wanted out.

A part of her, Hadley knew, should be relieved. They hadn't had a real marriage in far too long. So long, in fact, that it had become harder and harder to remember the good times. Nay, she thought as she settled the bolts of fabric down in the demonstration area.

The easy times.

They'd had those once. Life wasn't perfect every day but she'd never doubted what was between them and she didn't think Zack did, either. Even at their very worst, during those horrible days she still shuddered to remember, they hadn't had such a hard time talking. Being with one another. Or simply finding cordial, caring words to speak to one another.

Where had those gone?

Did it matter any longer?

Hadley stared around the demonstration area, the wide gleaming counters a taunting blend of accomplishment and censure. As her job had grown and grown, her world getting bigger right along with it, her marriage had grown smaller and smaller.

So small that a simple conversation with her husband was impossible to have any longer.

And oh, how she wanted that once again.

Did a person use up their luck? Was it actually possible that when one area of your life resulted in life-altering dream fulfillment, all others had to fail? She'd always been hesitant to believe that, convinced instead that a true partner saw your accomplishments as well as your failures, and understood all that went into reaching a goal.

But, as the past few years had grown bigger, more and more of her professional dreams coming true, she'd increasingly begun to think she was wrong. It wasn't that Zack begrudged her the work. In fact, the one civil thing he'd continued to say to her, mixed in and among all the other less civil things they found to be angry about, was how proud he was of her. She knew it wasn't lip service, too.

She'd overheard him and his father one day, a few weeks before Zack had initiated "the talk" with Charlie.

"It's amazing, Dad. The whole production. I know it's a pain in the ass to have everything disrupted with the people and the cameras, but it's like nothing I've ever seen. And it's all about Hadley."

"She's something."

"That she is. I knew she worked hard. I've always known that, all the way back to her 5:00 a.m. wake-up calls to work the bakery and coffee shop in town when we were dating. But what I've seen her build? Create out of her own imagination. It's incredible."

She'd warmed at her husband's words that day, nearly interrupting them before quietly stepping back out of the stables. Zack's praise had given her hope and she'd nearly burst from the excitement of it.

Maybe there was a future for them. Something they could continue to craft and mold and build together.

They'd had a few good days after that. Quiet words at dinner that weren't fraught with animosity or the deeper, unspoken thoughts they both held at bay. They'd even made love that week, the quiet kind that held all the things they didn't say instead of what sex had become over the past year.

Perfunctory.

Stilted.

And, while still deeply consensual between them, tinged with an anger she couldn't understand, even as she gave herself up to it, over and over.

She wanted her husband. And in the stillness after sex, she'd come to accept that whatever they'd had before . . .

Whatever they'd had was gone.

ZACK DROPPED TWO pieces of bread into the toaster and looked around the kitchen. The calf had held up well overnight and Gray was convinced they'd have the animal back out with its fretting mama in a few hours. With the vet's sharp instruction still ringing in his ears to go in and shower and get some down time before they reintroduced the animals, Zack had finally headed back to the house.

And five thousand square feet of empty.

He'd showered off the prior day's sweat and dirt and anger, only to find a fresh brew of resentment waiting for him as he changed into clean jeans and a flannel.

Where was Hadley?

It had only been on his arrival back down in the kitchen for a bite that he'd seen the note. The instruction that she was spending the day at the Trading Post and to text her if he needed anything while she was out.

Polite. Unfailingly so.

And about what he deserved after his early morning request in the barn.

Why'd he bring up the California trip? He didn't even want to do the damn thing, yet here he was, talking about it when he was bone-crushingly tired.

Why?

Hadn't he decided, albeit grudgingly to himself, that doing the event was good for both of them? Both their businesses benefitted. Even if he hated dressing up in a monkey suit, the benefits far outweighed an evening of his time.

Only he had gone there.

It was almost as if the quiet in the barn and that weary sense that he'd never get his marriage back—the one he'd had where he and his wife talked and laughed and loved—had pushed him onward. Because weary and tired needed a place to land and his wife made a damn soft spot.

"More like easy target," he growled to himself as he headed for the fridge.

Hadn't it been good once upon a time? There were days he barely remembered it and then there were others—fleeting moments, really—when he remembered it with such clarity he hurt clear down to his marrow.

They'd lived in that perfect state, once for a while, where everything just seemed to *work* when they were together. It was like a decorated Christmas tree. Or newly fallen snow. Or the fresh glow of sunlight after a hard rain.

That perfect state that sort of shimmered there, like a mirage, only for them it had been real. One hundred percent real.

They'd had that once.

And what they had now was a sort of separate existence, even if the world around them thought they were together. Their marriage was the real mirage. One that would have been cloying and oppressive under any circumstance, but under the glow of bright klieg lights and TV cameras, had become suffocating.

The toaster popped, pulling his thoughts away from all they'd lost. Hadn't he spent enough time thinking about it all, already? Hadn't he traced it back in his mind, trying to find the moment that would explain it all? His thoughts drifted, as they did so often, to Jessica. She seemed like the obvious reason, but each time he tried to fit his mind around it, he stopped himself. They'd survived losing their baby. Had grown stronger, even, in the midst of those dark days.

He rubbed a hand over his chest as he turned to get the cold cuts out of the fridge. The easy dismissal of that loss always left him feeling empty and he avoided thinking about it. And what those feelings said about him as a person.

And as a husband.

But *damn it,* he slammed the container of ham on the counter. What else could it be? Because they *had* come through that time. And he had been grateful for it.

Hadn't he been supportive enough of her career? He knew the show was important to her and he was proud of her. Damned proud. Sure, he'd laid down some stipulations on the network, but if he hadn't, they couldn't still safely operate a working ranch. Each of his demands had been agreed to by the show's producers and they'd found a way to work in and around his schedule and those of his ranch hands.

"Zack! Hadley!" Carter Jessup's voice traveled the length of the house from where he hollered at the back door.

"Kitchen!" Zack hollered back, surprised to hear the tapping of heels on the hardwoods. And even more surprised to find Bea Malone tottering forward on her usual spikes, her arms full with what looked to be a heavy box. Zack rushed around to relieve her of it, just as Carter entered behind her, his hands doubly full, a box in each arm.

"What is this?" Even as he asked, laying the box down on the counter, Zack knew his words held more censure and guilt.

"It's Hadley's cookbook," Carter said. "Mailman just delivered them."

"Let's open them." Bea was already reaching for the tape when Zack stopped her.

"Hadley should be here to open them."

"She already did." Bea stopped and stared at

him, blinking. "The first few copies came last week."

Whatever he might think of Bea—and Zack had come to care quite a lot for the drill sergeant–slash–TV producer over the past four years—he knew her to be quick. Sharp, with an ability to read the room faster than anyone he'd ever met.

And it was that skill on full display as she backed away from the counter. "You're right. These books are Hadley's accomplishment. She should definitely be here to open them."

Those heels tapped a few more feet as she edged toward the door. "I also know last night was a long one with the calf so I'll leave you to your lunch."

Remembering his manners, Zack extended a hand. "You don't have to leave. There's plenty here for everyone."

"I'm good." She waved a hand. "And I need to get ready for a quick trip home in a few days anyway for annual network meetings. It's been busy getting the plans done for the last few shows of the season, then getting us wrapped up and I haven't even thought about packing. I'll see you before I leave."

Before he could stop her, Bea was gone, in her usual swirl of activity. But it was the look of deep longing that painted his foreman's face that drew Zack up short. "Carter?"

"Hmmm?" Carter turned back to the counter, his blue eyes clearing quickly as if he caught himself. "Oh. Yeah. Where do you want me to put these?"

"Over by the table's fine. We'll move then when Hadley gets home and can put them wherever she wants them."

"I guess the season will be done soon." Carter's back was to Zack as he settled the boxes where directed, but that odd longing still echoed low in his voice.

The outdoor shots had already been completed, leaving them to wrap up two remaining episodes with only the indoor kitchen scenes left. "Most of the outside crew is already gone. All anxious to get home, I assume."

"Oh yeah. Sure." Carter straightened and turned back to the counter. "I'll leave you to it as well. I, um, have some stuff to do. Before we head back out to get the calf situated."

"Have you eaten?" Zack pointed toward the ham. "Help yourself."

"Nah. I'm good. I need to get going."

Before Zack could stop him, Carter was already heading back the way he came, his fast retreat broken only by a quick goodbye. "I'll meet you over at the pasture in a bit. Help you get that calf back to his mama."

"Sure."

Zack's agreement met nothing but air. Carter was already gone, his pace as fast as Bea's.

Did he still smell? Zack wondered as he spread mustard on his toast. He'd been distracted and tired in the shower. Maybe he'd missed a few spots.

Since Carter and Bea had both run off like the hounds of hell were at their heels, Zack shook it off and took a bite of his sandwich. His gaze drifted to the large box that still sat on the edge of the counter. He was curious to look inside. To see the proof of his wife's accomplishment.

More, to celebrate it.

Only she'd already seen it herself. And clearly hadn't seen fit to share it with him.

Chapter 5

Bea hotfooted it to her car and silently cursed her Stuart Weitzmans. She loved these boots. Hell, she could still remember the day she'd bought them at the Shops at Columbus Circle. She'd spied them in the window and had fallen in love with the butter-soft leather and the way it curved around her calves like a lover's hands.

Which was a hell of an image to have since the thought of a lover brought her right back to Carter.

Nearly four years in Montana and she'd done zero fraternizing with the locals. She knew that wasn't the case with the entire crew, but she'd held herself apart. She'd believed her responsibilities to the show and to her company outweighed getting naked with the cowboys around Rustlers Creek.

Not that there'd been a line of cowboys waiting for her, Bea admonished herself as she sidestepped a large puddle in the driveway outside the house, but she'd felt her responsibilities all the same.

Until that night . . .

Nearly five weeks ago, after a day spent reflecting on all the things she didn't have, including a husband and children. A situation she'd long believed herself used to, until she'd seen a Facebook post from her last single college friend, announcing her elopement in Vegas.

Bea had whipped through her small rented apartment in downtown Rustlers Creek in a cleaning frenzy but even a manic scrubfest with a package of Mr. Clean Magic Erasers hadn't expunged the suddenly massive hole in the pit of her stomach.

Nor had an hour with her production plans for *The Cowgirl Gourmet*. Nor had a tear-filled rant to her younger sister who'd murmured soothing words and hadn't gone down the annoying path their elder sister would have, pressing yet again about how hard Bea worked and how she needed to do online dating.

In addition to her long-standing acceptance that a husband and children were increasingly not in her life plans, she'd long ago accepted that the only avenue married people could come up with for meeting someone was online dating or church singles.

When either of those suggestions failed to meet with shooting, streaming sparks of joy in response—as was often the case with her and Molly—the conversation inevitably shifted. Just like the last time she'd been home and gone to lunch with her sisters.

"You had a chance with John Teasdale, Bea. I still don't know why you let him go."

"Um, because aside from the fact that we weren't particularly well matched, I caught him getting a blow job from my coworker at the office Christmas party."

"He liked you, Bea. He wanted a relationship with you."

"Which he clearly showed by getting his dick sucked off by Kayla Martin."

Even as the words filled the air between them, Bea could have scripted her sister's response.

"And where has all that judgment gotten you, Beatrix?" Molly's exasperation had dripped so hard over her chef's salad Bea was quite sure it would curdle her sister's ranch dressing. *"He liked you."*

"Do we even have the same definition of that word?"

Molly ignored the response, steamrolling merrily into her favorite set of proof points. *"So sitting home instead is the answer? Or roaming around Montana with a bullhorn in hand?"*

Stephanie had quickly jumped in and changed the subject before their lunch completely derailed, but it had left a sour taste.

Not that it was either of her sisters' responsibilities to fix her situation, but if all she was going to get were annoying and judgmental platitudes, she'd rather talk about something else.

Anything else.

Memories of that conversation had haunted her long after Bea would have liked and, combined with the infamous Facebook scroll and the lingering sadness of her crying jag, she'd found herself at loose ends and unwilling to sit home on a Saturday night.

Twenty minutes later she was on a bar stool in the Branded Mark in downtown Rustlers Creek. It was meant to be a quick drink—a chance to get out for a bit—but it had turned into so much more.

That impulsive decision had changed her life.

"Bea!"

Carter's voice closed the distance between them barely before his long, long legs did and she turned around, refusing to cower.

"Carter."

"I'd like to talk to you."

Not "we need to talk" or "can I have a minute?" Just standard nice-guy Carter. Firm. Direct. And leaving no room to deny him.

"Of course. What's going on?"

"Besides you ignoring me for the past five weeks?"

"I'm not—" She broke off because whatever else she might be, unwilling to confront her own petty behavior wasn't it. "Yes, I have been."

"And?"

"And what?"

"I think I deserve better than that." He moved in another step, his impatience telegraphing off the hard lines of his body, along with delicious waves of heat she wanted to reach out and touch.

Or lap up with her tongue.

Pushing down on *that* image, Bea focused on the difficult conversation she didn't want to have. Because it would lead to more difficult conversations when all she really wanted to do was curl up against him, wrap herself in his arms and let the world fall away again.

Since that wasn't an option, she swallowed a bitter pill and started in.

"You do deserve better. But I don't have better to give you. I enjoyed our night—" She broke off, correcting herself as memories of nearly thirty-six hours in his arms filled her mind. "Weekend, together. But it's over."

"It doesn't have to be."

"I don't live here. And in a few weeks, I'll be back home permanently in New York until next season starts shooting."

Home.

Even though it hadn't felt fully like home in quite a while. Which was ridiculous because she was a born-and-raised Brooklynite and hadn't ever seen herself anywhere else. Certainly not Montana. And certainly not in a job that was, by design, ephemeral and temporary, no matter how much time she spent in one place.

Montana wasn't her home. And before long she'd be in her real home, watching the months stretch out in front of her as she grew round with Carter's child.

"I don't care where you live."

"Well I do. I enjoyed our night together. But it can't happen again and talking about it isn't going to change anything." *Oh, and by the way, I think you're wonderful and amazing and if I let myself I could see how easy it would be to blindly fall in love with you.*

"You think I'm only standing here because I want to sleep with you?"

"Don't you?"

"Hell yes. But that's beside the point. I like you, Bea. I enjoy spending time with you. That includes time when neither of us is naked." He did grin then, a cheeky smile that made her knees buckle. "Although if you want to talk to me about the merits of klieg lights versus key lights in nothing but those sexy, silky purple panties of yours, I'd hardly argue."

On any other man it would have been insulting. But on Carter, it was just . . . not. He was a gentleman to the core and the fact that he thought she was sexy was intoxicating. And in that moment, with that cheeky grin and mischief riding high in his eyes the color of a Montana summer sky, Bea nearly gave in.

She wanted to.

Oh, how she had wanted to for thirty-three miserable days.

But images of all that was still unsaid between them stopped her.

She needed to tell him about the baby. He deserved to know and she *would* tell him. But first, she wanted to go to her gynecologist she'd gone to since she was eighteen. She'd made the grand mistake of researching pregnancy stages and when the words *geriatric mother* flashed at her from her laptop screen, a large pit had opened beneath the butterflies she'd been carrying since reading the bold YES on that little pee stick.

So she'd do a quick trip back to New York. She already had an appointment with Dr. Crandall to understand fully what to expect from her pregnancy. She was determined to have this baby, but she needed to know all the possible challenges before telling Carter. She had several other meetings at the network which had prompted the trip in the first place.

Then she'd come back.

And she'd tell Carter all the things he deserved to know.

HADLEY PULLED INTO their cavernous garage and cut the engine. The snow had just started on her drive back from town and she was ready to hunker down with a bowl of the chili she always kept in the freezer. Maybe she'd whip up some corn bread and see if Zack wanted to join her.

Assuming he even wanted to.

A part of her thought about just heading straight upstairs, avoiding him—and the conversation they needed to have—altogether. But he'd also said they'd save it for once they were home from California, so like the impending threat of hail, she was now on perpetual guard for when the skies of her marriage opened up and rained down destruction.

Which made the sight—and smell—that greeted her in the kitchen a massive surprise.

Zack was already at the stove, her big pot on the burner, the distinct scents of chili wafting her direction. A bottle of her favorite red wine sat on the counter, open and breathing, and a large mixing bowl held the dry ingredients for what she was pretty damn sure was corn bread.

What had he done?

Or, maybe more specifically, why?

"Hey." Although she'd stilled when she walked in, he'd obviously heard the garage door and he turned to face her. "I hope you're hungry. I think I went a little overboard on the chili."

She walked toward the counter, affirming that yes, those were the dry ingredients for homemade corn bread. "It's in preportioned containers."

"I opened all of them."

She did a quick tally of what was in her industrial-sized freezer. "You opened six packs of chili?"

"I made the mistake of starting dinner when I was hungry."

His boyish grin, lighting clear up to his warm brown eyes, nearly had her stumbling and Hadley grabbed for the counter to steady herself.

Was she dreaming?

What had happened to her frustrated, angry husband? A state that she'd learned to live with, even as she knew it wasn't even remotely the correct description for the Zachary Wayne she used to know. "How's the calf?"

"He's doing great. Gray checked him out, pronounced him on the road to recovery."

"The vigor of youth," she mused, suddenly aware of the reason for the good mood. "That's great the little guy's okay. News well worth celebrating."

"It is great. But that's not what we're celebrating." He busied himself with pouring the wine and Hadley felt the panic open in her stomach like a wide pit.

The anger that had churned all day, about his casual order they discuss what comes next, erupted.

Was he actually celebrating the end of their marriage? He wanted out that bad? Like this was some sort of farewell meal? How could he ruin her favorite wine and corn bread and chili like that?

Zack handed her a glass, then lifted his. "To your new book."

"My what?"

"The cookbook." He tilted his head toward the kitchen table and the boxes she hadn't noticed. "It arrived today."

Throttling back on the waves of panic that had launched rockets throughout her nerve endings, Hadley fought to compose herself. With a solid sip of wine, she took in the stack of boxes before turning back to her husband. She searched his face but saw nothing other than excitement and overwhelming support lining his smile and filling his eyes.

"Oh. Of course."

"Go on. Open them. I left the scissors next to the boxes."

With one more fortifying sip of wine, she crossed to the table. What had prompted this change? When she'd walked out of the barn at three o'clock this morning, she'd believed her marriage over.

And now?

Now he was acting like nothing had happened, they'd never had words and it was more than two years ago when they were happy and easy with each other.

She slid the scissors through the tape at the top of one box, the move rough and jerky as the barrier gave way easily. Taking hold of herself and trying desperately to stem the twin tides of confusion and assumption, she set the scissors down and reached for the cardboard flaps. Only to find her own face smiling back from her kitchen, standing nearly in the same place Zack was right now.

"Well, bring it over."

Hadley lifted out a copy. She'd already seen the book a few weeks ago and now that she held a copy in her hands once again, she felt petty about that.

Sorry, really, that she'd failed to share that initial moment with Zack.

Nothing to be done for it now, she thought as she handed over the copy.

"You look beautiful." He looked up from his perusal of the cover before opening the book and flipping through. That crisp scent of new paper greeted her and suddenly at a loss for something to do, she pulled the bowl toward her and reached for the eggs. Cracking them into a separate bowl for the wet mixture, she got to work.

Zack stopped on a page and stared up at her. "You included my grandmother's chocolate silk pie."

Hadley had no idea why she felt so exposed, but in that instant, standing across the kitchen counter as they had so many times before, she felt naked. Without protection or armor or any of the multitude of defenses she'd employed as their marriage had shifted from loving support to one of combat and mutually assured destruction.

"Well, yeah. It's your favorite. And it's—" She stilled, her gaze going to the small block of copy at the top of the recipe page still facing up to Zack.

"The one you made the night I proposed."

She let out a heavy breath she had no idea she'd been holding. "Yeah."

Although she hadn't told that specific story in the pages of the book. The night he proposed was still a memory she held tight to her heart, unwilling to share it with the public who seemed endlessly fascinated with her marriage.

Because *that* night. The one that had cemented a future for the two of them. It was all hers.

Or theirs, really, and not for public consumption.

She'd nearly given in when working on the written passages in the cookbook, waffling back and forth on whether she should share those details, wanting desperately to hang on to those happier times. Some strange, abstract thought that if she wrote it down she might be able to will those good times back into her life.

But in the end, she'd opted for something else, choosing to keep close the memories she still held in her heart of the night she'd made his grandmother's recipe. Mamma Wayne had assured her that it was Zack's favorite.

She wasn't nearly as competent in the kitchen then as she was now, but her skills had been coming along. The double boiler portion of the recipe had needed a bit of extra attention, but when the recipe had come together on a practice run, Hadley knew she wanted to make it for Zack.

It had been a surprise for him—one made with love—and it had ultimately set the backdrop for his proposal.

Something she hadn't known as she'd made the pie but which had become evident when he'd jumped up from his seat at dinner, moving around the kitchen in agitated strides. She'd been half convinced she'd curdled the eggs and he was trying to figure out a nice way to let her know when he'd dropped to one knee beside the chair.

The look in those rich dark brown eyes she loved so much had nearly laid her bare.

Longing and love and need and joy. It all mixed in a dazzling swirl richer than the chocolate in her pie and far, far sweeter.

It was that look, one she still saw daily in her mind's eye, that ultimately had her holding back, keeping the proposal out of the cookbook.

In the end, she'd recounted Mamma Wayne's special recipe instead, and how Zack's grandmother had used it to snag her third husband. Because if the public was hungry for stories of her and Zack, they were nearly as eager for stories of Zack's grandmother. A family tale Hadley had recounted in the first season had shot the social media comments through the roof.

Surprised at the sudden interest in the woman who was Rustlers Creek's very own version of Annie Oakley, Hadley had peppered in a few comments two shows later, to the same surprising outcome. Bea had taken the idea and run with it, ensuring a few shows each season had a scene with Zack's wily grandmother. Her publisher was equally interested, already talking about making a Mamma Wayne cookbook companion when this current version went into paperback.

The fascination in Charlie's ninety-two-year-old mother hadn't lessened, either. It seemed to delight Mamma Wayne and it amused Carlene to no end that her mother-in-law had become an overnight sensation as an octogenarian. But in the past three years, America had become almost as enamored with the family matriarch as Hadley was.

"That sassy red head of hers is only going to get bigger, you know." Zack shook his head as he set the book down on the counter. "And won't that be fun to watch."

Although he always spoke of his grandmother with a mixture of fondness and good-natured exasperation, Hadley never failed to hear the love that laced it all.

Which only brought another wave of confusion. What had changed his mood so drastically?

Hadley didn't want to comment on it for fear of picking a fight, but the man standing across the counter from her was vastly different from the one who'd sat opposite her across a cold barn stall the night before.

Do you want to pick a fight or do your own part to appreciate his efforts and enjoy each other?

Oddly buoyed by the internal admonition, Hadley filled muffin tins with the corn bread mixture and walked around to pop the tray in the oven.

And turned around to face the man she still wanted with a passion that scared her at times. The one she wanted to look at her with longing and love and need and joy.

Because after too many days and months and now years of fighting, those were the emotions that still filled her own heart every damn day.

ZACK WASN'T SURE what had changed—or shifted, really—but something had come over him after talking to Gray about the calf. He wanted to lay it at the feet of relief after a hard day of labor and a night spent worrying about his stock that things felt like they were back on the right track, but he knew that wasn't it.

He wouldn't call himself a pessimist, but raging optimist was never a moniker anyone would lay at his feet.

After ruling out worry for the calf, he'd spent the rest of the afternoon wondering about that weird, charged atmosphere between Bea and Carter. There was something about knowing Hadley had seen that cookbook a few weeks ago and hadn't shown him that bothered him. A fact Bea had clearly recognized.

These were the things he and Hadley used to share. Together.

And now they happened with other people in their lives, cold and devoid of any sense of the pride or accomplishment they used to feel when they experienced them together.

Wasn't he guilty of that the night before? She'd come out to the barn to help him. To be his partner, even if it was just to wait it out and see if the calf was okay. And how had he repaid her for the partnership?

Suggesting they needed to take a trip he really didn't want to take and then talk about their future when they got home.

Dick move, Wayne.

He owed her an apology for that one. He'd even been working up to it as he put the chili on to cook and uncorked the wine.

Only now . . .

He snuck a glance her way, at the soft sweep of hair that fell behind her ear, brushed back as she set plates at the table. God, she was beautiful. Luminescent, really.

He wasn't a fanciful man. He knew the land and the earth and nature and was a realist about it all. Seasons changed. Animals—and humans—got sick. Sometimes they got better and sometimes they didn't. People aged.

But Hadley was special.

She was his partner. He'd understood that from the first moment he'd met her, everything inside of him shifting as he realized this was a woman he could share all those things with.

The change of seasons.

His work.

His life.

Was he going to compound last night's jerk-fueled attitude by bringing it up now? And screw up what felt like the first good mood between them in far too long?

Hell no.

Instead, he pushed those lingering feelings of frustration down with all the other things they left unsaid and did his best to continue on as he'd begun.

With the desperate hope that he could share an evening with his wife.

That things weren't so far gone between them that they couldn't get them back.

And while chili, corn bread and wine wasn't exactly a lover's feast, it felt safe.

Comfortable.

And a place he wanted to return to with his wife.

Chapter 6

"The entire pan of ranch chicken. On the ground in the front yard?"

"All of it." Hadley nodded, laughing at the incredulity painting Zack's face as she shared the memory of their first week of shooting the season they just wrapped up. "I thought Ted was going to sob. And I didn't think strong, grizzled TV directors born and raised in Secaucus, New Jersey even knew what tears were."

"You made extra, though, right?"

"Not for that shot. So we used what was in the freezer. Which"—she reached for her glass—"nearly made your father cry when he went hunting for a casserole later that week and couldn't find his favorite."

"He does love his ranch chicken."

"He made do instead with the tater tot breakfast casserole your mother forbids him to eat."

"For his dinner?"

Hadley considered her wine and what she was comfortable sharing. She knew Charlie and Carlene's marriage wasn't an easy subject for Zack. But backtracking on her story now would call unnecessary attention to that fact, even as she was loathe to have a repeat of their harsh words the night before in the barn.

"I assume so," she said. "He mumbled something as he dug it out of the freezer that he was going to eat what he wanted to eat."

"That sounds just like him. And more evidence of his old man spite that he didn't just go home and have dinner with Mom."

Hadley considered her wine for one more moment before deciding to go for it. She and Zack had always known how to talk to each other and the foundation of that was that they'd always been honest. If it backfired on her then so be it.

"Deep down, I think he knows that. And he's stuck because he doesn't know how to make amends for his behavior."

"Which only makes the last six months worse."

Zack's ready agreement bolstered her, and she took heart that their nice evening might remain on track.

"He should just apologize and be done with it," Zack continued. "This pouting and hiding from Mom is getting real old."

"He'll come around."

She didn't miss the skepticism that clouded

Zack's gaze but he said nothing as he poured the rest of the wine in their glasses.

God, how she'd missed this. Just sharing time at the end of the day. As their simple meal had progressed, the conversation flowing through any number of topics, she'd forced herself to calm down and enjoy it. Those shots of panic that had lanced through her nerves when she'd walked in had finally faded, the easy conversation, good food and rich wine going the rest of the way toward relaxing her.

Yet even as she thought it, Hadley knew that wasn't quite true.

It was Zack.

For all the reasons he knew how to set her on edge, he also knew how to take smooth those edges away. He was her refuge and her calm in the storm and when she was with him, things were just better.

More, somehow.

Like she was exactly where she was meant to be.

Their conversation tonight had only reinforced those feelings.

Still steeped in the glow, she tilted her head toward the far side of the kitchen. "Speaking of goodies I store in the freezer, I have one of those chocolate silk pies stashed away in the fridge. It was supposed to go in the freezer this morning and I forgot to wrap it up."

"You do?" Zack's dropped mouth and the sudden avarice that lit his deep brown eyes had her laughing. "How'd I miss it?"

"Probably because it's stuck behind a bowl of brussels sprouts."

"Did you do that on purpose?"

She shot him a side-eye on her way to the refrigerator. "What do you think?"

"You're as bad as my mother."

Although the comment was in clear reference to Charlie, Hadley heard the humor in Zack's words. "Special things are no longer treats if we have them every day."

He'd followed her to the large counter, his gaze waiting for hers as she looked up from settling the pie on the counter. Something had shifted.

No, she corrected herself.

Something had *heated*.

That avarice was still there, but it was edged with the marked signs of desire. "I think you underestimate my powers of appreciation."

Shocked by the answering tug low and deep in her belly, Hadley turned back to the fridge and the large carton of whipping cream in the door shelf. She'd never stopped wanting Zack but something in that dark, swirling pull of desire scared her.

To want him so badly. To feel that answering pull of desire so clearly . . .

Damn it, but it put a woman at a disadvantage.

And while she'd never kept score where the two of them were concerned—and most certainly not in the bedroom—she also needed to keep her head. She was operating on a sleepless night and the assumption her husband wanted to file for divorce in a matter of weeks. It would be easy—God, so easy—to abandon those worries and just take what was being offered. Here. In the moment. With Zack.

"Chocolate silk pie *and* whipped cream?" Zack slapped a hand to his chest. "Why'd you let me eat so much chili?"

Hadley allowed her gaze to drift over his chest. The long-sleeved T-shirt did nothing to hide the broad chest and shoulders. And she already knew the hard cut of muscles over his stomach could handle a bit of an extra indulgence when it came to rich chocolate and even richer cream. "Like you're going to turn it down?"

"Hell no."

"That's the hardworking cowboy I know and love."

As the word *love* lingered between them she busied herself with getting the metal mixing bowl and whisk she used to make whipped cream by hand. She did love Zack and she knew he loved her. The bigger question—one she'd avoided thinking too hard on over the past year—was if he was still *in* love with her.

A wildly different state that spoke of action and feelings and a sweetness that outweighed any dessert.

Conscious that her mood was at dangerous risk of turning very, very sour, Hadley headed for the cabinets, only to find Zack beat her there. His large body blocked her way, the oversized bottle of vanilla she'd been in search of in his large grip.

"Thanks."

He bent his head ever so slightly and her breath caught in spite of herself at his nearness, as hints of saddle leather and fresh air lingered beneath the simple scent of soap. "You're welcome."

She headed back to the counter, making quick work of the carton of cream and the vanilla, avoiding the usual addition of sugar she normally put into whipped cream. The pie was sweet enough and years of making the cream for it had proven that lack of sugar made for the best accompaniment.

Only she'd suddenly stopped thinking about complementing the pie. Instead, all she could envision were dabs of that whipped cream all over her husband's abs.

Not that that was a bad thing, per se, but why now? She had spent the entire day miserable, contemplating her life without him. Now she was considering jumping him? After a few glasses of wine, a bowl of chili and some corn bread?

Ignoring the twisting emotions, Hadley began whisking the thick liquid.

When she was in the kitchen, she felt in control. When she was handling food, she always knew what to do. Like an underlying instinct, it was the one place where she never doubted herself.

She knew when to mix and when to leave something to rest. How to temper eggs or melt chocolate in a double boiler or braise meat. Just how much sugar to add to yeast and warm water to jumpstart Mother Nature.

Here, she was in control.

Something that had become increasingly necessary as the rest of her life had slipped out of control.

"I can do that for you if you want." Zack's voice broke into her thoughts.

"You want to make cream?"

"Nah, I just want to be a big manly man and show off my forearms." With a wry smile on his face, he shoved up the sleeves of his T-shirt, exposing all that tanned expanse of skin.

Hadley laughed in spite of herself, the forearm thing a running joke between them ever since the show had taken off.

"Joke all you want," she said pushing the mixing bowl and whisk toward him across the counter. "But there are actually several websites and Facebook fan pages devoted to your forearms."

The comment had its desired effect as a distinct shade of red crawled up his neck.

"Where do people get the stuff?"

"Oh, I don't know." She eyed the muscles flexing in those much-rhapsodized about forearms. "You are nicely built, Mr. Wayne."

"I spend all day outside, handling animals in the neighborhood of half a ton or more. I'd better have some muscles."

That blush had only grown deeper, his motions with the whisk harder and more erratic against the metal of the bowl. Although it was fun to tease him, she had to admit his reaction was a bit unexpected.

"Why does that conversation always make you nervous?"

"I'm not—" He broke off, staring down at the peaks of whipped cream that had formed in the bowl. "Yeah, I guess I am. It's weird, is all."

"Most men would enjoy it."

"Preening assholes who don't have to get ribbed about being a pretty boy while they try to run a ranch, maybe. Not me."

She should have realized it bothered him. They'd joked about it and she'd always sensed he had a layer of discomfort about it all, but here, now, she saw a new side. And with it, Hadley finally recognized the truth. Zack might have an ego as healthy as any other man, but he wasn't—and never had been—an attention seeker.

"I leave that public bullshit to Jackson," he'd told her in their early days of dating when his younger brother was in the midst of a hard-core college football recruitment campaign that had brought any number of scouts and reporters to their small town.

"Aren't you excited for him?"

"Sure I am. He's worked damn hard for this. But it seems like a lot of fuss for someone to have to put up with. Too much of it can mess with your head if you're not careful."

Hadley hadn't fully understood it at the time, but she'd come to see the truth in those words. Her life had grown bigger than even her wildest imaginings over the past five years. Yet through it all, she was still herself.

Hadley Wayne, maiden name Allen. She was a wife and sister, a daughter and a born-and-bred Montanan. The same girl that liked the smell of doughnuts frying and the Tilt-A-Whirl at the summer county fair and Christmas morning and the first Montana snowfall each year.

The attention that had come with her show wasn't simply unexpected, it was foreign, somehow. Like a version of herself she watched from a distance.

"I'm sorry, you know."

"Sorry for what?" Despite the direction of their conversation, he seemed genuinely confused by her apology as he swiped a finger in the bowl to take some whipped cream.

"All of it, Zack. The silly fan websites. The attention. That stuff that gets so out of control."

He took his index finger from between his lips, his Adam's apple working around the helping of cream. Acknowledgement reflected from his eyes, a gentleness layered beneath.

"I know none of that is your fault." His voice was low, quiet, but the sexual heat that had tinged their conversation had faded. In its place was simple, raw honesty. "Your dream comes with a lot of strings, and I understand that. Most of the time, it really doesn't affect me."

"Doesn't affect you?" She stared up at him, curious that this was his take. "It affects you all the time. We just finished a long shooting schedule that had people crawling the property from one end to the other. Strangers come to town and people try to come out to the ranch and poke around. To our home. Now we have to take a trip to California in the run-up to the holidays." She could only continue staring at him, unable to fathom his sudden casualness. "It affects you, Zack."

"Yeah, but it's not that bad."

Hadley knew she had been off-kilter since she'd walked into the house but damn it, she was confused. The distance between them that had felt impassable, nay, impenetrable, for the past few years had seemingly faded for the evening. She didn't know why, and she was so afraid to lose it.

But she also needed to see this conversation through.

"Of course it's that bad. Isn't that we've been dealing with for the last two years? Isn't that why you and I barely speak to one another half the time?"

Isn't that why you want to leave?

It was on the tip of her tongue to say the words, but Hadley held them back. Somewhere, in the deepest recesses of her heart, she was so desperately afraid to put *that* into words.

Just like all the other things they held back from one another.

Like the family they'd wanted once. That was a conversation that never seemed to land, flitting away like a frightened bird when they got too close to it.

How many moments had they lost to anger and frustration by the simple act of leaving so much unsaid?

All the touches they'd never get to experience, lost in a sea of reckless resentment and unspoken antagonism that confused even as it seethed and roiled between them.

And worst of all, Hadley admitted to herself, all the wasted time they'd never, ever get back.

ZACK KNEW HE'D overstepped but had no idea why. He'd told her things weren't so bad. And he meant it. The show was a pain in the ass, but it wasn't awful. And it had brought a lot of good things to Wayne and Sons as well as to the entire damn town of Rustlers Creek. Hadley had *built* something here.

Something that had roots and a foundation and seemingly endless creativity that allowed it to keep growing and changing, evolving and becoming . . . *more*.

Why was she suddenly mad about it all?

And worse, why did she seem so nervous? They were an affectionate couple, always had been. But each time he'd moved in close she'd skittered back, like a colt shying away from its handler.

Which was ridiculous because his wife wasn't an animal, nor was he someone who needed to "handle" her.

Only . . . Zack faltered for an answer to the strange impressions swirling through his mind. Because no matter how he tried to come up with another image, it still felt that way.

The familiar resentment churned, and Zack forced it back. Bitterness and irritation had become a toxic brew that he'd given far too much air to and it had to stop. Wasn't that what had really bothered him all day?

He wasn't a dick but his behavior in the barn last

night suggested otherwise. And then the sight of her new book—one she hadn't shared with him—had only cemented the feeling. He played a part in what was going on between them and it was about time he owned up to that. But damn it, he was *trying* to make amends. Hadn't he'd spent the whole night trying to make it better?

Where had he fallen short?

Because as he stood there, staring down at the woman he loved with everything he was, all he saw was hurt. And, if he were totally honest, a mirror image, reflecting back at him from deep in those gorgeous green eyes, of all the things he pushed down or waved away or just flat out refused to acknowledge.

The marriage he wanted wasn't the one he had.

How had it all happened?

While it was convenient to blame it on a camera crew crawling the ranch and a busy schedule, that wasn't really the problem and Zack knew it. It was simply an excuse.

"Why are we fighting?" Her voice was low, edged with a hoarse laugh. "I thought we were on the verge of sex yet we're right back where we always end up."

His pulse spiked at the mention of sex, but he pushed that back as well. Sex, while complicated, was easy all at the same time. It was a binary act. You had it or you didn't.

But talking?

Sharing?

They'd obviously danced around far too many conversations that needed to happen.

"I don't want to be fighting, Hadley. I want to be talking to you. Sharing something with you."

"Why now? What changed tonight?"

He nearly stopped right there. And, if given the chance, would have gladly faced down another herd of upset mamas outside in the pasture to avoid this conversation.

But she deserved it.

And damn it, so did he.

"What changed was I came home this afternoon to find boxes of books you created and when I wanted to wait for you to open them Bea mentioned you'd already gotten an advanced copy a few weeks ago."

"Bea was here?"

"She and Carter came into the kitchen with the box. Earlier, after I came back in from the sick calf. She let it slip that you got a copy a few weeks ago. Something you'd created and should be proud of and I hadn't seen it. And—" He stopped, that edgy feeling that always precipitated a fight swelling in his chest.

Once again, he willed it back. Like the sex, anger was easy. It was a whip-quick emotion that fired out, setting a blaze over everything in its way. But it was a coward, too, hiding the real root of the problem.

And she deserved better.

Hadn't that advanced copy of the book proven it?

On a hard exhale he added, "And you didn't share it with me for a reason."

"I'm sorry."

"It's fine." When she made to argue, he pressed on. "It is fine. It's not the end of the world and a lot of stuff goes on around here in a day. But it felt like a neon sign, you know?" He edged a finger at some cream that had stuck to the upper lip of the bowl. "Like I wasn't paying attention to the important things."

Hadley moved closer then, the hesitation he'd seen over the past few minutes fading as she laid a hand over his chest.

"Why do we keep coming back to this place?"

"What place?" His voice was scratchy in his ears and even as he knew what she asked, somewhere inside he needed to hear her say it.

Needed to know she was as miserable as he was. As confused as he was why all they'd had together had seemingly vanished.

He nearly asked if it was because of the baby but stopped himself. They didn't talk about those days and, if he were honest, they'd moved past that loss. Their marriage hadn't started going downhill until after their lives became so chaotic. After The Cooking Network took up part-time residence on their ranch. After they'd healed together from losing Jessica.

Somewhere in all that time, as he'd puzzled through the challenges in his marriage, he'd begun thinking of Hadley's miscarriage as a cop-out or an excuse if he tried to lay their problems at the feet of an innocent life.

So he kept it to himself, never giving voice to the question.

And waited to see what she'd say.

"This place where we don't know how to talk to each other anymore, Zack? Where we don't know how to *be*?" The emphasis on that last word was nearly his undoing.

Hadn't that been the miracle of their relationship? All his life, he was the eldest son. The heir to a ranching dynasty. The one who wanted to follow Charlie Wayne into the business.

And he had wanted that.

Wayne and Sons was a part of him. The land his family had ridden for four generations was so deeply embedded in his blood there were days he didn't know where the land stopped and he began.

But with Hadley . . .

With her it had all made sense. Those things were a part of him, but they didn't define him. Or better said, they didn't have to be the only mark of who he was. With her he could be goofy or serious or even a raging asshole and she was still there to navigate life with him.

Until she wasn't.

Until it became patently obvious they couldn't breathe the same air without sniping at each other.

And until he'd had to admit that the things keeping them tethered together were memories instead of day-to-day living.

She moved in closer, her arms settling on his shoulders before her hands met at the nape of his neck. "When did we stop just being?"

He bent his head, his forehead pressing to hers. "I don't know."

"Can we stop trying to figure it out for a little while? Can we just have tonight? Chili and corn bread and good wine and chocolate silk pie?" She shifted so that their gazes met, steady and still. "And sex without all the baggage we keep carrying around?"

His hands tightened at her waist, his fingers flexing and fisting in the material of her jeans. God, he wanted that.

It wouldn't erase all that had come before. And it wouldn't fill all the conversations they still needed to have. But couldn't they both take this?

Just for a little while before the world intruded once more.

"I'd like that."

"Me too."

And then her lips met his and what had been gentle, even tentative, shifted in a flash of heat lightning.

There were still things left unsaid. Lots of things. But he had his wife in his arms. And maybe he could show her all the things he couldn't find the words to say. The ones that clogged his throat and lay buried, somewhere in the vicinity of his heart.

Hesitation and caution vanished as if they'd never been, as heat and need and something elemental and raw took over both of them. He'd felt the insistent tugs of exactly this emotion the other day, when they'd been shooting outside and he'd kissed her over the barbeque. He'd felt it again, sitting there across from Hadley in the barn.

But here.

Now.

There was nothing in the way of seeing those emotions through. Not a horde of people, each and every one with their eyes trained on them, not to mention three cameras capturing their every move. Or a hundred-and-sixty-pound sick calf between them. Or even his parents and all the other individuals who made up life on a working ranch.

Right now it was just the two of them.

And Zack was determined to take.

To take the moment for both of them.

He tugged the material of her blouse from her jeans, heat rising off her skin where his fingers slipped beneath the hem. He skimmed lightly over her flat stomach, the quiver of flesh beneath his fingertips as much an answer as the light sigh that feathered against his lips.

Those sighs turned deeper, hotter, when his hands drifted up to cup her breasts, his fingers caressing the hard points of her nipples through the thin silk of her bra. Zack felt his control slipping, shifting dangerously into the overexcited lust of a teenager, at finally having Hadley back in his arms. Willing himself to slow down, he drifted his hands once more, settling on her hips before lifting her up to sit on the edge of the counter.

He was going to take this slow, damn it. Set the

pace of a mature man who knew how to pleasure his woman.

"Zack?" Hadley purred his name against his ear, her seat on the counter giving her the height advantage. One she quickly used to wrap her legs around his waist.

"Hmmm?" He hummed his answer against the soft, tender skin of her neck while his hands began a return trip to her breasts. She answered in kind, pressing the fullness of her flesh into his palms, even as she continued to croon against his ear.

"I can't wait. Not now. Not tonight."

He looked up at her then. Desire filled her green gaze, evident in the inky blackness of her widened pupils. Her hair fell around her cheeks before falling over her shoulders in a luscious tangle, that brilliant red haloed by the overhead lights in the kitchen.

He'd give her anything in that moment.

Save one.

"I don't think so."

Hadley tightened her legs around his waist, the move drawing her core even closer, the jean-clad apex of her thighs fitted tight against his stomach. His own body hardened even more—a feat he hadn't believed possible—as he felt the heat rising off her body and transferring against his like a brand.

Her hands brushed against his as she reached for the hem of her blouse. She shot him a saucy side-eye as she began to draw the material up her body. "You don't think so?"

He stilled her movements then, his hands covering hers and stopping the upward progressing of her blouse. "I have a better idea."

Before she could even ask, he was in motion. The blouse—one he knew she had in a different shade—was bunched tight in his fists. He pulled hard, the material splitting down the middle, leaving nothing but gorgeous flesh open to his view.

"Zack!" His name came out on a hard rush of surprise, but he caught no anger there. Just a subtle bemusement as her widened eyes maintained their hypnotic grip on his.

Without warning, something flashed in his mind's eye. A juxtaposition, really, to the disheveled state of his wife, her thin blouse hanging in two over the pert rise of her lush breasts and that same heartbreaking face, smiling back over the same expanse of counter, on the cover of her book.

A book he hadn't seen until today.

It was cave man in the extreme, but for the life of him, he couldn't stop the insistent need that pushed him into motion. Couldn't stop this damned insistence that he make her moan, wild with need.

For him.

Only him.

Right here, in this very spot.

It was raw and elemental and maybe it had to be, Zack considered as he sought the button of her jeans. With deft movements despite the trembles in his fingers, he unclasped the button and had the zipper down, his hand dipping inside the opening of both jeans and her panties. Her breath caught on a hard rush as his fingers unerringly found her hot, slick center. Suddenly mad with it, he pressed in one finger, followed by a second, caressing those hot folds.

The demanding woman in his arms changed, shifted, *transformed* really, as his fingers worked her flesh. Her demands increased, even as her breath grew shallow and her head fell back with the increasing pressure he built inside of her.

He knew this woman. Knew her laugh and her smile, her moods and her ire. He also knew her body. Nearly ten years together had taught him what she liked and what made her feel good and what made them feel good together.

But this . . .

Zack watched as Hadley took her pleasure. He inhaled her, the intoxicating scent of her arousal adding to the sensual feast playing out beneath his fingers. He pushed her on, as if he could somehow brand this moment on every one of his senses, erasing the feeling of emptiness and embarrassment he'd had earlier, looking at that damn box of books.

The bright lights of the kitchen overheads hid nothing. This was no quiet lovemaking in the dark or even a fun romp out by the pool on a summer's night. This was raw and real and he could see it all as it happened. As it unfolded, brilliant second by brilliant second.

The subtle tightening in the muscles of her neck as he pushed her harder, pressing for the pleasure he wanted to see with his own eyes. That he wanted to feel, wrapped and pulsing around his fingers. That he wanted to hear in her increasingly ragged moans.

The pink flush over her pale skin, visible in her face and neck and over that pretty expanse of cleavage he'd exposed, growing deeper as the threads of desire tugged harder and harder inside of her.

The dropped lids of her eyes, masking and shielding the vulnerability at his ministrations.

It was that last that he couldn't allow.

Not when he felt so raw and achy, in control of the moment yet so out of control in his skin. So desperate for her he could only be thankful he had the hard, immovable pressure of his zipper and the hard press of the counter against his hips.

He wanted to be buried inside of her so damn bad, yet he refused to stop watching her, even for a moment. He needed to see her come.

Right here. On the counter where America watched his wife cook and bake and talk about their ranch life like it was some magical fairy tale.

He needed *this*. His own damn fairy tale. With the wife he loved so much beyond himself he didn't know how to live anymore.

He wanted the life he'd had *before*. Before the things he couldn't name and had no words for or even a fucking idea of how those things that had broken the two of them had existed.

He wanted . . .

Hadley's scream of pleasure punctuated the moment, raw and satisfying as her interior muscles fastened around his fingers, her body bucking against his palm where he cupped her. Zack wrapped his other arm around her, holding her close, even as her trembles of pleasure shook hard against him, trapped between his chest and the forearm holding her in place.

And there, in those bright lights, he held her as her pleasure crested like shock waves in the suddenly quiet kitchen.

It was only as that quiet continued, like the sudden deafness after a bomb blast, that Zack recognized what he'd done. What he'd shit-stirred beyond all reasonable imagining.

What had begun as mutual enjoyment and pleasure between them had altered, once again. Only this time, it hadn't been words or silence, it had been action.

Selfish action that claimed her pleasure for his own, without any of the mutual benefits of lovemaking.

He'd branded her, but he hadn't made love to her.

And he fucking knew it.

And so did Hadley.

"Did you get what you wanted, Zack?" Her quiet words were scratchy, still laced with the throes of passion. Only underneath it all, he also heard the hurt. "You finger fucked me to prove a point, right?"

"Hadley, no, it's not—"

Remorse sharp, he removed his hand from her body, gently slipping past the elastic of her panties. He was about to say it wasn't like that, only it was exactly like that.

It hadn't begun that way, but it sure as hell had ended that way. And now he had the overwhelming need to pull her close but she was already slipping from his side, scooting aside before jumping off the counter. He didn't miss that her legs were shaky as she sidestepped her way around the counter, but he said nothing more as she slipped from the room.

Even if he couldn't take his eyes off the stiff lines of her slim back as she walked through the doorway. Or as his gaze lingered on the space where she'd been.

They'd wanted each other and even in the midst of all that churned-up need and desire, he'd still managed to mess it up.

Dropping onto one of the stools they kept against the counter, Zack braced his hands on the marble of the countertop. When he came into contact with heat, still lingering from her body, he dropped his head to the counter, willing some of it to enter his cold heart.

Fuck, shit and damn.

Why had he thought sex was easy?

Chapter 7

Hadley lay in the spare room bed, her eyes on the ceiling for the second night in a row.

Oh, who the fuck was she kidding? It was her bed and it had been her bed for nearly two freaking years. Calling it the "spare room" was nothing more than hurt pride.

And since she was nursing a whole damn heart full of it, she might as well give it a name.

The correct name.

It's real name.

She was sleeping in *her* bed, in a room that wasn't also her husband's because he slept down the hall. It was high time she started to admit it because the disaster of an evening she'd just had was solidly imprinted on her mind.

And, damn it all, on her body too, based on how her clit still throbbed from his touch.

Her husband had given her the world's greatest orgasm, all to prove a point.

It hadn't started that way. In fact, things had progressed between them *because* the evening was so familiar. Achingly so.

How things used to be. When they could both seamlessly shift from talking to each other to laughing together to loving one another. She'd seen it in his eyes. In the relaxed set of his shoulders. Even in the way they'd talked about his father without it becoming some sort of red flag for all her own ambitions somehow luring his mother to work at the Trading Post.

Even the sex had started out mutual. Very mutual, she admitted to herself when she considered the hard press of his body where he'd fitted between her legs.

Zack had wanted her. Until he'd needed to prove something.

Wasn't that what hurt?

Or is it that you took and took because it felt good and you wanted to prove a point, too?

Those words slithered beneath her anger like some sort of truth serum. And once she acknowledged them, Hadley had to finish the thought because the one person she hated lying to the most was herself. And she'd been doing a damn fine job of it for the past year.

Her phone dinged, the face lighting up with the incoming message. Although she wasn't interested in talking to anyone she snagged the phone off the end table almost in reflex.

YOU UP?

Her sister, Harper, had impeccable timing, as usual. She could ignore the message, but the older sister in her refused to leave her baby sister hanging.

YEAH. YOU WANT TO TALK?

The phone rang almost as fast as Hadley had hit Send on the message.

"Hey. Sorry to bother you and Zack. I realize it's getting late." Harper's voice spilled out of the phone, all rapid efficiency and no nonsense.

"I'm good. I mean, it's fine. I can talk."

"How is your hot cowboy?"

It had been a joke between her and Harper since Hadley had gone on her first date with Zack. Even before, if she were honest. When she was working at the coffee shop downtown he'd come in and flirt with her and the hot cowboy moniker had been how she'd first described him and had somehow stuck between the sisters. Long before the rest of the world had created Facebook groups fussing over how hot her husband was, Hadley had done the very same.

"Oh, he's as hot as ever."

Liar, liar pants on fire, that little voice taunted her again, even as a bigger part of her wanted to break down and confess all to her sister. Because lying or not, she *was* dealing with a serious case of pants on fire and was having a hard time coming up with any answers on how to solve the problem on her own.

"Are you okay?"

Harper's question was sharp and on point and Hadley fought being mad at herself for answering the phone. "I'm fine, why?"

"You sound all throaty. Like you were crying."

"I'm not crying." Which was entirely true, even if she'd spent the past hour wondering why she hadn't shed a single tear over her sex-gone-sideways with Zack.

Even as she wanted to fake her way through it, she weighed the idea of just giving voice to her feelings and talking to Harper about what was going on. Of just letting out all the ire and upset and damned sadness it felt like she'd been carrying around forever.

"You sure?"

The temptation passed and on an inward sigh she refused to give air to, Hadley added, "Yes, I'm sure. I had some wine with dinner and my throat's a little dry."

The answer seemed to be enough to satisfy her sister because the take-no-prisoners tone suddenly changed, Harper's voice thickening on the other end of the line. "Oh, Hads. I'm done out here."

"Done? Done with what?"

"Work. The job. The endless rat race that never gets any better and really is just full of rodents."

It wasn't a new conversation between her and Harper, but for the moment, Hadley was happy to have something else to focus on.

"So what do you want to do about it?"

"I did something about it. I quit."

Hadley sat straight up in bed at that bit of news. "You did?"

"Yep. Marched in three days ago and resigned. Handed in my laptop and my badge and told them I wasn't coming back."

"What did they do?"

"Called security and showed me the door."

"No way."

"Yep. Almost a decade of my life and it ends with a security escort off the property."

Hadley considered what little she knew of her sister's job. It was easy to say "she worked in tech in Seattle" but that sort of covered half the population of the city. And try as she might, Harper usually got about as far as the words *cloud computing* and *server farms* before Hadley's mind spun. That one time Harper had mentioned something called *Kubernetes* Hadley thought her head might have actually exploded just a bit. She admired her sister and her amazing brain, but she had no idea how it worked or how Harper kept track of the various items that rolled around in there.

All she did know was that Harper had left Montana almost ten years ago and hadn't looked back. She'd buried her heartache in software and technology and had made a damn nice life for herself.

A happy one, Hadley wasn't quite sure.

But a nice one all the same.

She'd judged that lack of happiness for a while, until her own life had started to come apart at the seams. And in those fraying strings she'd begun to understand her sister in a different way. There were a lot of paths to experience heartache. And some days, Hadley admired the way Harper had simply walked away from it, removing herself from the source.

Removing its power over her, too.

"You there?"

"Oh yeah. Sorry. And wait," Hadley said, coming back to the conversation. "You said three days ago. What have you been doing since then and why haven't you called me?"

"Um. Well. Because I did a thing."

"What kind of a thing?"

"A bit of a gamble."

Although she didn't know exactly how much her sister made and didn't need to, she knew Harper was well compensated and had a nice life in Seattle. A condo downtown and a luxury SUV and, best as Hadley could tell, a nest egg courtesy of all those late hours and cloud computers.

Or software for cloud computers.

Did computers sit in clouds?

She shook her head, ignoring the usual mind scramble at the details. "Please tell me you didn't go blow your future in Vegas. Because you might have had fun but I'm the one who is going to have to listen to Dad gripe about it."

"I didn't go to Vegas and I'm not talking about blackjack or roulette." Harper took a deep breath. "I bought a coffee company."

"Don't you live in the place with the biggest coffee company in the world? In fact, can't you see their building out of your living room window?"

"Only on a clear day."

"Smart-ass." Undeterred, Hadley pressed on. "And haven't you always said that Seattle is obsessed with coffee and that there was a cup to be found on every corner?"

"I did. But mine's going to be better."

"How?"

"Because I'm going to make it better. And I'm going to use all that technology I know about to figure out what my customers want."

"With coffee?"

"Yes."

Hadley wanted to ask more questions but, aside from Zack, the only human in the world she wouldn't bet against was her little sister.

But coffee? In Seattle? Wasn't that like starting an ice business in the dead of winter?

Even as she considered the risk, Hadley already recognized the reward. It was in the lighthearted happiness she heard in Harper's voice. Something she hadn't heard since the days when her sister still lived here and had been in love.

With Gray.

With her own bitterness from the disastrous sex—almost sex?—with Zack still lingering on her skin, Hadley settled back into the pillows.

If there was one thing the Allen girls had figured out in spades, it was their entrepreneurial spirit. Maybe if she listened to Harper's ideas she could figure out a way to help her sister get her new venture off the ground. She needed a signature blend for the Trading Post, after all.

Might as well start close to home.

And if talking to her sister and planning a business venture took her mind off her hot cowboy and his damned clever fingers, all the better.

ZACK DIDN'T KNOW what to do with himself. He'd tried TV but he'd never been a huge baseball fan and had zero interest in the two teams engaged in a playoff battle. He considered watching his brother's football game, recorded from the previous Monday night, but his little brother usually put him in a ripe mood, even if it was just watching him prance across a TV screen.

He loved Jackson, don't get him wrong, but most of the time he didn't like him all that much. His relationship with his brother was his biggest failing outside of his rapidly disintegrating marriage and Zack wasn't up for revisiting one more fuckup this evening.

Which was how he found himself heading for the stables, with its welcoming smells of hay and whickering horses the only place in his mental list of things he could do to waste time that managed to stick. He briefly considered saddling up Lucy or Ethel but thought better of it. The mares were strong, even-keeled mounts, more than willing to roam the property in the dark, but he wasn't up for a ride.

He wasn't up for much of anything except

spending the evening with Hadley but he'd gone and fucked that up to hell and back.

And why?

Why had that damned book bothered him so much? And why, when he'd gotten his wife in his arms after what felt like forever, did he let something so stupid and worse, insanely prideful, stand in his way?

"It's awfully late to do paperwork." His father's voice radiated out from the depths of the barn as Zack made his way down the long row of stalls.

"What are you doing up?"

"What I've been doing for the last six months. Killing time."

Zack didn't miss the hints of remorse in his father's voice, or how dangerously close Charlie's plans for the evening were to Zack's own, but he left it alone. He loved his father and could tell his old man anything, but tonight . . .

Tonight, something held him back.

He hadn't spoken of his marital problems with anyone and with his emotions this close to the surface he wasn't about to start now. But he did recognize a kindred spirit in Charlie Wayne's rheumy gray eyes, staring back at him across the remaining length of the stable.

"You want a drink then."

Something lit in his father's gaze. "You have hooch in here."

Zack couldn't hide his surprise at the question. "When haven't we had hooch in here? You always had a bottle of good Scotch in your bottom drawer." Zack shrugged coming up beside his father. "I've just carried on the tradition."

Charlie laughed at that. "I *used* to have a bottle of Scotch in my drawer until your damn fool brother broke into it with his friends. Threw up six ways to Sunday with that dumbass Tommy Claridge all over my stable floors."

Zack considered his earlier thoughts of Jackson and decided to let the comment slide. He was aware raising children wasn't easy and figured raising six would tax even the most patient soul, but Jackson had given his parents a full-on run for their money. If he didn't have a ball in his hands, occupying his time, he was doing something irritating, ill-advised or flat-out reckless. Where Zack had always found his solace with the animals and the wide-open spaces of the ranch, Jackson wasn't content with any of it.

And after a while, that lack of contentment had morphed into a clear veneer of resentment.

Not for the first time, Zack figured his brother was exactly where he needed to be, more than fifteen hundred miles away in Houston. It would have been nice to have a relationship with him—to have him closer—but maybe that wasn't in the cards for the two of them.

Or for any of them.

Pushing the weight of it all to the back of his mind, Zack went to the oversized oak cabinet in the corner of his office and opened the thick varnished doors. The bottle of Pappy Van Winkle he kept stashed in the back seemed like a good choice for this unexpected chat with his father and he pulled it from the cabinet.

"Woo-hoo, look at you, fancy pants." Charlie let out a low whistle as he caught sight of the label. "That's not just hooch. That's a felony waiting to happen sitting in here in an unlocked cabinet."

Zack shrugged even as he remembered opening the expensive gift from Hadley the prior Christmas. "It's just a bottle of booze. If someone needs it that bad they're welcome to it."

Funny enough, he meant it. Sure, the liquor was expensive, but it was still just an indulgence. A lovely one, to be sure, and especially thoughtful as it came from Hadley. But it was an indulgence all the same. A momentary enjoyment that their professions had wrought. He appreciated it, but if someone felt the need to take it, he wasn't losing sleep over it.

That bottle sure as hell wasn't keeping him warm in bed tonight.

"That's awful generous thinking." Charlie nodded. "And it's also a sign of what a good staff we have here. We've got a few loners, and that's fine. A man's entitled to keep his own council. But it's a good team overall."

Zack considered his ranch hands. He knew them all by name and made a point to get to know each and every one, but he left much of the day-to-day management to Carter. The man knew how to hire well and he also knew how to nip small problems before they became big ones.

"That we do. A fine credit to Carter, it is."

Since Zack never quite knew what version of his father he was going to get if they talked about ranch business too long, he switched to one of the few safe topics between them. Crossing back to his desk, Zack settled the glasses and the bottle on the aged wood. "I haven't watched Monday night's game yet. Heard it was a good one."

"Real good. Bishop's having a kick-ass season so far and he's been spreading the ball around. Jackson had a few really good catches, though not as many as he should have." Charlie frowned as he reached for the glass Zack had filled with a generous pour. "No TDs this week, but still, a solid game."

Since his brother usually got more than "a few good catches" he nearly probed for more details but opted to leave it alone. It would only lead to questions about whether or not he was watching the games this season and he'd missed a few.

"To solid games and their path to the playoffs." He lifted his own glass and tipped it against his father's. "To a good season."

"To a good season." Charlie took a sip, his eyes closing on that first, solid taste. "Wow, this is really something."

"Hadley got it for me for Christmas."

"She's quite a woman."

Zack stared down at the amber liquid filling his glass. "That she is."

"So what the hell are you doing out here with me instead of sitting inside, cozied up with her?"

Zack considered confessing all—or mostly all, he amended to himself, his sex life with his wife nothing he'd share with anyone. But something held him back. Talking about it meant he'd have to speak the words into existence about what an asshole he'd been lately and he just couldn't go there.

Not when he knew just how in the wrong he was.

So he did what he usually did when either of his parents crept too close to the edges of his marriage.

"We finished up dinner a little while ago. She needed to get a few things done and I headed out here."

"There was a time you never left that house after dark."

The comment hit way too close to its intended mark and Zack fought to keep his voice even.

Level.

As if it was no big deal he was sitting out here shooting the shit instead of doing all that cozying up to his beautiful wife. "Yeah, well, life and work gets in the way sometimes. For both of us."

"I suppose it does." Charlie glanced down at his glass. "Sorry if I'm keeping you from something."

"A drink with my father's a lot of something." Zack smiled across the expanse of the desk where they'd both taken seats. "And time well spent."

"Well then." Charlie coughed and Zack didn't miss the slight mist that veiled his father's eyes.

They sat quietly, enjoying the company and the very stellar liquor, the sounds of the horses a gentle backdrop. It was nearly out of his mouth to bring up what had been bothering him when Charlie started in.

"Heard you were heading to California."

"Yeah. It's a trip Donnelly set up. He sold a line of our grass-fed prime to Total Foods. He's been aiming for their fresh gourmet section for the past few years and got in after Archer and Mead pulled out."

"Amateurs." Charlie shook his head, no small measure of disgust setting his lips in a straight line. "Archer's been screwing around with his product for too long. Finally caught up to him. And that's damn public, losing an account like that."

Zack considered his father's words, disappointment spearing through him at the way things had been ever since he told his father he didn't want him physically working the ranch. This was what he wanted. A business partner who understood the industry and its players as if the details were as easy as breathing air. *This* was what he needed Charlie doing. Not fretting his ass off that he couldn't ride the ranch, roping heads of cattle.

But like everything else in his life, he left it alone. They were having a nice moment and flagging the reasons he valued this conversation to his father would be akin to waving red in front of those very same heads of cattle.

"That may be so, but his bad business is our very good business. Bryce has been waiting in the wings for this opportunity and swooped in the moment he saw an opening."

"Sounds like Donnelly closed the deal. What're you going for?"

"It's a two for one."

Zack took a sip of his drink, willing his tone to stay even and level. Casual.

Very casual.

Because his old man might be rather chilled-out tonight but Zack knew his father missed nothing.

"They worked out a deal to do an exclusive on Hadley's new cookbook with the same retail chain. We're both going to be a part of Total Foods' annual sales conference and managers meeting. Hadley's book will be featured in all their stores with an exclusive promotion for their shoppers."

"Look at you, my boy." Charlie slapped his knee, his smile broad. "Don't know what I'm worried about an expensive bottle of hooch for. You and Hadley are playing in the big leagues."

"I guess."

Charlie leaned forward over the desk, his grin broad and a lightness flashing in the depths of his eyes that Zack hadn't seen in far too long.

"You guess nothing. You're playing in the big time. I'm proud of you. Both of you."

"Thanks, Dad."

"You don't need to thank me." Charlie waved his free hand as he lifted his freshly filled glass. "But you do need to listen to me."

"About what?"

"You and Hadley."

"Me and Hadley what?" Again, Zack fought to keep his voice casual, even as he was pretty sure he'd missed that mark by a mile.

"You get that girl to California and spend some time away from here. It'll be good for you. For both of you."

"Good to leave home? Our home?"

"A home can be a prison if you spend too much time in it."

Charlie leaned forward then, all hints of a smile vanished as if they'd never been. "It's about damn time you did something about it. Something away from prying eyes and cameras and too many well-meaning family members who don't know their heads from their asses."

"It's not like that."

"It's exactly like that." Charlie lifted the hand that held his glass, the amber liquid flashing all sorts of gold in the dim light of the office overhead. "Which is why you have to go. Fix this before you end up like me. Old, nasty and stuck sleeping in a bunkhouse instead of with the woman you love."

Chapter 8

Zack zipped up his dopp kit and dropped it into his rollaboard. He nearly had the suitcase closed when he remembered the tie he'd wanted from inside his closet. Crossing to the large oversized monstrosity of a closet that currently sat three-quarters empty with all of Hadley's stuff down the hall, he easily found the bow tie that went with his tuxedo.

Fix this before you end up like me.

His father's words had rattled around in Zack's mind like hail in April, a near-constant drumbeat since they'd had their talk in the barn.

Since the night he'd managed to fuck up sex with his wife, insulting her beyond measure.

Since the night he'd had to admit that his father had seen far more in Zack's marriage than he'd given the old man credit for.

It was a humbling piece of advice and one he'd

had no ability to put into practice because Hadley
and Bea had spent days turning the kitchen upside
down with recipe ideas for a live holiday special
the network decided to do at the last minute. Three
days of the most amazing aromas of cookies and
pies had morphed into a late-breaking trip to New
York for a week of prep meetings and visits with
advertisers.

The most he got out of all of it was something
about boosting ratings, but as far as he could tell,
all it seemed to do was boost stress levels. Didn't
TV networks plan their Christmas schedules further in advance than six weeks?

Apparently not, when advance sales for a holiday cookbook topped even the strongest, most
bullish projections, Zack had come to discover after a hallway discussion with an unusually fraz-
zled Bea.

Which meant the apology he'd worked on, over
and over in his mind, for the jerk move on the
kitchen counter never manifested. And now here
he was, staring into a wasteland of a closet with a
fucking tie in his hand.

One he hoped like hell his wife would deign to
tie for him because he had no earthly idea how to
do it himself. A situation that hadn't improved despite an hour with four different YouTube videos
the other night.

He'd nearly called Donnelly three times over the
past two days to cancel, claiming a ranch emer-
gency. It had only been the knowledge of how
damned hard Bryce worked for Wayne and Sons

and the extraordinary opportunity he'd landed for
them with Total Foods that had kept Zack from
making the call.

That and the idea that he was actually going
to get to spend time with Hadley. Enforced time
where they had to be nice to one another because . . . of course, there was an audience.

And if it chapped his ass that they had to have an
audience to muster up something close to détente,
well, it was what it was.

And it was still better than his nasty ass deserved.

"Zack!" Hadley's voice drifted back toward the
closet and he left the cavern of disappointment,
snapping off the lights as he went.

She stood by the open doorway to the bedroom,
waiting for him.

"You can come in."

"Oh. Okay."

They'd exchanged the basics over the past three
weeks and she'd texted him each day from New
York, but they hadn't actually spoken beyond polite platitudes since that fateful night over chili and
corn bread.

And here she was, asking if she could enter
her own bedroom? Every time Zack thought he
couldn't be surprised or hurt by their situation,
something new reached up and grabbed him by
the throat.

She glanced toward the open suitcase. "You
look ready to go."

"Just about. We're heading out early tomorrow."

The grocery chain had offered a private plane

for him and Hadley but taking that level of luxury didn't sit well with him. The chain was carrying Wayne and Sons beef, which meant he stood to profit well from the arrangement. If he wanted to fly private that badly he could pay for it himself.

In the end, it hadn't mattered. Hadley took care of their tickets and had them on a 9:00 a.m. out of Billings. It was first class—her notoriety had increasingly limited their ability to fly coach—but it was still commercial.

"Which makes what I'm about to ask that much harder. But the guys really want to take us out for a little bon voyage drink."

Zack had already talked to Carter and had considered heading over to the Branded Mark for a few beers. His team had been working hard and they were all excited about the opportunity with Total Foods and what it meant for the ranch.

"You want to go?"

Hadley shrugged and Zack couldn't ignore the shot of attraction that curled in his belly at the slim rise of her shoulder. Nor could he miss how her blouse slipped to the side, showing the edge of a silk bra strap. "I hadn't really thought about it, but Bea seemed pretty insistent that I go."

"Bea wants to go out?"

"I know, right?" Hadley's smile grew wide. "You can't get her to sit down for two minutes at a clip and suddenly she wants to go out for the evening. But she's been working so hard with this last-minute show the network threw at her. I feel bad to disappoint her."

Something small and petty lodged in his throat. She didn't want to disappoint Bea but spending more than a week out of the house and another week buried in work was okay?

And once again, you've descended into alpha asshole territory. Worse, Zack corrected himself. *Alpha asshole with a toddler tantrum complex.*

His gaze alighted on the tie where he'd tossed it onto the top of the pile of clothing in his open suitcase. He'd spent the past three weeks feeling bad about his behavior to Hadley. He'd topped that off with a miserable hour spent attempting to tie his tuxedo tie, his hands about as graceful as an ape's.

Yet here he was, with an invitation from his wife to go have a few beers, and he was going to pick a fight or consider turning her down? To do what? Sit home alone?

A home can be a prison if you spend too much time in it.

As his father's words floated through his mind's eye, Zack nodded, a sudden lightness hazing over that ill-timed shot of bitter. "And I feel bad disappointing Carter. So I guess we're going out tonight."

Hadley's smile was bright in return.

"I'll get my purse and meet you downstairs."

How do you expect to hide a pregnancy in a bar?

That question had taunted Bea through the afternoon, as she wrapped up emails to her boss, to the network brass and to one of the Cooking Network's sales leads who was near to closing a deal with a major packaged goods company to sponsor Hadley's holiday show.

Bea smiled to herself at their latest request, on top of the discount their ad agency was pushing for. Bea didn't want to do the sales team's job for them—and avoided sales meetings as often as possible for that very reason—but she'd run the traps as requested, confirming with Hadley if she'd be willing to use three of the company's ingredients in one of her segments.

Her favorite TV star's easy going "yeah, sure, I can make that work" made the email she had to send back a simple-enough chore. But she couldn't resist making a point to confirm that the use of the ingredients—and their presence on Hadley's famous kitchen counter—should offset any further price discounts for the in-show placement.

Satisfied she'd done what she could, she turned her attention to her wardrobe, a series of "why am I drinking a club soda" excuses floating through her mind.

She could use the excuse that she had to fly tomorrow. Her flight was technically two days away but if she got home from the Branded Mark after midnight it wouldn't be an outright lie. She could also try the whole "my liver's already going to get a workout from the work holiday party" to snag a pass.

"Or you can be a grown-up and have a club soda if you damn well want one," Bea muttered to herself as she dragged one more outfit out of the closet.

Although she wasn't showing yet, she had felt a thickening around her middle. Her clothes still fit, but they were increasingly snug. Opting for a flowy blouse she'd picked up for that upcoming holiday party, she pulled it on, then reached for her jeans.

"They *will* fit," she muttered to herself as she pulled them on. Even if they were the loosest pair she owned. With a quick twirl in front of the mirror, Bea considered her image reflecting back. Her high-heeled boots would go a long way toward lengthening her out and, thankfully, the Branded Mark didn't go in for major overhead lighting.

She wasn't even sure why she was going, only everyone at the ranch wanted to send Hadley and Zack off before their trip to California. And much as she wanted to find an excuse not to go, Carter's insistent purr in her ear for those two minutes he got her alone in the big house—that she join them or risk leaving Hadley as the only woman stuck with a table full of cowboys—had seemed reasonable at the time.

Eminently reasonable.

Even if a series of sparks had erupted the length of her spine, nearly setting her clothing on fire.

Or maybe that was just her traitorous body?

The pregnancy hormones were a bitch. She was either crying or so damn horny she wasn't sure who she was any longer.

"You're Beatrix fucking Malone," she muttered as she trekked back to the bathroom to retrieve her favorite lipstick. "You're cool, calm, collected and accomplished. You can *do* this. You'll handle it all, just like everything else in your life."

Even if big fat tears kept cropping up, unbidden and plopping onto her pillow as she tried to fall asleep each night. The ones that kept company with the whispered questions of "how" she was going to do this.

All of it.

The baby. The job she couldn't find a free breath around. The crushing weight of desire she had for Carter . . .

The swift rap on her front door was a surprise—and a welcome distraction from another round of tears—and she snagged the lipstick off the bathroom counter, hotfooting it back to the front room of her small apartment. Had Hadley swung by to get her? They'd agreed to meet at the bar, but that would be just like Hadley to think of her, keeping her from walking over to the bar alone, even if it was only a few blocks.

Bea pulled the door open, shocked to find the object of her desire, framed in her doorway.

And oh, what a sight it was.

Carter Jessup stood there, in all his cowboy glory. Long jean-clad legs. A chambray shirt that looked so soft she could literally feel it beneath her fingertips. And a twinkle in his eyes that made the sun-grooved edges crinkle along with his smile.

She'd never considered herself drawn in by the mythos of the American cowboy. She had never even seen a Western and, if she were honest, she'd even questioned the initial offer of producing *The*

Cowgirl Gourmet, thinking she was better served managing one of the network's food competition shows or the other location shoot offered to her, a behind-the-scenes show set in a trendy Chicago kitchen.

In the end, it had been Hadley's enthusiasm and charm that had won Bea over and she'd found herself on her way to Montana, a place she'd never even thought she'd visit in her lifetime. A place that wasn't nearly as full of wilderness as she'd expected, but which was well and truly "the West," from the Western wear shops that greeted her at the airport to the wide-open land that housed the Wayne and Sons ranch.

And it's foreman, Carter Jessup.

"Hi." That lone word came out a little breathy and Bea fought a grimace, instead searching for an excuse. "Sorry. Ran from the back of the apartment."

Those crinkles grooved a little deeper as Carter made a show of looking past her. "It's such a long way to run, too."

And damn the man, she thought, with no small measure of frustration. He knew exactly how large her apartment was because he'd been inside it. The same weekend he was inside of her.

Since that train of thought wasn't going to get her anywhere productive, she cleared her throat. "Yes, it's small but I still ran in my heels."

"An impressive feat." That smile never wavered but he did extend an arm. "You ready to go?"

"Go where?"

As answers went, it might have sounded like a cop-out, but in Bea's defense, she had no earthly idea what he meant.

A fact punctuated by Carter's frown. "To the bar. Zack and Hadley's bon voyage."

"Oh. Yeah. Right." She waved a hand, the nearly forgotten lipstick still in her fist. "That's why I was running. I almost forgot my lipstick."

"That would be a tragedy." His smile dipped slightly. "You shouldn't run, though. It's dangerous."

Bea had nearly turned to grab her purse from a small table by the front door when his question caught her up short. Did he know? About the baby? What did he mean?

Was it possible he'd figured it out?

She ran a self-conscious hand down the side of her blouse. "Dangerous? How?"

"You run around in those heels like you're on a mission. One of these days, you're going to fall."

"I've got good balance."

Carter moved in then, his large frame seeming to take up all the space around her. Beside her. Next to her. "You sure about that?"

He never touched her. Yet in that moment, caught up in his gaze, Bea felt her world tilt.

It had done so nearly two months ago. Hell, it had happened the first time she'd laid eyes on him.

But here.

Now.

Those heels she was always so sure of—and so self-assured on—began to wobble.

"See?" His hand came up to grip her elbow, holding her steady. "Dangerous."

Her chest squeezed once more, that lack of breath far more dangerous to her health than four-inch heels.

Tell him.

The urge nearly overwhelmed her, right there in the hallway, where they'd kissed and touched and stripped each other of their clothes.

But she couldn't do it now.

They had Hadley and Zack's impromptu party. And she had the sudden pressure of a live show to produce. And . . .

And she was stalling.

Because despite the fact that she was carrying a very healthy baby, courtesy of the most amazing man she'd ever met, she still hadn't figured out a way to tell him.

So with a small smile, Bea stepped back, planting one foot firmly behind the other until she'd put a bit of distance between them.

"Danger averted," she said with a bright smile before turning to get her coat.

Well aware she'd avoided more than just a fall.

HADLEY WAVED IN the direction of the scarred wall-length bar at the back of the Branded Mark, the quick shouts of "hello!" and "'bout damn time!" and "look what the cat dragged in!" greeted her and Zack as they made their way inside. The shouts were all friendly and a solid reminder of just how long it had been since she'd been here.

Since she'd been anywhere, really, where people actually knew her. *Her.* Hadley Wayne. Not The Cowgirl Gourmet.

Not that she was complaining, but it wasn't until peanut shells crunched underfoot and the distinct clacking of pool balls meeting rose up into the air that she realized something so simple.

When was the last time she'd gone out? With people she knew to a place she knew? When was the last time she and Zack had done anything together?

Although she still wasn't over the events that led up to—and came after—her kitchen counter orgasm, the time since had given her some distance from the situation and that immediate smack of emotions. And while it was all well and good to stay pissed, she owed it to herself and to Zack to have it out about what happened in the kitchen.

About all the ways it went wrong.

Which there hadn't been time to do with the live holiday show and running off to New York. But they had time, these next few days. And she'd be damned if she was leaving California without having this discussion.

"You want a drink?" Zack leaned in, pressing his lips to her ear to be heard over the noise.

"Yeah." She nodded, even as a wave of heat flooded her veins. Even with the lingering anger she'd nearly shaken off, her hot cowboy could still get to her. "A beer. Whatever they've got on tap."

He nodded before heading off to the bar and she saw Bea waving from a large table the guys had gotten in the back.

Gar had a seat opposite her, but his attention was firmly focused on the rousing game of pool taking place at the baize-covered table next to them. One full of trash talk and a lot of boasting, even evident from across the bar. Hadley headed her way, hoping to relieve Bea of the unrelenting testosterone pulsing around her.

"Look at you, sitting here with a passel of cowboys."

Bea stood and gave her a quick peck on the cheek, a wry smile lighting the angles of her face. "If my friends in New York could see me now."

"I think they'd be jealous."

Bea's gaze drifted over the group of men, all collected together around the pool table, as she sat down. With Hadley's arrival Gar got up to join them and, Hadley had to admit, they made quite a sight. "I think you're right."

Hadley still remembered her first meeting with Beatrix Malone. She'd convinced herself that the street-smart, sophisticated New York producer was going to take one look at her and run. Bea's reputation as an up-and-coming talent at the Cooking Network was stellar and Hadley had been prepared to develop a working relationship only.

Which made the friendship they'd built— together—that much more surprising.

Bea was everything she had expected. Street-smart. Tough. Hard-driving. She was also warm, kind and endlessly funny. She had a wry, slightly sarcastic temperament that never veered to nasty or unkind.

And she had just enough moxie and storytelling ability to keep them all in stitches. When she wasn't, of course, marching around in four-inch heels, bullhorn in hand. Although even then, she managed her fair share of zingers, just at twenty-five decibels higher than normal.

The juxtaposition of Bea's city life with the wilds of Montana was an endless amusement. An amusement that had been visited back on Hadley with her trip last week to New York. To take Bea's place in the fish out of water scenario the woman had found herself in for the past four years.

"I'm glad to see you tonight, but I'm surprised you came out. The last few weeks have been sheer madness."

"I figured it was time to let off a little steam. And despite having so much still to do, I'm not sure I can take another night of staring at my show notes."

Not for the first time, it struck Hadley how overwhelming Bea's job could be at times. Something she'd observed over the years, since beginning *The Cowgirl Gourmet*, was the great satisfaction that suffused everyone when a show wrapped. It was something she saw in the crew. A sort of jubilation at a job well done.

A job that was finished.

But as executive producer of the show, Bea's job was never really finished. And while Hadley's circumstances were somewhat similar, she also recognized she was not only paid a hell of a lot better as the person front and center to the public, but she had the luxury of having a lot of people do a lot of things on her behalf.

"Do you ever just want to walk away?" It was serious conversation and probably not particularly well-placed for a fun evening out of the bar, letting off steam. Only now that the question was out, she couldn't exactly pull it back.

"Not walk away, per se." Bea's face was serious as she chose her words. "I'm incredibly grateful for this job. I know that I'm lucky. And it's something that I want. Something I've worked for for a long time. But I'd be lying if I didn't say some days were harder than others."

"Or some seasons?" Hadley asked with a grin when she reached for her beer.

"Yeah." Bea smiled. "Some seasons is right. And a kick-ass cookbook for Christmas definitely qualifies as one of those."

"People seem really excited about it."

Bea grabbed a handful of peanuts from a small pea green bowl on the table. "The early feedback on the cookbook is through the roof. You should be really excited about this. It's next-level sort of stuff."

Next-level.

Which was what the roller coaster of her life had been for the past four years. Not that she was complaining. Like Bea, she fully recognized how lucky she was.

But there were some days where it felt like blowing up a balloon. She kept pushing air in and in and in some more.

Wasn't it going to pop?

"The marketing people have been beside themselves," Bea continued on. "And thank you for agreeing to that ingredient list. Sales texted me they closed the deal with that packaged goods company and your agreement was what stuck the landing."

"That's great."

Hadley considered the meetings in New York, conjuring up the handful of people who'd sat around the Cooking Network conference room. "Were they the ones on Tuesday or Thursday?"

"Tuesday. They had that really serious research guy who kept going on and on about your demographic."

"Oh yeah!" Hadley took a sip of her beer, remembering the man in really tight pants and a skinny black tie. "He kept talking about panks. I had no idea what that meant so thanks for reminding me. I've been wanting to ask."

"It's me. I'm a PANK."

"Excuse me?"

Bea smiled, but it was easy to see how it never reached her eyes. Hell, Hadley amended, it was actually more of a grimace.

"It's an acronym. Professional Aunt, No Kids."

"Oh." Although the two of them could—and often did—talk about anything and everything, Hadley saw the red flags immediately. And while she knew she needed to tread carefully, the low simmer of outrage at such a name overrode her willingness to keep quiet. "It seems rather insulting. Why was he so insistent on bringing it up?"

"It's a trendy marketing term right now. The toy companies love it and all market to the demographic, too. They claim these women buy a lot of the expensive toys. Clearly out of the depth of their professional pockets and the lack of buying them for the children they don't have."

"Okay, I was vaguely insulted before. Now I'm sort of grossed out by skinny-tie marketing guy who can shove his sexist demographic up his too-tight pants-clad ass."

"Be careful now." Bea dropped an empty peanut shell onto the table, the grimace fading as a fierce smile took its place. "You, my dear, are wildly popular with PANKs."

"I prefer to think of them as strong, kick-ass professional women who require no definition and buy whatever the hell they want. For whomever they want, including themselves." Hadley took another sip of her beer as the acronym ran through her mind once again. "Wait a minute. What about men? Aren't there professional uncles, no kids?"

"Punks?" Bea asked, the smile back in full force.

"Well, yeah," Hadley said, even as she started laughing at the name. "There should be punks if there are panks."

"I've yet to find one." Bea brushed her stack of peanut shells to the floor. "They're all either married or fucking their way through Tinder."

"There's nothing in between?"

Bea's gaze shifted quickly—so quickly if Hadley hadn't been engaged in the conversation she'd have missed it—to the heap of cowboys over at the pool table. "Nope."

Hadley hadn't walked a mile in Bea's incredibly awesome shoes and if she'd recognized a red flag she was willing to barrel past before, she did slow down for this one. Hadn't Harper talked about similar frustrations?

Frustrations Hadley didn't understand because they'd been so far from her own experiences. She'd begun dating Zack in her early twenties; had known of him even longer with both of them growing up in Rustlers Creek. Even with their age difference, she *knew* him.

What would it be like? To look and look, yet continue hitting walls that held no answers?

Bea was more than a demographic. So was Hadley's sister. And so were all those "marketing quintiles" skinny pants had rambled on and on about as he coveted their disposable income.

So were she and Zack, Hadley realized, as her gaze drifted to the team assembled around the pool table. Hadn't she spent nearly every event over the past decade—with family, friends or professionals—being asked when she was having a child? When she and Zack were going to have a family?

They'd tried and, like Bea's and Harper's own brick walls, run into one of their own. A terrible, awful wall that still caused a layer of bone-deep fear and sadness she had trouble even thinking about, let alone attempting to scale once more.

So she'd found new dreams. New outlets. And in the process, she'd found herself again.

Even if she'd increasingly lost Zack.

Or what they'd had when it had just been the two of them. When the pressures of their jobs and lives and dreams were enough.

Before the questions. Those endlessly repetitive ones that seemed like a lighthearted tease but instead poked and jabbed and damn it, *hurt*. For Bea it was terms like *PANK*. And for Hadley it had been those social moments of intrusion and inappropriate, misplaced curiosity about when she'd start a family.

"Those pants really were a fashion monstrosity."

Bea's comment was enough to pull her out of the increasingly sad thoughts, even if Hadley hadn't quite caught the swift change in conversation. "What pants?"

"Skinny-ass marketing dude." Bea made a face, her eyes crossing as she stuck her tongue out.

"Yeah. Well." Hadley picked up her drink, lifting it in a toast. "Fuck him and his marketing spreadsheets. Let's toast to real women with real lives and a shit-ton of ambition."

"Here, here!" Bea reached for her own drink, lifting it in a gesture of toast, and Hadley registered what looked like club soda in the tall bar glass. It was a surprise, but she quickly lifted her own glass higher and clinked. Bea did consume alcohol. Hadley had seen plenty of instances of that over the past four years—but kept any question about today's lack of drink to herself. Alcohol was a surprisingly personal subject far too many people made public. Just like those obnoxious event questions she hated so badly.

But still . . . Hadley wondered.

And as she considered the lack of drink, had to admit that Bea had avoided any drinks the prior week at their work dinners, too. She'd made a vague comment about a late night of work ahead of her on one occasion but hadn't mentioned it on the other.

But she hadn't been drinking then, either.

As that thought hit, another knocked her back even harder. One that began to take shape and form as Bea's gaze caught Carter Jessup's once more across the wide expanse of the pool table.

Chapter 9

Hadley was practically quivering as Zack dropped another round of beers off at their table. He'd had his last already and had switched to Coke in order to take the responsibility of the drive home, but since he'd agreed to being designated driver for the evening, he'd been more than happy to snag his wife another draught.

And the way she kept catching his eyes, attempting to telegraph something, had him laughing to himself.

Just like old times.

Even if he had zero idea what she was all keyed up about.

"Yo, Wayne. We know she's a looker but are you going to keep making eyes at your wife or are you going to play pool?"

Zack turned toward one of their newer hands, Drake Washington. The man had proven himself immediately invaluable since joining Wayne and Sons, working the long hours without a complaint and having a way with the animals that was nearly spooky, he was so gentle yet firm. He had a good-natured attitude and sense of humor to boot, which had quickly ingratiated him with the team. "Can't I do both?"

The man's face split into a wide grin. "I really do like your style. Which is why I'm going to do some multitasking myself."

"How's that?"

Drake nodded toward the corner of the bar as he moved up to take his position at the pool table. "Way I figure it, if I keep smiling at that bachelorette party over there, I might see what happens with that sexy, fit bridesmaid. She looks like she's going to need consoling after holding the bride's hair back in the bathroom."

The bride-to-be had belted back a significant number of shots already, so Drake's outcome was rapidly heading toward a fait accompli, in Zack's estimation.

"You're a giver, Washington."

"I am, I am." Drake proceeded to knock three balls in from various angles, his swagger around the table growing more pronounced with each successful drop in the pocket, before tanking a corner shot.

"Sucks to be you, Washington." Zack took his place at the pool table, his gaze drifting unerringly back to Hadley. She had her head bent toward Bea's and they were talking animatedly about something.

It was only as her eyes caught his, just before he was about to line up his shot, that his breath caught.

Held.

And he had the oddest moment of drifting outside his body. Above it, really, as the tableau of the bar spread out around him. He saw that bachelorette party in the corner. Saw his ranch hands, all gathered around the pool table in various conversations of their own. And he saw Hadley, her conversation with Bea momentarily halted as he met his wife's gaze, the two of them reconnected across the darkened space that smelled of beer and peanuts and heat. A sensory trifecta overlayed with the pounding beat of a band, coalescing into a sweet sort of Saturday night ritual.

All that had consumed him for the past few years had been about what they'd lost. But maybe he had looked at it all wrong. Maybe, somewhere, they'd stopped trying.

He certainly had.

"You've really got it bad, my friend." Carter's deep voice was low, likely unheard by others in the midst of the din, but it was enough to pull Zack from the reverie of the moment.

"I what?"

"You've been lining up that shot for about a minute now. Why don't you make your excuses and get the hell home?"

"You afraid I'm going to kick your ass at pool?"

"Nah." Carter slapped him on the back. "No chance of that tonight."

As if to prove otherwise, Zack tore his gaze off

his wife and lined up his shot. The ten ball was primed and waiting for him where Drake had already lined it up.

Nice. Easy. Simple.

Zack pulled back and nailed the cue ball, leaving a light dusting of green chalk on that ivory white surface.

And sent the eight ball straight into the right side pocket instead.

The hoots of laughter were swift and immediate, a fitting punishment for the social sin of unmitigated arrogance and pride-fueled boasting.

He should have been embarrassed. Hell, a younger version of himself likely would have been.

But when he saw Hadley's head thrown back, laughing along with the rest of them, he could only join in. With easy movements, he tossed his pool cue to Carter—a move his foreman caught easily—and headed for his wife.

Hand extended, he stared down at her where she still sat next to Bea. "You ready to get going? We've got an early day tomorrow."

Her laughter had faded, but the broad smile hadn't. And in that moment, he felt something he hadn't felt in far too long.

Hope.

"I think that's a good idea."

She reached for his hand and as his fingers closed around her smaller one, their palms meeting, that hope unfurled a bit more.

It was only as she stood, wobbly on her legs, that she reached forward with her free hand to steady herself against his shoulder. "Whoops. Those draughts were good."

"I'd think so since you had four."

The smile drooped to a frown as her forehead wrinkled in thought. "I had three."

"You had four," Bea hollered after her. "And two whiskey chasers."

Zack saw the look of unholy glee on Bea's face, where she remained primly perched on her own seat. She didn't look drunk at all and that's when he realized there wasn't the same line of empties in front of Bea as there were in his wife's now-vacated seat.

Interesting.

And in that moment, he had a vague clue what Hadley might have been eyeing him about.

"You ready then, Whiskey Chaser?"

Hadley's hand hadn't left its perch on his shoulder. "I thought you'd never ask."

CARTER JESSUP CONSIDERED himself a patient man. Partially, it was a quirk of his nature, a product of genes and upbringing and who he was meant to be as a human. It also was a quality that made him good at his job. Although animals needed a firm hand, there was a degree of unpredictability about them that could never be fully accounted for. Patience went a long way toward handling that unpredictability.

And while he had no interest in comparing Bea Malone to a cow, he had to admit the quality had come in handy with the woman as well.

Patience, however, had its limits. And he was about done with his.

The bachelorette party had directed increasing interest in their direction, enough so that various members of his party had moved over to begin mingling with the women as female ritual and rite of passage gave way to a normal Saturday night out on the town. It gave him the perfect opportunity to mingle with Bea under far less scrutiny.

"Glad you came out tonight. It looks like you and Hadley had fun."

"We did." She had already stood and was making a show of gathering her purse and coat from behind her chair. "I appreciate the invitation tonight. It was a lot of fun. But I should get going."

"I'll walk you then."

"You don't have to. It's only a couple blocks."

"You really want to argue about this?" He quirked a brow at her, maintaining that damnable patience even as it chafed to have the argument at all.

Precisely because she wasn't an animal to be handled, it bugged him that she seemed to have developed this skittish reaction to his presence. And it bothered him even more now that there was so much more to be said.

"No, I don't want to argue." Bea smiled and the gesture reached her smoky gray eyes, even if her light sigh was audible.

In minutes she was bundled up and they were walking back to her apartment, snow lightly falling around them. "Thank you for walking me home. Even if the news didn't properly prepare me for this snow eventuality."

"That's because you're not producing it."

She shuddered, slightly bumping into him with the movement, and Carter didn't think her reaction had anything to do with the sudden blast of cold. "News? No thank you."

"Not a fan?"

"Of watching it? When necessary. Of producing it? No way."

"How come?"

"News producers get minimal sleep, they have to check and recheck sources and they broadcast endlessly depressing topics. Not my jam."

"So cooking is?" He reached out for her hand, tucking it in the crook of his arm as he stared down at her. "Your jam, that is?"

Bea nearly stumbled again and he was pleased when she didn't remove her arm. He wanted to touch her, pure and simple. But the snow had already slickened the ground and her heels were basically pointy death traps as they walked down the sidewalk. *Thanks, Mother Nature.*

"For starters," she said as she looked up at him, beginning to walk again, "cooking wasn't so-not-fun news. And it was also the internship that worked out after college. Cooking Network always hires a crop of summer interns and I got lucky."

"Luck is college debt and an unpaid internship in New York City?" At her surprised look, he said, "I'm no expert on the entertainment world, but coveted jobs are usually incredibly hard to come by."

"That they are. So yeah, I got lucky and my paycheck was proof of that."

"Minimum wage?"

"Not quite with all the overtime. And it was an opportunity and a chance to prove myself."

"Which you're still doing. Admirably, I'll add. I've seen ranch hands after a day of branding cattle that haven't worked as hard as you."

Bea came to an abrupt stop, tugging hard on his arm. It was enough to catch him off balance and he held tight to her as he righted himself on the slick sidewalk. "You okay?" he asked, concerned.

"I'm shocked, actually. That you noticed me working around the ranch."

"How could I miss you? You and Hadley are like the TV dream team. You're moving faster at eight at night wrapping up a day of production than you are when it all starts at eight in the morning. I've questioned whether or not you sleep." He decided to go for broke and lowered his voice to a whisper, bending his head so that his lips brushed her ear. "Even if I was lucky enough to see proof that you do."

She pulled back slowly, but where he expected to see frustration, he saw something else. The mirror to his own need as she stared up at him.

Was he surprised she was attracted? No. The chemistry between them was palpable and he knew it. But it was the inevitability that limned her gaze that really caught him.

And then he was simply mesmerized as her hand lifted, brushing snowflakes off his hair.

"I didn't go out tonight so things would end this way."

"I did."

Her eyes widened at that but he pushed on, taking full advantage of the quiet moment between them. "I'm not going to pretend, Bea. I like you. Hell, more than like you and I'd like to see you again. I don't want to intrude on your life and if you want me to back off just say it. But until you do, I'm not inclined to take your silent treatment as proof we should ignore what's between us."

"It's impractical."

"Life's impractical. If that's your only excuse I think we can work around it."

"I live in New York and you live in Montana. That's real, Carter."

"So's the baby you're carrying. My baby."

Time seemed to stretch out and then fold in on itself as she stared up at him. Her face was so clear to him in the light of the overhead lamps on the main thoroughfare through Rustlers Creek. A street he'd grown up knowing, just as he knew all the other land that surrounded them. Memory after memory imprinted itself in his mind's eye from the street they stood on to the gazebo in the heart of the business district to the annual fireworks they set off in the big field barely a mile outside of downtown.

But none of those memories would ever compare to this one.

To the moment she confirmed what he'd begun to sense and, after her alcohol-free evening, now *knew*.

He was going to be a father.

"How?" Her question was a quiet whisper, but it held power. Meaning. Consequence. "Is this because I didn't have a drink tonight? Why is it a woman can't go out for an evening, not have a drink and not have people think it means something?"

"A woman can do that. So can a man. But when she regularly indulges in at least one glass of wine or a cocktail on every other occasion, it leaves a man to wonder."

She crossed her arms, her disgust evident. "To wonder what?"

"To wonder if his questions about her suddenly flowy clothes and the overheard early morning retching in the bathroom off the kitchen meant more than just an off day."

"Oh." She glanced over her shoulder, tilting her head in the direction of her apartment. They were barely a storefront away from its entrance over the town coffee shop. "Why don't you come up? We can talk."

He nodded but said nothing, following her instead. Their steps were so similar to their evening nearly two months ago when they'd first gone back to her apartment. It had been a revelation, that night. A coming together that had been about mutual need, yes, but it had also been about so much more.

And it had created so much more.

He followed her into her apartment, that night shimmering to life in his mind.

"Are you sure this is okay?"

Bea nodded. "It's better than okay." She stared up at him, her gray eyes dark in the heat of the moment and the dim light reflected off the small lamp she'd left on in the window. "And, um. Well. I just think you should know that I haven't done this with anyone else. Since I've been here." A light blush tinged her cheeks. "For a long time, actually."

The hunger that had risen steadily in his body—from his gut to his chest to his raging bloodstream—spiked even harder, if that were possible. He expected no explanation for how she lived her life, but now facing one, he couldn't deny how powerful it felt to stand there with her and know he was the only one.

And it made his own personal decisions over the past few years that much more rewarding, too.

"Me either."

"Really?" The serious look that covered her face faded slightly, replaced with a decided glint in her eyes. "But you're Carter Jessup. A true fan favorite."

"Which is nice and all—"

"You're considered hot and an in-demand bachelor. You even get suggestive fan mail."

"Which I returned, by the way." A fact that didn't help the blush that crept up his neck even now as he thought about the lurid photos that he'd inadvertently opened over breakfast in the bunkhouse. "I'd've preferred to burn them, but I thought it was better if she had them in hand to destroy on her own. There's no mistaking my intentions that way."

"Hadley said you mailed a thank-you note. It's sweet."

His blush spiked harder at the evidence Zack had

shared his handling of the unwanted fan mail. "I'm going to kill my boss."

"Don't be mad." Her voice drifted over him, low and husky in the dim light of the room. He felt it envelop him, and as the length of her body pressed against his registered once more, Carter knew a new truth.

There was nothing sweet about him, but there was everything sweet about this moment. A craving that would finally be satisfied, with a gorgeous woman.

"Oh, I'm not mad. Even if I am going to find a way to stick Zack in the squeeze chute on branding day."

The widening of her eyes at that news nearly put him over the edge. There was an innocence there, one he didn't normally associate with the incredibly competent and confident Bea Malone. And, coupled with her news that she hadn't found her pleasure with other ranch hands, brought him decidedly back to the moment.

"I want you, Bea. Very much."

Those expressive eyes shifted once more, from that sweet naivete to an intense, feminine knowing in their smoky depths.

"I want you, too, Carter."

The memory winked out as Bea tossed the keys on the small table in the hall. "Do you want anything to drink?"

"After we talk. Right now I want to know what's going on."

She led him to the small loveseat and chair that made up the living area of her one-bedroom apartment. Whether by design or happenstance, she took the chair, leaving him the couch.

Just far enough away they couldn't touch.

"I am pregnant."

Although her lack of denial outside had suggested as much, the simple truth in her words hit him.

Hard.

His third year working on the ranch, he mistimed a bull they were preparing to brand. It was a dumb mistake and one he'd made being careless, and probably cocky, too. Even now, all these years later, he could easily conjure up the feeling of having his breath knocked out of him and the real, tangible fear that life as he knew it was about to change.

A part of him wondered if this wasn't the same thing.

Only when faced with a thousand pounds of raging bull, it had hurt.

And this . . . didn't.

"When did you find out?" He kept any censure from his tone, more curious to know the answer. He had no interest in adding to the grooves of worry and stress that set subtle lines in her forehead.

How had he missed that?

He always looked at her. Over the years it had become as commonplace as breathing. But now that he looked at Bea with fresh perspective, he saw what he hadn't been able to put a finger on over the past few weeks. "You're not happy about it?"

"Are you?"

As answers went it was vague and damned hard to decipher. It also shot a wave of panic at him that maybe his initial burst of happiness at the news hadn't been a match for her own reaction.

"Babies are happy news."

Something hovered there in her gaze. Carter couldn't quite read it but knew his words had lightened the storm clouds. "For people planning on having them maybe. Other times . . ." She trailed off before taking a full breath. "Other times the news isn't quite so welcome."

It still didn't give him a sense of what she thought, but he couldn't worry about that right now. He was happy about it and it was time to double down on this conversation. "Plans change all the time. That's part of what makes life interesting."

An inscrutable light flashed in her gray eyes once more before she seemed to stop herself. "It's not something I planned. Or you planned, I'm sure," she quickly rushed on. "And I know it takes some getting used to. But I do want this baby. I've been to the doctor and he or she is healthy. Even if I'm—" She stopped, her mouth thinning to a small, straight line. "Old, Carter. I'm thirty-nine."

"And I'm forty. But the baby's healthy. And you're doing well, right?"

She nodded, a small smile edging her lips. "Aside from the morning retch sessions off the Waynes' downstairs hallway bathroom. I've taken to carrying Clorox wipes in my tote bag."

Although there was distance between the chair and couch, Carter shifted to the end and reached for her hand over the small expanse. The warm curve of her palm fit neatly against his and he added a small stroke of his thumb along the tender skin of her hand. "It does take some getting used to. Life-changing news usually does. But we'll figure something this wonderful out. Together."

He had no idea where the steady calm came from. Some small part of him, way down deep in his gut, kept flashing like a neon sign that he should be upset about this. Or nervous. Or hell, running for the hills. Yet even as he considered it, he discarded the panic.

Their situation wasn't easy or neat. A child was a responsibility beyond measure and her slip about her age suggested Bea had fears that went beyond the awe-inspiring prospect of motherhood. Yet even with those two solid truths, he couldn't stop the steady shots of joy that enervated his blood and ticked just beneath his skin like a live wire.

He was going to be a father.

Chapter 10

Hadley's eyes popped open and she struggled to sit up straighter, suddenly wide awake in the passenger seat. She had something to tell Zack. It was a secret, but she had to tell him anyway. Or so she thought as his truck bumped over the last few miles to home.

"You okay?" His deep voice floated across the small space.

"Sorry. Did I fall asleep?"

"Just a little nap. You've been burning the candle at both ends."

"Did I snore?"

"Never."

She heard the smile in his voice and landed a light punch on his arm. "Liar."

He loved to tease her about her snoring and it was only now, as she realized how long it had been since she'd slept in his presence, that she felt a shot of sadness at that fact.

One more reminder they weren't okay. A fact they'd been dealing with for years but which had imploded in startling fashion a few weeks ago. Only tonight . . .

Tonight he was teasing her about snoring and she was punching him in the arm. And tonight, she'd had a date with her husband.

Her *hot* husband. And she knew he was hot because, well, because he was. With those sexy broad shoulders and jean-clad hips and oh, when he had a few days' scruff on his face he was . . . sexy. Vibrantly, achingly so.

And then there were his eyes.

A dreamy sigh bubbled up in her throat and she heard it escape before she could check the impulse. His eyes were that deep, rich brown and when he looked at her, he fully *looked* at her. Consumed her, really.

That had done her in from the very start.

When Zachary Wayne put his attention on you he gave you his whole focus. It was powerful and heady and more than a little intoxicating.

"You have a really hot ass. You know that, right?"

"What?"

"The bridesmaids were all talking about it."

"When did you talk to the bridesmaids? You and Bea were as thick as thieves tonight."

Bea . . . Was Bea the secret? The thought flitted away before she could grab it. "What was I saying?" she asked, the thread of their conversation seeming to vanish from her mind.

"My ass, I believe."

"Oh yeah." She smiled, supremely satisfied by the remembered words she'd overheard from inside of a bathroom stall, surrounded by giggling bridesmaids. It was hardly classy and she wasn't particularly keen on objectifying anyone, let alone her husband, but hell, she had eyes.

And to be fair to the bachelorette party, they all had eyes, too.

And Zachary Charles Wayne had a supremely perfect ass.

"Well, they're right."

"Thank you. I think."

"Damn straight." She didn't even realize she'd lifted her hand in a fisted "yeah right" move until she saw herself, illuminated by the lights of the entrance to the ranch's property.

"What were you and Bea talking about?"

"The show. And some funny stories from the trip last week. Some weird research dude came to one of our meetings." The heady waves of her buzz and impromptu nap faded as she remembered the look on Bea's face when she described the various marketing terms the guy had used. "Only it wasn't really funny, actually. What he said."

"What did he say?"

Hadley didn't miss the careful question, or the way Zack's tone of voice suggested he barely leashed his temper.

"Something really insulting about single women

with disposable income. Like he has a right to tell them how to spend it. Or worse, that he's so greedy to get his grubby hands on it. But that wasn't the only part that made me mad."

"What else?"

"It's this idea that people are objects. Or worse!" She settled on an image that seemed to fit what she and Bea had talked about. "It's like they've taken people and put them into groupings like they're our cows. Like they move in a herd and all do the same things and are led around with some sort of poking device.

"I mean, I know it's my business and all, but I want people to watch the show or buy the book because they want to. Because they are willing to share their time with me and feel I have something to say. Not because I'm talking to them like they're objects."

She let out a hard breath, not sure why the discussion with Bea had upset her so badly. Only as she tried to dimensionalize it, a weird, shocking sob escaped in a hard rush.

"What's wrong?" Zack slowed in front of the garage, reaching up to hit the opener where it perched on the visor. He put the car in Park and turned in his seat to face her. "What has you so upset?"

"I'm not doing this for money. I know our life is a product of that, but it comes from me. For fun. For entertainment. And to make people realize they can make good things themselves. Good cooking and baking doesn't always have to happen outside your home or be done by other people."

"That's why you're successful. Right there." Zack reached over, his thumb gently brushing the unexpected tears off her cheek. "That passion and excitement and belief in what you're doing. That's what people are responding to. That's why they want to watch your show or buy your book. It's you, Hadley. You make the difference. In your passion they see themselves."

That all-consuming stare drew her in, and just like always, being the object of that full focus was heady.

Intoxicating.

And far more potent than a few whiskey chasers.

But as they sat there, parked in front of the home they'd shared since they got married, she wanted to relive some small pieces of their old life. Their night out was a start. The teasing about her snores was another. And while she knew they needed to talk about what happened on the kitchen counter, for one single moment, she wanted to take what was right here beside her.

Anticipation beat between them and, unwilling to check the impulse, she leaned in, pressing her lips to his. The move was expected—she knew it, he knew it—and Zack was right there waiting for her.

His arms wrapped around her, over the console between them and it was perfectly awkward as he pulled her close in the confined space. Deliciously so. It made the leaning and the twisting and the strained press of their bodies feel ever so slightly out of reach.

Hadley sank into the kiss, the blend of memories and urgent, needy heat of the present moment crashing into her. His mouth was perfect, the insistent play of lips and tongue over hers familiar and somehow, *not*.

Because while the man kissing her might be her husband and might have been the only man who'd kissed her for more than a decade, there was something new underneath the aching familiarity. Almost as if the distance of the past two years meant they had to somehow start over again. Not quite strangers, but people who'd lost touch and moved down different paths and didn't quite fit any longer.

Even if the kiss was explosive.

And more than a little wild as the air heated around them in the relatively small space of the truck cab.

"Zack," she whispered, pulling her head back. "Let's go inside."

The sensual blaze still flared, hot and high, but his slight frown quickly dampened some of the flames. "I think—" He let out a hard exhale, his hands tightening around her briefly before he shifted back into his seat. "I think you had a lot to drink and we have an early morning and . . . Aw fuck, Had—" He leaned his head on the rest, closing his eyes. "We just shouldn't."

It was a rejection. And it should have felt like a rejection. Only somewhere between her request to go inside and his "aw fuck" she sensed the truth. It was the only thing keeping her from feeling well and truly rejected, that knowledge that the incident a few weeks ago still hovered between them, blinking like a Vegas-sized neon sign.

"What happened the other night?" She asked the question, half expecting the need to clarify what she meant.

But the raw pain in his dark eyes as he opened them and turned his head toward her was the proof she didn't need to clarify anything. "A few weeks ago? After we had dinner?"

"Yeah."

She'd wanted to ask and didn't need beer and whiskey to do it, but now that she had the mix of liquor and self-righteous anger from her conversation with Bea, not to mention a raging case of lust, it felt like the exact right time to address it.

Like those things were just enough armor to work through the hard things they had to say to one another.

"I'm sorry. For all of it. You deserved better and you deserved something mutual between the two of us. And that's not what I did. And I'm so—" He let out a hard sigh. "I'm so sorry Hadley."

If the hitch in his voice caught her by surprise, the absolute misery lining deep grooves in his face speared her heart.

"I did have an orgasm. A damn good one, as a matter of fact."

Instead of lightening the mood, that misery only seemed to grow deeper. "Don't make light of this. You're not an object, Hadley, but I treated you like one. I took my frustration and my anger out on you in the worst way."

"Wait." She waved a hand. "Wait a minute. I was there. In that same moment with you."

"And I took advantage of you."

The mix of memory and need and anger and sadness swamped her before she could stop it. "I'm not . . . I mean . . . I don't feel that way."

But she *had* been upset after that night and a lighthearted tease wasn't the right response to his apology. Nor was a make out session in their driveway with the issue still unresolved between them.

But damn it, neither was this a disaster between them. She refused to allow that.

Reaching out, she laid a hand over his where it fisted on his thigh. "Before we take this to a place where we don't hear each other, it's important to me that you understand this. How I feel. What I feel."

He nodded, his gaze never leaving hers. "Okay."

"I wanted you. I wanted to have sex with you. In the worst way. And we were. And then something changed. Like the whole event became a competition instead of something mutual. I'd like to understand why. I want to know what upset you."

The storm clouds never left his eyes, but he didn't evade the question, either. "The book. I was upset about the book."

"The one I wrote?" She realized she was still sporting the earned effects of alcohol consumption, but their conversation and that heat-drenched kiss had her rapidly sobering. Yet even with that, she still had no idea what he was talking about.

"No. I mean yes, that one. The new cookbook."

He shook his head, before laying his free hand over their joined pair. "It's important that you understand this, too."

She nodded, as her own words came back to her.

"I'm proud of you. Damn proud. I want you to make TV shows and write books and be interviewed and whatever the hell it is you want to do. I love that you've found such amazing success. It doesn't upset me or threaten my masculinity or whatever damn Google search anyone's done on how I might feel about it."

"Who's googling anything?"

"I overheard a few of the show staff talking about it one day. That all your success might hurt my pride."

The same threat of violence she'd heard in his voice when she spoke of skinny-pants researcher hit a fierce chord in her own chest. There were more than sixty people on the ranch during any given shoot and it would be impossible to know who said it. But it still stung.

Like all the other stuff she and Bea had talked about.

All the damned assumptions.

"But it's not my pride. Or it was my pride, but not because you wrote a book. That's great. But it's what we talked about. The fact I didn't see it first is what sucks."

Hadley might still be processing the gossiping show staff, but the hurt in his voice was solely a result of her actions. And as she considered it from his perspective, she could see what had bothered him.

There was a time when they'd shared everything. And as time had passed, their lives growing further and further apart, they shared very little of the day-to-day realities of living.

Zack might have been talking about the book, but couldn't they say the same about so many aspects of their life?

Hadn't she offered the job at the Trading Post to his mother without telling him? The contract extension she'd signed the prior spring for *The Cowgirl Gourmet* came up and she'd handled it, no conversation required. Even the trip to New York the week before had been issued as an edict for him to agree to, not something she'd considered discussing with him so close to their trip to California.

Why?

Because if you don't tell him those things you also don't have to tell him the big thing. The one that will well and truly break you both.

A baby.

She'd wanted Jessica and had grieved the loss of their daughter in the worst way. In every way. But she had moved on. Or maybe better said, she'd moved past. Into the after.

And on into a new life where the reality of having a late-stage miscarriage was a part of her. Both a blessing for having had the experience of that life touching hers for the briefest of moments and a scar that was a reminder every day of what she'd lost. She'd never be over the loss of her child, but she had accepted living a childless life.

The Cowgirl Gourmet didn't define her, but in the drive and purpose and determination to find some joy in her life after losing Jessica, she'd found that after.

But if she said the words, the after she'd worked so hard for—the one where she couldn't imagine a life without him *or* a life that included a child—would vanish, too.

So she'd said nothing. And hadn't said nothing for so many seasons it had caused a rift in their marriage neither knew how to fix.

But worse, a rift for which Zack had no knowledge of the origins.

Just like the book . . .

"I didn't think about that. I don't know what to say, other than I'm sorry."

So many "I'm sorry"s between them. It was healthy and needed, but was that all there was between them anymore? Just an endless litany of apologies for the way they kept fucking up?

"Don't you see, Had? That's the problem. It's not about an apology. It's about us. There's a time I would have been the first person to see it. And now . . ." The hand that laid over hers squeezed lightly, like a physical way to soften the blow. "Now I'm not."

ZACK TAPPED THE wheel of his truck, considering all that had been said—as well as all that hadn't—the night before. He'd enjoyed the evening out, with his wife, with his ranch hands. No, he amended. With his friends.

When was the last time he'd done that?

He didn't miss the carefree days of his early adulthood. He'd enjoyed himself, but he'd never reveled in it as other people—both male and female—had always seemed to. Whether it was the responsibilities of the ranch or just who he was and how he saw the world, Zack wasn't sure, but he'd enjoyed himself and when it had been over, he'd been happy to see that time pass. Had been even happier to find Hadley and move into the stage of his life where he shared it with another person.

An old soul, his mother had always called him.

And maybe that was it, but he'd always believed it was a bit more. He hadn't had to stare longingly at a troop of bachelorettes, hoping for his shot at the pretty one who'd caught his eye, because he already had the best woman by his side. The one he wanted to make and share a life with.

He still remembered, vividly, the first day he'd noticed Hadley. Really noticed her. The way a man notices a woman.

She was working at the small bakery downtown, Frosting, and he'd walked in to pick up a cake for his grandmother's birthday. He noticed her immediately, the big smile, pretty green eyes, and hair a shade of red that had captivated him then and every day since.

He knew of her. Hadley Allen and her sister, Harper, had been several years behind him in school, but they had been there around the same time his sister Charlotte had gone through. They didn't run in the same circles, but Rustlers Creek was small enough that everybody knew everyone.

So why hadn't he noticed her before?

That thought had kept him company as she walked him through the merits of cream cheese frosting on carrot cake or the decadent delights of an Italian cream cake. Even as he'd asked himself, he knew the reason. When she had been young enough to be running around with his sister, he wouldn't have given her a second thought. But now, staring at her over that bakery counter, something clicked.

Hard.

He flirted his way to getting her phone number and had texted her while sitting in the driveway of his grandmother's house.

Everything had rolled forward from there. She'd been a little hesitant at first, claiming their nearly four-year age difference was big. But he managed to push past her resistance, sweet-talking her into a date, and then another one, and then another one. They had been inseparable from that third date on.

Maybe that was the problem, Zack wondered. Did people really get that sort of easy love story? That simple knowing, that one day you were apart and the next day you were together?

Forever?

He had never questioned his good fortune. Never considered that there'd be a time in his life when things no longer clicked. They were Zack and Hadley, Hadley and Zack, and he liked it just fine.

More than fine.

He was happy they were together and he'd never had the sense that he'd missed out on sowing his oats or enjoying the fruits of his youth. He'd never wanted anyone else after the two of them got together and he'd never wondered if there was anyone else out there.

Which, if he were honest with himself, wasn't actually a problem. He'd hit the jackpot—he'd found someone he wanted to share his life with—and had never once worried about betting on a new hand.

So when had he given up on them?

That thought perched uncomfortably on his shoulders, heavy and unwieldy and unbearably sad. And as he sat there, warming up the truck while he waited for his wife, Zack let that weight settle, bearing up under it.

Because at the end of the day, he didn't want to leave. He didn't want to give up on them. He wanted more evenings out and more days together and many more make out sessions in his truck that he didn't feel honor bound to walk away from.

Because he sure as hell didn't want to walk away from her.

When had he forgotten that?

Like a punctuation to his thoughts—and a hardy punch to the chest—Hadley came out the interior door of the garage. Her red hair seemed extra vivid in the sunlight as it blew around her face in the breezy morning air and the cold added a zip of pink to her cheeks. She juggled a large bag on her arm, her rollaboard dragging behind her.

Zack jumped out and raced around to meet her. "Here, I've got that."

"Thanks." She looked up at him, her smile sweet and a little shy.

Shy?

Was it because of their discussion last night? Her frustration from her conversation with Beam flaring high on the ride home after her slightly tipsy evening. Or something else?

Something she refused to tell him.

Which brought him right back around to his thoughts while waiting for her. Hell, for roughly the entire last two years. When had their life become about all the things they didn't say to each other any longer?

Even as he asked himself the question, another thought followed quickly on its heels.

It didn't have to be this way.

And as his hand brushed hers as he took the handle of her suitcase, he let that idea take root, way down deep.

If they chose to say unpleasant things, they could choose *not* to say them, too. It was simple, and a bit of a silly revelation, but it was still true all the same.

"How are you feeling this morning?"

"I don't quite need the hair of the dog, but I am looking forward to something greasy and bad for me at one of the fast-food places at the airport."

"Who knew you needed a hangover for one of those?"

Her laughter followed in his wake as he opened

the back door of his crew cab, stowing her bag inside.

And if her smile had been shy, her laugh was vintage Hadley.

Zack turned, his own smile broad as he stared into that laughing face. The urge to touch her—to pull her close and kiss away that smile until, just like last night, something more urgent took its place—tugged at him, but he held back, keeping his hands at his sides.

But he did hold her gaze, allowing it to arc there between them in the frosty morning air.

And as he faced the prospect of three days away from here, Zack knew that he was looking forward to every single moment of it.

Chapter 11

Bea nestled in deeper against the very warm, very strong chest that lay against her cheek, unwilling to wake from the dream. She was warm and content and surprisingly sated, which made no sense since she had a ton of work to do and an impending flight to New York and . . .

Her eyes popped open, and she stared up, straight into the knowing gaze of Carter Jessup.

A small squeak escaped from the back of her throat as she struggled to sit up. To get away from all that warm, welcoming, *sexy* heat. Even if her movements only made him hang on tighter, his arms cradling her with a strength and assurance she'd only ever imagined in her dreams.

He'd stayed. And they'd made up for almost two months of wanting and had sex.

After they'd talked about the baby. After he'd made it clear that he would be a part of his child's life. And after he'd assured her, over and over, that he'd be there for her every step of the way.

As if to prove it, he was still here. And they'd actually slept together, if falling asleep at four in the morning could be considered sleeping.

If she'd scripted the perfect outcome for telling a man she barely knew that she was carrying his child, this certainly would be it.

And if she were fair, they weren't exactly strangers. She had known him for four years.

But not like this.

And certainly not in a way where she was waking up, snuggled securely against his chest after a night of amazing sex and deep understanding of what she needed emotionally right now as a hormonal pregnant woman.

She had to get away.

Nothing in life could be that perfect. Things just didn't work out that way.

"Oh God, Carter. What did we do?"

Seemingly undeterred by her less-than-kind greeting, his smile only grew deeper. "You use that term a lot."

"What term?"

"The 'Oh God' part. You sure said it a lot last night."

She smacked him on one very solid biceps before struggling to sit all the way up. She didn't even have the excuse of a hangover for her behavior since club soda could hardly do the devil's work after an evening out. She was about to tell him that very thing when her stomach pitched a fit, immediately launching a revolt at the sudden shift in her center of gravity.

"Oh God!" She slammed a hand over her mouth and, struggling out of his hold, raced toward the bathroom ignoring the fact that she was completely naked.

The nausea roiled and swirled and she cleared the doorway and had the lid up on the toilet just in the nick of time.

Misery swamped her as she threw up, a cold, clammy heat suffusing her body. She flushed once before dropping to her knees, having been through this enough times now to know that once wouldn't be enough.

But it was the strong arms that wrapped around her, holding her hair as she leaned forward once more that brought the tears. Great gulping sobs that started just as soon as her stomach cleared its meager contents.

Without saying a word, he pulled a nearby towel off the rack and settled it over his lap, then pulled her against him. "Shhh. It's okay."

The sobs suffused her and all the fear and anxiety she'd carried for the past two months seemed to well up and spill out along with them. How was she going to do this? She lived over two thousand miles away from her child's father. And no matter how much she enjoyed being with him, they came from two different worlds and had two vastly different lives.

How did you reconcile that?

Especially now that a child was involved.

Bea laid her head against his chest, the nausea still there but calming after the abrupt rush to the bathroom. "It's really not okay, but it's sweet you think so."

"Yeah, actually it is. Want to know how I know?"

She closed her eyes and leaned into him, allowing that deep voice to drift over her. "Tell me."

"Because babies are miracles, no matter how they arrive. We're having our own miracle, Bea. We'll figure it out."

Oh, how she wanted to believe him.

And as she sat there, cradled gently in his arms, Bea decided to give in to the fantasy. In a place where she had no show notes or demands from a high-powered job. No pressing requirements beyond allowing her empty stomach to settle while wrapped in the arms of a big, strong cowboy. And no fear at all about the future.

It was a lovely dream and, for a few blessed moments, she reached out to take it, holding on tight.

HADLEY WASN'T EXACTLY sure what had changed, only she knew something had. Was it the conversation on the way home last night? She had been tipsy, for sure, but she still remembered everything she'd said.

And everything they'd done.

Most especially, though, their discussion about assumptions had lingered with her, an odd counterpoint to the overheated needs of her body. All that desire was amplified by the fact that she could *also* talk to Zack about her thoughts and her reactions to things and her hopes and dreams.

In the cold light of day it seemed a bit trivial to get so worked up over that dumb marketing guy she and Bea had spoken about, with his charts and some presentation he kept calling a "deck."

Only last night, in the moment, it hadn't been trivial at all. Nor had it been misplaced pride to share all the reasons why she loved doing *The Cowgirl Gourmet*. Even the fierce anger that some of the show staff would question Zack's attitude and what it might imply about his masculinity felt right. Real. And *still* a surprisingly large irritation, even in the cold light of day.

But what had dominated her thoughts, as she tossed and turned all evening, was the discussion about the cookbook. What it implied about all the things they no longer shared.

In all those hours of tossing and turning, she had only seen last night's discussion as something hopeless. One more sign of all they'd lost. But this morning, with the open, laughing greeting in his eyes and his warm breath escaping through smiling lips in cold puffs of air, she got a different sense.

A sense of . . . renewal? If that was possible.

The urge to dissect it was strong, but the deeper urge to revel in it was even stronger.

Seeing that light in those dark brown depths made her happy. And maybe it was time to just reach out and take the happy.

They'd had precious little of it of late.

"I think we have a free afternoon today, after we land. Nothing until tonight's dinner."

"Anything you want to do?" He took his eyes briefly from the road, before turning back to the highway.

"Nothing offhand, but then I thought it might be nice to do a little bit of shopping. I haven't even started Christmas yet."

The few items she'd ordered online did *not* constitute Christmas shopping, no matter how busy life was. But that also presumed there was going to be much of a holiday to shop for. She and Zack had been faking it in front of their families for a while now, but were they even going to have a standard Christmas with Charlie and Carlene fighting?

It would be silly to think that things would just magically resolve themselves. Which sort of burst her own bubble of happiness when she considered her and Zack.

Was it equally silly to think a few days away would make a difference?

"That's a good idea." Zack's ready agreement bolstered Hadley's spirits a bit and she tried to brush off the suddenly dour thoughts. "Maybe we can find something for Charlotte and her business."

Zack's sister had started her own PR firm a little over eighteen months ago and, while she'd mentioned how she would still be "bootstrapping" it for at least the first three years, from Hadley's perspective her sister-in-law was well past that.

Charlotte had a good idea, an amazing work ethic and what appeared to be a ready slate of clients already. She'd tapped into a market that was hungry for her services—companies that wanted a smart, sharp PR work with a Western tone and sensibility in the way they were presented to the public.

"I'm sure we can find something that fits the bill. And the triplets will love anything that comes from LA."

"So true." Zack nodded, his fond smile widening at the mention of his youngest sisters. "Everly stopped in to see me yesterday and I believe she dropped the words *Rodeo Drive* and *Beverly Hills* no fewer than eight times."

"What about your brother?"

"He can buy his own shit on Rodeo Drive."

The third rail that was the usual discussion of Jackson Wayne didn't disappoint and Hadley considered how to play it. "Has he done something?"

"You mean recently?" Zack shook his head. "Nah. Unless you count egging Dad on about his fight with Mom."

The revelation that Jackson had even paid enough attention to take sides was new news, and Hadley couldn't hold back the surprise. "He what?"

Zack nodded. "He's firmly Team Charlie. Which is fine, he's a grown-ass man who can pick sides in this ridiculous fight between our parents if he wants, but what I don't appreciate is that he's poking into the situation without having any real knowledge of what's going on. One weekend home during his Bye week does not make an understanding of what the hell is going on between the two of them."

"No, it doesn't."

And while Jackson's lone weekend home each fall was full of big smiles and flashes of grandiose family time, it did give him the benefit of an outside perspective. A perspective of her own she knew Zack wasn't ready to hear.

Carefully, she asked, "Do you think he sees something we don't?"

"I think he saw an opportunity to poke at me and pal around with the old man. To give him any more credit than that is a mistake."

Oh yeah. Definite third rail territory.

"I'm sure he's not against your mom's point of view, either. And it's hard to see Charlie and Carlene fighting like this."

"Like two junkyard dogs circling each other for dominance?"

"I was thinking like two children on a playground, but we can go with that if you want."

Zack's hard laugh had her shifting her casual attention off the road in front of them, the sign for the Billings airport announcing they'd be there soon.

"What's so funny?"

"You've been more than generous about both of my parents. And I know you want to look like you're not taking sides."

"I'm on their sides. *Both* their sides. And before you tell me I'm trying to ride two horses with one ass"—Hadley held up a hand—"hear me out."

"Shoot."

"They're both right. Which is why they're both wrong."

Zack's jaw hardened and even though his gaze had returned to the road, Hadley could picture the small line that bisected his forehead when he was working through a problem. "That makes an odd sort of sense, but why don't you spell it out for me?"

"She's entitled to her life and to do whatever she wants. Charlie doesn't care that she's at the Trading Post, no matter what he says."

"He doesn't?" She didn't miss the ready skepticism but couldn't see his expression because he was focused on navigating the exit ramp.

"Not really. Have you ever known that man to deny her anything?"

"I suppose not."

"And at the same time, your father's going through a life transition. It's hard and she could be a bit more sympathetic to that."

"He's such a pain in the ass that—"

Hadley cut him off before he could really get going. "He's a pain because he's upset. And because he doesn't know what to do with himself. And he's embarrassed."

"What does he have to be embarrassed about?"

Hadley took pity on Zack, and the obvious incredulity that sparked beneath his words. "He's embarrassed because he can't do the things he used to. How would you feel?"

"I—"

It was a hard thing, watching the people that

you loved change. She'd seen it in her father, although Martin Allen's journey was different. Her mother died when she and Harper were young, so her father's major life change had been about raising two daughters through their teenage years, navigating life as a widower and finding a new normal for all of them.

But Hadley saw him slowing down, too. Her father wasn't quite as old as Charlie, nor had he spent his adult life in the same sort of active lifestyle. While she would never call the town's high school principal someone who sat around on his ass, Martin Allen had also never spent eight hours a day on a horse.

"I'm not excusing his behavior, Zack. But I am saying this is hard on him. And while he doesn't have a right to take it out on your mother, I don't know that she fully appreciates his side in this."

And that was all she was saying, Hadley thought as Zack pulled up alongside curbside check-in.

Because if there was one thing she knew, it was that you couldn't judge someone else's marriage.

Hadn't she learned that the hard way?

ZACK STRUGGLED WITH Hadley's words, running them over and over in his mind. All through check-in, while waiting in the lounge for their flight to be called, and even after several well-wishers came over to say hi and take some selfies.

Oh, he did what was expected of him, smiling and running the "aw shucks" cowboy routine. Yet the whole time, he kept thinking of his father.

Had he been too hard on the old man?

Sure, he understood it was a point of pride for Charlie that his responsibilities around the ranch were reduced. But what about the other side of that, Zack wondered.

There was help he genuinely needed—and consistently brought up—asking Charlie to be part of the back-office operations of the ranch. Wasn't that part of what pissed him off so badly every time Jackson flitted in and out?

The ranch was called Wayne and Sons. Plural. But Jackson didn't care about any of that. So how come it was okay that his younger brother got to come in, dust things up for forty-eight hours and then go back on his merry way to Texas?

It fucking wasn't.

"You okay?" Hadley leaned in close, her voice urgent against his ear.

"Yeah. Why?"

"Because I've said your name three times and you haven't heard me."

Zack keyed back in to his surroundings, their first-class cabin shimmering back to life in front of him. He'd missed it all, from everyone boarding to the round of flight instructions from the crew. "Sorry. Yeah. I'm fine."

"You look upset. Was it the selfies?"

"What?" Her anxiety registered loud and clear. Was this really what she expected of him? That every quiet moment was an explosion waiting to happen.

If the news about his father had knocked him

for a loop, that revelation threatened to drag him beneath an emotional undertow.

He laid a hand over hers, where it rested on the seat arm between them. "Of course not. It was fine."

"They were really excited to meet you." A merry smile settled on her face while an unholy twinkle lit her eyes. "And I love seeing how flustered people get over you."

Zack felt the same embarrassed tug as the night before when Carter ribbed him about the pool game. "They were sweet. Although I swear they get younger all the time."

"No, it's just us who keep getting older."

"Hmm, maybe, but I think they were disappointed we weren't on the same flight." Determined to erase her concerns, he added, "I was thinking about what you said. About my dad. About how he feels."

"And?"

"And maybe I have been a bit hard on him."

"You have a right to be upset. He's been miserable to everyone and you've borne the brunt of it. But I don't think he's doing it quite as intentionally as it seems."

"Yeah. I think you're right about that."

She was right, and she had also given him something to think about. A new view to a situation he thought he understood. Yet one more thing that had been missing from his life as his marriage continued its gradual decline.

Hadley was his partner, in all things. And while

he had spent time thinking about what they had lost between the two of them—laughing, intimacy, sharing—this discussion about his father was one more stark reminder of all the other things they'd lost.

Marriage wasn't just sex, or nights on the couch watching TV, or dinner dates. It was also conversations about loved ones, and the tough talks that often went with it. It was sharing anger and frustrations, that even if well-earned meant having a partner who could objectively hold a mirror up to them.

Who could give you a new perspective.

It was just one more thing they'd lost.

And as they headed toward California, Zack had to admit that it was everything.

HADLEY TOOK A handful of the pub mix on the counter in the airport lounge and considered her options. Their layover in Salt Lake City was extended due to a flight delay and she was debating the wisdom of attempting to do some Christmas shopping in the airport. And each time she considered it, she defaulted back to how nice it was to sit with her husband for a few idle hours talking about everything and nothing in particular.

And who wanted gifts from the airport?

"Isn't this great?" Zack dragged out a box of candy he'd beelined for on their walk through the terminal. "Carter mentioned these mint chocolates once and talked about how good they were."

"Our Carter?" she asked as she amended the

thought about airport gifts. Clearly her husband was in his glory. "The healthy and fit one?"

Zack snorted at that as he extended the box toward her. "Fit my ass. That man loves junk food more than my father."

Hadley took one of the treats and raised her eyebrows. "Now that's saying something. Especially since your father's been hoarding my tater tot casseroles. I swear he stole another one last week out of my freezer."

Zack eyed her, his gaze speculative as he chewed on a bite of his chocolate. "And you didn't maybe happen to put a few extras in there just for him."

Hadley sat up straighter and took a small nibble of her chocolate, avoiding Zack's gaze. "I'd do no such thing."

"You so did it!" Zack slapped a hand on his knee and reached for the beer before him on the bar. "Don't play innocent with me."

It was a bit early for drinks, but they were on vacation and she'd given it all a "what the hell" moment and ordered a Bloody Mary when Zack got his beer. Despite the lingering hangover from the prior night, the drink had gone a long way already to smoothing out any rough edges.

And sitting here staring at her grinning husband finished the job.

"Your father's entitled to a little treat now and then."

"I'm not sure a nine by thirteen dish of tater tots, copious amounts of cheese and a heaping of mayo qualifies as a *little* treat."

A hard giggle erupted in her chest and she leaned forward, lightly punching him in the arm. "I'm an enabler, what can I say?"

Zack stared down at her, his humor fading as something more intimate took its place. With one lone finger, he brushed a lock of hair back behind her ear, the two of them sharing the same air as they faced each other on cushy bar stools. "No, you're a temptress."

"I don't try to be."

"Nope." He sat back and reached for his beer again. "Not buying it."

"I'm not! I just like to feed people. It makes me feel useful."

And it did make her feel useful. Happy, too, to know that she'd put a small smile on someone's face or given them a few moments of enjoyment with her food. That was the real reason she socked away the casseroles for Charlie. He was in a rough patch and if a few extra helpings of processed potatoes and cheese made him feel a bit better then yeah, she'd own it.

"Useful?"

She shrugged as the pointedness of his question sank in. "It's a good skill to have. People like to eat. And they like to eat even more when it tastes good."

"There's more to you than being useful, Hads."

"Sure, but—" She broke off, not sure where the direction of their conversation had come from or why she'd even used a word like that.

Was that how she saw herself?

A *useful* tool that got things done on behalf of others? A conduit for other people's needs with very little focus on her own?

It was a silly thought and she wanted to wave it away before she got too far down a weird path. They were having a good time. Why mar it with something heavy and forlorn? Hadn't they spent way too many months acting that way?

Yet as she sat there, she had to admit that much of her life *was* about being useful to others. The way she'd helped her father and sister after her mother died. And the way she'd helped Zack with feeding the ranch hands when they first got married. Even now, she wasn't under any illusions that the Cooking Network found her to be anything more than a means to an end. That end being their ratings and profitability.

They'd made her a successful woman because of it, but she well knew anything that tarnished the image they projected on their TV programs and on their website would make her the next network casualty faster than she could say "boo."

So yeah, she might see herself through a rather utilitarian lens, but she was honest and realistic about it all.

"But what?" Zack pressed his question again, and she realized that this was her real chance to tell him how she felt. To put to words all the things she hadn't been able to say these past few years.

"I don't think being useful's a bad thing. I never saw it as a problem or as something I resented. Or

I didn't until you and I stopped finding a way to talk about stuff."

"Why's that?"

Hadley pushed on, suddenly determined to get it out. "With you I've always felt valuable just being me. No other reason needed."

"That's still true, you know."

"Is it?"

"Of course it is. You don't need to be anything for me or try and be something you're not. You just need to be yourself."

His words were honest and in them Hadley heard his genuine conviction and belief in her. He was such a good man. For as mad as she'd been over the past few years, nothing had ever diminished that belief in his innate goodness and decency as a human being.

But as his gaze sought hers, seemingly trying to will her to understand, Hadley knew the truth.

Zack might believe he didn't need her to be more, but that was only because she'd been hiding a large part of herself for the past two years. A part he'd clearly sensed based on the increasing distance between them, even if he couldn't put it into words.

The woman he loved lived in his mind as a wife and a mother.

And she had no desire to be both any longer.

Chapter 12

"I owe you big time, Zack." Bryce Donnelly had said something similar about five times already, but Hadley just smiled through it, already expecting the effusive praise when he turned to her. "You too, Hadley. I'm sure it wasn't easy to juggle your schedule."

"I wouldn't miss it, Bryce."

With their shopping plans derailed by the flight delay in Salt Lake City and significant traffic snarls on their drive from the airport to the hotel, Hadley had taken the glass of wine Zack poured from the minibar and raced off to get ready for the evening. Bryce's arrival to their suite had kept her from saying much else to Zack, but she hoped their discussion of something as pedestrian as usefulness didn't make a return trip.

As for her and Zack?

Hadley took a fortifying sip of wine and vowed

to worry about her somber thoughts about the two of them later.

"So Bryce, tell me a bit more about the people we're having dinner with."

Even though she'd already had a full overview of who they were meeting with as well as the plans for the entire trip, the shift in direction was enough to get Bryce onto a new topic. And what a topic it was. If she had tried to script it, she would never have come close to the drama that was promised for the evening.

"Susan Edgar is the chief marketing officer of Total Foods and her brother, Louis, is the president, CEO and de facto head of the chain. Louis's wife is about twenty years younger and Susan is not a fan."

"Why would his sister care who he's married to?" Zack asked, the ice in his own glass clinking as he gestured at Bryce.

Bryce shrugged. "Family dynamics? Worries about the family money? Irritation the wife can sit back and bask in all the family hard work? Total Foods has been on a hot trajectory in the past five years and Susan is responsible for most of it. What started out as a family business that catered to a certain customer has hit the big time with its organic approach to food sourcing and curated shopping experience inside the store. Her marketing work has driven that."

"Sounds like Louis is no slouch, though. He's obviously known how to run the business to keep up with the promise of marketing," Zack said, adding in another option to Bryce's list. "You can run as many commercials as you want, but if the operations aren't behind it, that shit falls flat."

"Total Foods *is* her business," Bryce stressed. "And the woman misses absolutely nothing."

"We'll just make sure the women are at opposite ends of the table," Hadley suggested, envisioning the intimate dinner Bryce had planned for tonight. It would be her and Zack, Bryce and two of his team members, and then Susan and Louis and Louis's wife, Madelina.

"It doesn't help that Susan isn't married," Bryce added. "Total workaholic."

Although she had built a particularly unfavorable impression of Susan Edgar due to the woman's disdain for her younger sister-in-law, the discussion Hadley had with Bea at the Branded Mark the night before came back in full force. "Maybe she likes what she does."

"Sure, maybe." Bryce shrugged again. "Maybe work fills the time. Who knows? If my wife and I didn't have any kids, we'd have a hell of a lot of time." He grinned broadly at Zack and Hadley. "Like you two. You're jet-setting in here together, not a care in the world."

Hadley was prevented from saying anything by the knock on the door, but she couldn't help being struck by Bryce's casual dismissal of Susan's life. The worst part, she admitted to herself, was that Bryce likely had no idea what he'd said was dismissive.

Sort of like skinny-pants marketing guy and his discussion of demographics.

And hell, she admitted to herself, she could complain about it all she wanted, but wasn't Total Foods taking on Wayne and Sons grass-fed beef because they had a *demographic* that wanted that sort of offering?

Didn't her show reach specific *demographics*? Cohorts of people who'd made her very successful, in fact.

Why did it seem so overtly obvious and maybe even necessary in business and so frustratingly one-sided when it came to thinking about actual people?

Because no matter how she spun it in her mind, that lingering conclusion that seemed to hover in the air left her feeling at odds. According to the rest of the world, if you didn't have children, something was wrong. Whether it was how you filled your days, or how you spent your time, or even the perception of how much time you had available to you.

Zack set his glass on the small bar area of the suite before extending a hand for her wine. She gave him her glass, still stuck on the questions swirling in her mind.

Why was she so worried about this?

And why had the conversation with Bea bothered her so badly?

She should shrug it off. People thought lots of things and none of it meant they truly understood what another person was living with. Yet the threads of that conversation continued to swirl, like a frustrating storm hovering on the horizon.

It's an acronym. Professional Aunt, No Kids.

It's a trendy marketing term right now.

They claim these women buy a lot of the expensive toys. Clearly out of the depth of their professional pockets and the lack of buying them for the children they don't have.

If she didn't have Zack, she'd be a PANK. Or would be one when Harper had children. And based on the deteriorating direction of her marriage, it was suddenly a possibility that seemed starkly real and tangible.

Was that what had her so bothered?

Even as she turned that over in her mind, she admitted that the term troubled her, regardless of the current issues in her marriage. She was angry for Bea. Angry for the women who were in the same boat. Angry that their love for the children in their lives felt exploited instead of being seen as gestures of love.

Even the fact they'd been categorized as a group who liked her show and responded to her work troubled her. She wanted people watching because they enjoyed what she had to share, not because they were some sort of free bank account that could be tapped into by advertisers.

So no, it wasn't just concern for her own future.

Because married or not, she no longer wanted children. And the world didn't know what to do with that.

"You okay?" Zack nodded toward the door. "Looks like the car is here."

"Yeah." She tried to muster up a smile but didn't

think she got much past a small grimace. "I'm good."

He laid a hand on her shoulder, his gaze direct. In his eyes she saw the shimmering truth. Zack hadn't missed Bryce's reference to children, either.

That knowledge hovered there between them, neither of them saying anything. Like always, neither she nor Zack were willing to put voice to the very real truth they both knew. The truth that stretched out between them like a wide-open canyon.

Because once they did put it to words, there was nothing to save them from the drop into that abyss.

THE RIDE TO dinner was relatively short, at least according to Bryce's team members who lived in LA and were joining them for the evening, but Zack couldn't deny the all-star views out his window. They'd left their hotel in Beverly Hills, joining up in the limo Total Foods had sent for to pick up everyone from Wayne and Sons. More than a half hour later they'd passed the Hollywood Bowl and, a bit farther on, the world-famous Hollywood sign. All in a distance that would have taken him about five minutes—ten tops—at home.

Had he ever expected to see or experience things like this in his life?

A small-town Montana rancher in Beverly Hills? It sounded like the title of a slapstick comedy, not his life. Only it was.

He'd come to understand a few years before that his wife was famous. It had taken some getting used to, but they'd both had the time to ease into the situation. Hadley's show had been a success from the beginning, but that success had built on itself, layer by layer. A core group of fans, that was then added to by those who enjoyed the show and told others, which was further added on to by those who found her through magazine articles or TV interviews or her books.

It was his own fame that had been the real surprise.

The idea that there were people enamored with him had been a strange truth to accept.

Hadley, he understood. She was warm, fun and beautiful. But him?

He spent his life around cows every day. What was so interesting about that?

Only people did find it interesting. Bea often talked about "the cowboy effect," and what his presence on the show, along with his ranch hands, did for ratings.

It had become the strange reality and while he wanted to say he was used to it, there were definitely moments when it overwhelmed him.

"I don't want to look like a noob"—Hadley leaned into him, her lips against his ear—"but the Hollywood sign looked really cool."

"I know. I noticed it, too."

"You can take the ranchers out of the country—" She left the comment hanging there.

"But you can never take the country out of the rancher."

"Amen."

They sat there together as time seemed to stretch

out, their faces turned toward one another on the limo's side bench seat. Zack felt something shift in the air between them—nothing more than a moment in a day full of them—but once more that persistent sense that he had something to be hopeful about shot through him like an electric current.

They were so often on the same wavelength. Or they had been, for so many years. And now, even after having lost it for so long, it was amazing how quickly they could find it again. How easy it was to sink back into those patterns, when he allowed himself to forget all his more recent frustrations.

And how pointless every one of those frustrations seemed as he sat there staring into his wife's eyes.

Pointless, but not entirely unfounded.

Isn't that what he was trying to reconcile? If he was fair, what they both were? All the small things each of them had kept inside had grown bigger. Wider. Until they pushed out all the air and had become big things.

"It should be a nice evening." Hadley's optimistic words hung quietly in the air, intruding on the questions his own thoughts had created.

And suddenly, he didn't want to think about the big things anymore. He was so sick of giving them all the room. Of allowing them to grow bigger and wider and all-consuming.

"Certainly an interesting one."

"Looks like you and I are going to run interference tonight."

"We are?"

A mischievous twinkle lit those green eyes. "You bet we are. Bryce wasn't just gossiping back there at the hotel. He was giving us the lowdown on the dinner dynamics."

A subtle panic skittered under his skin at her obvious enjoyment of what was to come. "What are we supposed to do about it?"

"We'll be the congenial out-of-towners who keep everything light, vivacious and fun."

"You're a celebrity. No one sees you as an out-of-towner."

She shrugged. "Fine. If I have to play that card then so do you, buster."

"Buster?" He couldn't hold back the small smirk.

"It fit the moment."

On impulse, he leaned forward and pressed his mouth to hers. The moment their lips met, the heat he'd kept banked for weeks flared bright and high, a volcano of need layered over a shocking rush of emotion.

Longing swamped him, a wholly unexpected reaction that should have been absolutely expected. Had there ever been a day since they'd met that he didn't want Hadley?

The taste of wine had lingered on her lips and he had the urgent desire to sip her slowly, savoring her and the contact between them.

If only . . .

Zack ended the kiss quickly, the audience in the limo more than he wanted for the first real affection he'd given his wife in weeks. As those long, endless days filled his memories, searing memories of the last time they were intimate played on a vivid loop in his mind.

The dinner. The kitchen counter. And his regrettable behavior.

Zack shifted his position, needing that focus of others to keep from dipping his head and tasting her mouth once more. Turning so they faced the center of the limo, he settled his arm behind Hadley's back.

And came right back to her questions.

I wanted you . . . And then something changed. Like the whole event became a competition instead of something mutual . . . I'd like to understand why. I want to know what upset you.

She'd been honest with him and more forgiving than he deserved. He'd already been determined to move past that night and apologize for his behavior, but she'd beaten him to the punch.

And in the face of that forgiveness he wanted to prove he was worthy of a second chance.

He wanted to prove to her that what they started that evening in the kitchen was a sign of what they could find once more.

Of what they could be.

So if she wanted to play celebrity mediators this evening, then that's what he'd be. Hell, he'd play the celebrity medium if it meant his wife would snuggle up against his side once more. Would whisper conspiratorially in his ear.

And would give him the sweet press of those lips against his each and every time they bent their heads together.

HADLEY HAD NEVER been particularly comfortable with the whole celebrity thing. She'd understood from the start it was a part of being the Cowgirl Gourmet and she had never forgotten how important it was to the person standing opposite her that she be kind, warm and approachable.

But she still struggled to understand it.

She was just herself. Same as she had been before. Even if others now saw her differently.

When she was on camera she was able to play her professional self. When she had the opportunity to do a book signing, she had the benefit of the table between her and others and the need to keep the line moving an essential part of the event. But in these situations, trying to talk to strangers and recognizing that she needed to be the one to put them at ease, had always proven the most challenging.

And also the most humorous.

Tonight was clearly going to be no exception.

The limo ride with Zack had gone a long way toward relaxing her. Those quiet moments after their brief kiss, so electric and fraught with all the attraction they both seemed strangely insistent on keeping banked, had buoyed her spirits. Like the night before when they'd headed to the Branded Mark together, they felt like partners going into this dinner.

The Edgars had selected a high-end steakhouse for dinner and, while an obvious choice, Hadley had to admit they'd chosen well. Even if the way they were seated for the meal when Hadley and

Zack and their small party had arrived had disaster written all over it.

The eight of them were seated at a rectangular table which, in Hadley's opinion, was the first mistake. A round table would have encouraged far easier conversation flow but the rectangle was a logistics nightmare even Bea and her bullhorn couldn't solve.

Louis Edgar had taken one head and Bryce was given the other, his team members relegated to the seats on either side of him. There'd been some quick scuffling about putting Zack there but Susan Edgar's hissed words to her brother that "she'd miss all the good conversation with Zack and Hadley at one end of the table" had shifted everyone around. By the time they had taken their seats, Hadley had the center spot opposite Susan, with Zack to Hadley's right and Louis's wife, Madelina at Susan's left.

And Louis was the only one smiling.

Obviously unwilling to miss the conversational upper hand, Susan dived in before anyone had their napkins unfolded.

"Hadley, you have to tell us about the new season. I also heard you've got a big holiday special coming up. The network marketing brass has already been courting me to participate."

Zack's light squeeze on her knee was fortifying—especially since drinks hadn't even been ordered yet—and Hadley pasted on a bright smile designed to rival Louis's.

"We just wrapped the season a few weeks ago.

And I'm excited to say we've got some fun surprises in store."

"Hadley's been channeling my grandmother," Zack chimed in.

"Mamma Wayne's going to be on?" Madelina's eyes lit up, her question eager.

"Believe it or not, she's so busy we could only manage her schedule for two episodes. But I've included several recipes in other episodes so she's there in spirit."

"I love her chocolate silk pie," Madelina added, her smile falling as her sister-in-law shot her a dark side-eye.

"The network's been talking nonstop about your ratings, Hadley," Susan said, taking control of the conversation again. "They're saying you're up three years in a row and have been instrumental in helping to drive their streaming services as well."

"You're very kind, Susan. The Cooking Network's been good to me. It's my privilege to help them grow their business."

"Just like Wayne and Sons is going to grow ours." Louis slapped the table, the move enough to shift the conversation to him as he lifted his glass in toast.

Susan's grimace was even darker than the side-eye she'd given her sister-in-law, but she didn't say anything. Which left Louis to say a lot. More than a lot, actually, when his verbose speech lasted from the toast until appetizers were delivered to the table.

"It is truly our pleasure to be working with

Wayne and Sons," Louis said, *finally* appearing to wrap up.

Obviously unwilling to take the risk the man had even more to say, Zack moved in smoothly. "The pleasure is all ours, Louis. I can't tell you how proud I am to be working with Total Foods, and I appreciate, more than I can say, your faith in us."

As far as conversation went, Zack was perfect. Jovial, kind and humble in a way that still left Louis the big man at the table.

It was an interesting skill, Hadley mused, the way Zack could seamlessly move from pure alpha male leadership at the ranch to humble business-man here at this dinner. On some it could be seen as disingenuous, but as she watched her husband work the table that wasn't a moniker that fit at all.

Instead, he recognized his own worth. His own value. And because of it, he was more than willing to let others shine.

I'm proud of you. Damn proud. I want you to make TV shows and write books and be interviewed and what-ever the hell it is you want to do. I love that you've found such amazing success. It doesn't upset me or threaten my masculinity or whatever damn Google search any-one's done on how I might feel about it.

She really needed to get over that whole Google thing, but with that memory came an unmistak-ably clear truth: He deeply understood that her success—or anyone else's for that matter—in no way diminished his own. He not only understood it, but he saw it with a clarity that was, sadly, all too rare.

It was yet one more thing she loved about him.

And despite those amazing qualities, Hadley saw the tornado whipping up as soon as Zack made his tactical error.

"Madelina, I understand you and Louis have three children. How old are they?"

Madelina lit up at the question about her children, her pretty features morphing into something particularly lovely. "Liam is six, Ella is four and Genevieve just turned a year."

Yet as Madelina sparkled, the conversation was enough to turn Susan's features from merely sour to darkly troublesome. And in that swift change, Hadley saw the other side of what Bea hadn't shared the night before at the bar.

How devastating it could be when your contributions to the conversation were seen as trivial or, worse, disregarded.

Hadley asked Madelina a few questions about each child, giving the woman a proper opportunity to share her excitement. And as the young mother spoke of her children, she ended up giving Hadley the opening she needed.

"They love their aunt Susan. They can't wait for her to visit and Ella's already been begging me to buy her a pair of high heels."

Hadley saw the first genuine smile from Susan at the mention of her niece. "She even knows who Jimmy Choo is."

"Jimmy who?" Louis asked.

The three women exchanged a conspiratorial

smile and Hadley shot a sassy quip in Louis's direction. "A girl's best friend."

If being a celebrity was awkward, it did have its advantages. The biggest of which was that people were loath to interrupt you because they seemed to think you were about to drop some sort of secret they'd never heard.

She'd never understood it, but in that moment, Hadley realized she could use it. Wield it, really. And before Louis could derail her, Hadley kept on. "Susan, I think the network brass has been holding out on you."

"Oh?" Susan glanced over the top of her wineglass, clearly interested but playing it cool at the mention of the network and the likely implication her professional pocketbook would be tapped. "How's that?"

"The network brass can't get you a front row seat in my kitchen for the live holiday show. If you want one."

Whatever bravado Susan had worn up to now vanished as she set her wineglass back on the table. "For the taping?"

"Sure. Your support of Wayne and Sons means a lot to Zack and me. It's only right that you come to the show as my guest." She waved a casual hand. "Forget the network brass."

Zack chimed in, his arm wrapping around her shoulders in a warm squeeze as he leaned forward conspiratorially. "It always pays to go to the source."

"I'd . . . I'd love to."

"Excellent. We'll get the details worked out." Hadley sat back, pleased as the tense tenor around the table began to shift. Conversation flowed more smoothly as the waitstaff arrived with their dinner. More wine was poured and Bryce told a joke that had everyone laughing.

But it was the quiet, grateful smile from Madelina Edgar that struck the sharpest chord in Hadley's heart.

Chapter 13

Zack hadn't expected to enjoy the evening quite so much, but Bryce had chosen well with Total Foods and the Edgar family. Once Louis calmed down and settled into the evening, the man had been quite congenial. He and Susan had a lot of stories about running a family business that Zack not only understood, but could contribute to with a few stories of his own.

And, subtly yet surely, as dinner had worn on, he and Hadley had stopped being the celebrity couple at the table and had become business partners and dinner companions for the evening. A contrast to the evening before at the Branded Mark, to be sure, but enjoyable in a different way.

Although he'd never dismiss the importance of spending time with his ranch hands—and considered Carter and the rest of the Wayne and Sons team like family—nothing changed the fact that he was the boss. It was a role he accepted, but it carried weight.

No matter how much they liked him or wanted to work for him, Zack was still their employer. And last night, he had no doubt after he and Hadley left, conversation had shifted toward more personal topics than anyone would ever mention in front of him.

There was still that distance this evening, but it was different, somehow. There had been a more equal exchange of ideas, balanced by the fact that Total Foods wanted the Wayne and Sons partnership, but Zack wanted it back just as much in return.

"You look happy." Hadley said as she walked back into the living area of their suite. She'd changed into a tank top and pajama pants, her face scrubbed clean of makeup.

The look of her struck hard and deep and Zack fumbled for a minute around his tongue. Enamored, he was fascinated to see how easily she'd shifted from competent professional to girl next door in nothing more than a costume change.

Useful my ass, Zack thought with no small measure of remorse that she even considered that moniker or that she might feel it was all she was.

Because unlike an actress, she wasn't playing parts. Each was her.

Professional businesswoman, because that's exactly what she was as the Cowgirl Gourmet. She was a show star, an author and, hell, a freaking brand all her own.

She was also a daughter and a sister and a friend.

And damn it, she was his wife.

And oh, how he wanted her.

"I am," he finally said in answer to her comment. "It was a good evening. I think Total Foods is going to be a really strong partnership for us."

"I agree. Once we got past that awkward start to dinner which, if I'm being honest, I expected, everyone really warmed up and had a good time."

"A reprieve before tomorrow night's event."

The conversation was banal and Zack wasn't sure why he couldn't find the smooth transition from enjoyable evening to more private time with his wife. They'd never had that problem before. Yet right now, standing here, he felt clumsy and awkward. Out of his element and not remotely sure what was the right next step.

Hadley shifted from one bare foot to the other. "You think tomorrow night is going to be crazy?"

"You can bet on it. Bryce told me it was supposed to be a two hundred–person event. But did you hear Susan? They topped five hundred with more people clamoring to get on the guest list."

"Yeah." Hadley sighed. "That'll be crazy."

They stood there, facing one another, with ten feet between them that felt like a mile.

Which made Hadley's leaping arc and the sudden armful of fragrant woman swamping his senses and soft pajama material beneath his hands the most amazing surprise. Hadley wrapped her legs around his waist and Zack settled his arms under her cute ass and held her tight.

"Crazy you say?" He couldn't hold back a smile. "Nothing we can't handle."

And then her lips were on his and his head was spinning and he couldn't believe the amazing gift of finally having his wife in his arms.

All of his wife. Zack couldn't help grinning against her lips.

He might have messed things up royally the last time he'd had the chance, but he wasn't going to make the same mistake again.

Without breaking the contact between their mouths, Zack walked them slowly to the large sectional couch that dominated the main living area of the suite. Hadley had already started working on the buttons of his dress shirt and by the time he deposited that sweet ass on the back edge of the main part of the sofa, she was dragging what was left of his shirt out of his waistband.

"What was in that dessert?" he teased her, murmuring the words against her lips.

"Forget the dessert," Hadley shot back, her fingers making quick work of his belt before cleverly dropping the zipper. "I'm far more interested with what's in here."

It was sexy and silly and Zack didn't care. They were here. Together. And he finally had a chance to show her all the things he hadn't yet figured out how to say.

Those clever fingers danced on, moving to the material of his shirt. She had the starched material down his shoulders and nearly off his back when they both keyed in on her mistake. The buttons on his cuffs weren't going anywhere and he was effectively locked in place with his arms behind his back, stuck in his shirt.

"I think we have a problem."

"We?" Zack used his position to press his bare chest against her, rubbing so that the thin material of her shirt teased her pebbled nipples. "I'm helpless here."

He dragged his chest against her again, satisfied when he got a light moan in answer.

"You're hardly helpless."

"Locked in place, unable to do"—he whispered against her ear as he brushed his chest over her once more and with harder pressure this time— "anything, really."

Zack nuzzled her neck, trailing his lips over that sensitive swath of flesh. He felt the hard thrumming of her pulse, and knew it was a match for his own. Her legs moved to wrap again around his waist, her arms matched around his neck. "Let's go to the bedroom."

He lifted his head just enough to stare down at her. "I thought you'd never ask."

HADLEY HAD LEFT a small side lamp on in the bedroom and she loved how the soft light bathed Zack's broad shoulders and chest. His arms were still stuck behind his back and she wanted to laugh at the awkward position. Would have if she wasn't still shivering from the arousal that layered in sharp electric bursts beneath her skin.

God, how she wanted him.

Needed him.

And if she'd just get him out of that shirt, she could have his hands back on her skin and could finally fulfill this desperate, achy need that nothing could quell.

"Turn around."

He shot her a saucy look but did as she asked. Her fingers trembled lightly as she undid the buttons, freeing his wrists and dragging the material the rest of the way down his arms before allowing it to fall to the floor. Zack wasted no time, spinning around and pulling her against him, dropping them both back on the bed. As that hard chest cushioned her, his arms strong around her, she braced herself on her forearms so that she could look down at him in the soft light.

"Hi."

"Hey."

Those deep brown eyes remained locked on hers, his gaze full of longing and sexual need and something that reminded her of a frightened animal, determined not to show it.

Was he as scared as she was?

Scared of not moving forward. Of not reaching out and taking this? And equally scared to make the move?

"I want you, Zack. More than I can say."

"Me too."

"And we're good? I mean—" She broke off, not sure how to navigate the strange mix of tenderness and aching need. "I want you. I want to make love with you. With you."

It felt like a fumble, but she saw welcome and understanding push the fear out of his eyes. "I know. I want that, too. And I don't want what happened before. It's us here, Had. You and me. Both of us in the moment. *Both* of us. Together."

That tense fear that she wasn't even aware of carrying lifted and she nodded. "Together."

He lifted his hands to frame her face before pulling her down for a kiss. The move was soft and gentle and welcoming, and in the tender press of his lips she felt yet another dimension of what it meant to love this man. Whether it was the sexy feel of his body against hers or the desperate, achy yearning that he could arouse in her so easily or even this sweet, tender gesture, he was all things to her.

Everything.

And he always had been, from the first.

"Yes," she whispered. "Together."

And in that yes, Hadley recognized another truth. Wasn't marriage about a lifetime of yes? For better or for worse wasn't simply a vow. And walking down the aisle might be part of a single day, but it led to a lifetime together.

A lifetime that depended on both parties continuing to say yes to those promises. Yes, to upholding those vows. Yes, to still loving one another.

She shifted to a sitting position, skimming the tank top up and over her body, sighing when Zack's hands came up to cup her breasts. He followed quickly with his mouth taking one nipple in and sucking deeply. Pleasure, raw and strong and unbearably deep shot through her.

She reveled in the sensations, her head thrown back as he focused on her body. And as he shifted his attention to trail kisses over her collarbone and on toward the sensitive skin of her neck, she made some moves of her own. She'd always loved the feel of his firm flesh beneath her fingertips. Loved even more the way his tight stomach muscles contracted as she pressed seeking fingers over those ridges, before moving even lower to grip the long length of him in her palm.

He didn't disappoint, those stomach muscles contracting before a hard exhale cooled the skin of her neck when her fingers wrapped, sure and firm, over the length of his cock.

How different this was from the night in the kitchen. Here, pleasure was shared. Passed back and forth and back again, a living entity between them that they owned together. A mutual passion, that lived and breathed entirely between the two of them.

A wholly reciprocal *yes*.

"Zack . . ." She breathed his name on a rush as his fingers slipped beneath the waistband of her pajama pants and her panties. Tender and gentle rapidly morphed, the already heated air growing electric with the intensity of her need.

Of *their* need.

His body strained beneath her palm and her own responded in kind, a hard, insistent demand to join with him. To breathe him in and allow his body to surround hers.

To surrender together.

No longer gentle, Zack shifted them so that he could slide down the length of her body, slipping the thin pajama pants off before returning and stretching them out fully on the bed. His crafty fingers—so strong, so knowing—once again found the intimate heat of her and the barely there thread of control she'd managed to hang on to vanished as he stroked her to orgasm.

The part scream, part moan had barely escaped her throat when he captured it with his mouth, his tongue tracing an erotic path with hers that mimicked the play of his fingers. Exquisite tremors shook her as everything inside of her exploded in a rain of starlight and barely leashed fire.

And then he was there, his arms cradling her as she rode out the conflagration. As all that bright, brilliant light settled softly inside of her, suffusing her with more of that glorious *yes*.

His hands were gentle as they stroked her hair, his lips soft where they pressed against her temple. But it was the hard, insistent press of his erection that had her smiling. That urgent proof of his need, so clear and sure, had her own rising once more, even more potent, even more demanding.

Even more necessary.

Turning into him, one hand snaked down to take possession of his flesh while the other wrapped around his neck, pulling him close for a kiss. "I believe we have some unfinished business, cowboy."

"I'm not quite sure I'd put it—" His hard exhale morphed quickly into a moan as she pressed just the right amount of tension with her palm and fingers.

"What was that?"

"Temptress." He half whispered, half moaned the husky word and Hadley took it as the highest compliment.

"You bet your hot ass I am."

For all his patience and all his tenderness, she knew the exact moment it all vanished. The moment when the urgency demanded by their bodies overwhelmed their words. Their teasing. Even their playful touching.

When satisfaction became the only answer to the question of what beat between them.

He shifted between her and Hadley opened to him, eager to welcome him home. And as his body filled hers and they began to move together, she felt the sure knowledge of familiarity and the amazing truth of how each time with him was new.

Fresh.

And a culmination of who they both were in that moment.

Here he was. The man she loved and the one she'd been emotionally apart from for way too long.

And as pleasure took its due—as the need for satisfaction reigned supreme between them—Hadley gave herself up to it.

Gave herself up to them.

And wished with everything she was that *this* yes—the one that was him and her—could be enough between them.

Zack floated on the satisfied haze of good sex with the woman he loved. He'd drifted in and out of sleep—they both had—making love with Hadley two more times in between the drowsy moments that seemed to suffuse them both.

Which made the fact that his eyes had popped wide open a mystery.

He glanced down but Hadley hadn't moved, curled up against him with her hair streaking over her face in strands of velvet fire.

So what had woken him up?

The distant ping of his cell phone went off again from the direction of the suite's sitting room, the now obvious reason he'd woken up. A glance at the bedside clock showed 4:00 a.m. which meant it was five back home. Carter might need him.

Zack disengaged himself from Hadley's soft form, hoping the jostling wouldn't wake her. When she let out a loud snore after rolling over, he couldn't hold back the smile.

Or the understanding that she wasn't waking up for a while.

He padded to the living room and grabbed his phone, expecting to see Carter's name on the screen face.

Which made the text from his brother—no, make that four texts—a surprise.

HOLY FUCKING SHIT YOU HAVE TO CALL ME BACK.

When that fifth text lit up his screen, Zack let out a long, dark sigh. And realized there was no ignoring whatever uniquely urgent Jackson-filled problem his brother had this morning.

Zack hastened back to the bedroom and pulled a pair of jeans and a T-shirt out of his suitcase. There was no way he was dealing with his brother while standing buck naked in the hotel. With a longing glance at Hadley, he headed back to the living room, opting to make Jackson hold on a few more minutes. Zack made quick work of a leftover coffee service that had been laid out for him and Hadley the day before. Snagging a disposable paper cup, he nuked what he'd hoped had turned into some seriously high-test brew overnight.

And then settled down on the couch to dial Jackson's number.

His brother answered immediately. "Where the hell have you been? You're always up at this time."

"I'm in California on a trip and I was asleep. What the hell do you want?"

"You took a vacation?" Actual confusion laced Jackson's question and Zack wasn't sure whether to be angry or sad that the mere idea of him taking a few days off could cause such puzzlement.

"Oh shit! There it is again. That fucker is big."

Zack was well aware his threshold for his brother's bullshit was woefully low, but nothing about this call made sense, from the time to Jackson's panicked voice.

"What the hell is going on with you?"

"I'm at your cabin in Jackson Hole and a fucking moose wants in. And this place is such a shithole, I think he might make it."

"You're where? Why?"

"Mom told me where you hide the key."

"How does she know?" Did he even know?

Zack scrubbed a hand over his face and reached for his coffee. "Start over. Why aren't you getting ready for a game today? And why the hell are you at my house, which I've never even seen, by the way."

He and Hadley had bought the property as a vacation home, sight unseen, the prior spring. He'd had every intention of going up to the place more than a few times, but something had always prevented him from making the trip.

"I had the Thursday night game this past week. And let me be the first to congratulate you, because you bought a royal piece of shit."

"I what?"

He knew he might have been out of it for the past year, but Zack *had* seen the photos of the cabin. It had seemed like a good investment and a nice idea, back when he was still thinking a vacation place was needed for him and Hadley to find themselves again.

"Why is Mom giving you the keys to my place? Or telling you," Zack muttered as an afterthought.

"Because you're spending so much time here?"

Zack gulped down the rest of the coffee, buying himself some time to settle his nerves. His brother was uniquely adept at riling him up and whatever was going on here needed focus.

And calm.

Two items in perpetually short supply with his brother.

"Jackson. What are you doing there? Why aren't you in Houston?"

"I needed to get away. Clear my head."

"So you flew to Wyoming? In the middle of the season when you're off to a great start and already in playoff contention?"

"Yeah."

Whatever irritation his brother could manage, and Jackson could manage a hell of a lot, Zack knew a problem when he heard one. That nonchalant tone, devoid of any of his brother's normal mischief and shit-stirring abilities—was the biggest clue.

"What is going on with you?"

The line went quiet but Zack had learned a long time ago how to wait his little brother out. It required patience and no small measure of calm, but he did know how to do it. And a lifetime spent working with large stubborn animals had given him a leg up on the practice.

He was rewarded when Jackson finally spoke.

"They brought another guy down here. He's been making plays and getting shit done and I'm no one's favorite anymore."

"And that's why you ran to Wyoming?"

"You don't understand the pressure, Zack. You don't understand what's asked of us. It's a fucking brutal beating we take, week in and week out. And now some young guy comes in here, just as I'm about to have a shot at the brass ring and suddenly I'm second fiddle?"

Zack wasn't entirely convinced that was all there was to it, but it did make sense. Jackson had made more than a few comments on his brief visit home recently about how old he was feeling. How different things hurt. And Zack had seen with his own eyes how hard Jackson pushed himself after an early morning run, coming back home drenched in sweat.

"What do you want me to say? It's biology, Jackson. You can't play football forever."

As soon as the words were out, Zack recognized his misstep. And unlike his verbal bomb the night before at dinner, bringing up the subject of Louis and Madelina's kids, this one didn't have Hadley right there beside him, ready to soften the blow.

Or redirect the conversation.

"Is that your welcoming way of telling me it's time to come home and ride the ranch with you? Put the plural in Wayne and Sons."

The argument was nearly as old as they were, Zack's insistent desire to go out on the ranch juxtaposed against Jackson's endless desire to have a ball in his hands. They hadn't reconciled it as kids and they had stopped even attempting to try as adults.

Scorched earth.

"It's me responding to what you just told me about the team. I've seen how hard you work and how much you push yourself. It's biology."

And it's just like Dad, Zack realized, even as he

knew well enough to hold *that one* back. Even he recognized Jackson wasn't going to take favorably to being compared to a seventy-two-year-old, no matter how much they both loved Charlie.

But it was an odd juxtaposition that both men were in surprisingly similar positions in their lives.

"Look, thanks for all the compassion in this little straight-talk therapy session, but I don't need you to go all big brother on me. I called you because you've got a fucking problem here."

Whatever calm he'd attempted to channel vanished. Zack got the stubborn and he even got the hurt at what Jackson was facing, but he wasn't a goddamn punching bag, either. "You want to stand the hell down a notch? You're the one calling me at four in the morning."

"Dude, you have a problem here. A big one. I'm not joking about the moose."

"What am I supposed to do about it? I'm in California."

"You better get here fast. I'm flying out later today, and I'll lock up before I leave. But you'll be lucky if this place is still standing when you get here."

"Great. Sure. Fine."

"Later."

"Yeah. Later."

The phone clicked off in his ear and Zack sat there for a long while, staring down at the face of his now-dark phone.

The house in Wyoming was a problem but it was just a house. They'd fix it. Or he would. After he figured out what the hell sort of shitty deal the Realtor got him for a house that was decrepit enough a six-foot-three-inch professional athlete was worried about a moose coming through the door.

What bothered him more was how quickly his brother had shattered his mood. That amazing sense of calm he'd floated on for a few hours with Hadley had well and truly vanished. In its place he had yet one more family member at odds with the direction of his life.

A direction that felt desolate and more than a little hopeless until . . .

Like wisps of smoke, the discussion he and Hadley had about his father filtered through his thoughts. Was it possible Jackson was experiencing a lot of the same things as Charlie?

He's a pain because he's upset. And because he doesn't know what to do with himself.

He's embarrassed because he can't do the things he used to. How would you feel?

How would he feel?

Here he was, coming off an amazing night with his wife. As the reality of what they'd shared filled him, it pushed out all the ugly thoughts about Jackson or his father or even the shitty reality of his own marriage for the past two years.

Because none of it could mute the truth.

He loved his wife. Now more than ever.

And for the first time in nearly two years—years full of bad communication and increasingly separate lives—he felt a spark of hope.

More than a spark, a conflagration.
He loved his wife.
And if they could still find the sort of connection
that had forged them last night, they could find the
way back to the life they both missed.

Chapter 14

"Do you remember that holiday party at the Cattleman's Christmas Ball? The year we got married?"

Hadley glanced up from the feast Zack had ordered from room service, her heart floating somewhere in the vicinity of her chest. It matched the same floaty sensation she'd carried out of the bedroom and on into the living room when the scent of bacon finally pulled her out of a dreamy sleep.

She'd made love to her husband all night.

And it had been amazing and glorious and transcendent and . . . "Oh! The one where that drunk guy hit on your sister Charlotte, which you stepped into and got a shiner for. And then later that night she punched Chance Beaumont because, as she recounted, he had the unmitigated gall to go after the same drunken ass for insulting her?"

"The very same." Zack reached for his coffee, a sly grin tilting the edges of his lips.

"What's so funny? That bruise stuck around for a few weeks as I recall, after turning a nasty shade of green."

"All I thought that night on the drive home was that the world had tilted on its axis."

"What changed your mind?"

"The mind-bending sex we had when we got home."

"Oh." A warm blush suffused her cheeks as she remembered that night. She and Zack had always had a good sex life, but there were definite moments in their marriage that stood out. That night, as she recalled, had produced a stunning number of orgasms in a relatively short window of time thanks to her indefatigable husband and an adrenaline high he managed to put to very good use. "I remember."

"Sort of like what we had last night."

The blush grew warmer, but her own smile met his across the table. "That we did."

"I've missed you."

"I've missed you, too." She extended a hand across the table, taking his, their fingers intertwining over the glass-topped table. "More than I can say."

"Funny enough, I woke up to an odd axis tilt this morning, too. Maybe I should start hoping for them instead of avoiding them."

Although the lightness hadn't faded, she knew him well enough to know there was something more to his comments.

"What happened?"

"Jackson called. At four this morning."

"I didn't hear the phone."

"He was blowing up my texts and the pinging finally woke me up. I called him after getting a series of panicked messages telling me our house in Jackson Hole is a piece of shit with a moose problem."

"Wait." Hadley waved her free hand. "Back up and start over. What is your brother doing in Jackson Hole?"

He had told her about the cabin and the threats of a moose—were moose that dangerous a problem?—but when she probed him on the rest of the conversation those light and airy hints of fun faded.

"He claimed he needed to clear his head and Mom mentioned the cabin to him. Even told him where the spare key was."

Hadley couldn't help her own frown at that. While she had no problem with Jackson using their home—or Carlene telling him how to do it— the entire situation was odd. She and Zack had only left Montana the prior morning. Why hadn't Carlene mentioned it?

Or was it more of the referee game she played between her two sons?

"If the house is as bad as Jackson says, we need to call the Realtor. I don't remember the photos being scary or even suggesting the house needed that much work."

Although both their jobs had been good to her

and Zack, they didn't spend money unwisely. But it had been out of character for them to buy a property sight unseen. Only they'd always loved Jackson Hole and when the opportunity came up to buy the house she'd jumped on it.

And the possible chance to use it as a getaway from the ranch for just the two of them.

With the thought that her imagined love nest was a house of horrors, she couldn't resist asking, "Why aren't you more upset about this?"

Zack popped a piece of bacon into his mouth, the grin that had faded at the mention of Jackson returning in full force. "I had great sex with my wife last night. What do I have to be worried about?"

"A ramshackle house with a moose problem?"

He snagged another piece of bacon. "We'll figure it out."

With their hands still clasped across the table, Hadley considered what she knew. Her loving but often uptight husband was basking in the glow of sex so good it overrode a possible million-dollar investment error.

And then she decided to stop worrying about it. This was what she'd wanted all along. Some sign that all wasn't lost between them.

"I guess we will."

He smiled at her bemusement and only reached for another piece of bacon. His other hand still held hers and something needy began to build beneath her skin at the way his thumb stroked over her palm.

"You still up for that shopping trip? The one we missed yesterday because of the flight delay."

"I do still want to get a start on your sisters' presents if we can. The events coordinator at my publisher booked us hair appointments for the evening but that's not until four."

"While I am in no way trying to refute the power of last evening"—Zack glanced at his watch—"if you make me walk Rodeo Drive for the next seven hours I might divorce you for spousal abuse."

It was a silly joke—one voiced at the prospect of shopping and which had no bearing on their current circumstances—but Hadley felt it all the same.

A small shot of reality in the midst of their morning after.

It shouldn't bother her. And she refused to say something, making more out of it than what it was. A joke.

His phone rang, jarring her out of the moment and the silly reaction to a dumb joke. Even if she did feel a bit empty when his hand dropped hers to take the call.

"Wayne."

He stepped away from the table and into the living area but she could already hear from Zack's greeting that it was Carter. She could also hear from Zack's side of the conversation that there was an issue with one of the horses that required a consultation with Gray in another hour.

Turning back to her breakfast, she poked at her scrambled eggs with her fork.

They lived on a working ranch and that work didn't take breaks or holidays. It was a needed call and she wanted to ensure their animals were well cared for and attended to.

But no matter how hard she tried for logic, another one of those perfect bubbles of joy she'd floated out of the bedroom on popped beneath her feet.

CARTER CURSED HIMSELF a blue streak that he hadn't checked on the horses the night before.

But he'd wanted another day with Bea, damn it, and that had included the night, too. Another day to make his case. To help her see that he wasn't just committed to raising a child together. That he wanted a chance for them to figure out who *they* were together.

Other than sex, she had shut down on any real conversation, keeping things light or sexy, but never giving him room to address all the things he wanted to say.

It was infuriating.

But he'd let his dick make his decisions and had merrily gone along with what she wanted. Which had resulted in an amazing day with Bea that had ended with nothing resolved between them and her on her way back to New York for a few weeks.

Just like overlooking the problem with Arthur's foreleg, he'd willingly overlooked all the things he needed to say to Bea.

Carter opened the door to Arthur's stall, giving the horse the room step out, only Arthur wasn't budging from where he'd backed himself into the corner. His big brown eyes were rheumy with pain and it shot straight to Carter's heart, tugging hard.

He hated to see anyone in pain, and it always hurt when the animals couldn't share their problems. He thought this was laminitis and hoped Gray concurred. Because if it wasn't, he had no idea what they were going to do. He'd pored over the texts he had on laminitis and if his diagnosis was correct, they could start Arthur on treatments and hopefully stop the problem in its tracks.

It wouldn't change the long recovery time, babying the horse and getting him back into working shape, but it would at least save the animal. They'd lost two horses the past season and he still caught a few of the hands shaking their heads or tearing up when they passed those empty stalls.

"What's going on?" Bea's breathless voice interrupted his thoughts and he whirled to find her there. Shocked, really.

"What are you—" He stepped away from Arthur's stall, unwilling to disturb the animal any more than he already was. "I thought you were leaving."

"I was. And then I saw Gray in the coffee shop"—she held up a hand—"where I was getting a decaf. But he said there was a problem with the horses and I didn't want to leave you."

"Why?"

"Because you need help."

Carter knew he was fast heading from dumbfounded, barreling straight on to flat-out stupid, but he still couldn't believe she was standing there. Bea Malone, right in the middle of the Wayne and Sons stables. "You don't know anything about horses. Or treating horses. Or ranches."

"So." She shrugged, but he saw something deflate a bit in her shoulders.

"So how can you help me?"

"I can be here. To support you."

Carter knew he'd lost the thread of the conversation pretty much immediately, still trying to catch up with the reality that she was actually here and not thirty-five thousand feet above him, flying her and their unborn child all the way across the country. But he did know, without question, he'd hurt her feelings.

"I mean, I'm glad you're here."

"It was dumb of me. Stupid. I shouldn't have come. Like you said, I don't know anything about ranching. And I sure as hell shouldn't have canceled my flight to come over here."

"You canceled your flight?"

Bea stared at him, her mouth dropping, and he also would've sworn he heard a light snort coming from Arthur's direction. "What do you think that means, Carter? I'm here, aren't I, and not on a plane?"

"You are."

"I shouldn't have come."

She turned swiftly on one high-heeled boot and the move was both vintage Bea and enough to jolt the fear of God into his heart. Especially when she slipped on a small patch of hay that had been nosed out of one of the stall doors overnight.

Carter ran to her, grabbing her before she fell, pulling her close in his arms. "I'm glad you're here. And we really need to get you a pair of sneakers."

"Not on your life."

He turned her to face him. "On our child's?"

Her face crumpled at that, tears filling her eyes. "Damn it, you don't play fair."

"Nothing about our situation is fair."

"I know." She nodded, the move enough to dislodge some of those shimmering tears so they fell down her cheeks.

"Then why wouldn't you talk to me this weekend? Every time I tried to bring up our future, you changed the subject."

"I changed the subject with sex."

"A delightful conversational maneuver, to be sure." Carter pressed a kiss to her forehead. "But it's not sustainable."

"What you want me to do? I'm scared, Carter. I don't live here. And you do. And the more time I spend with you the more I want to forget that deeply irrefutable fact."

"I could say the same about New York."

"Exactly! That's my point. My life is here when I'm working, but someday it won't be here. But you will be. You'll always be here."

"And we'll always have a child. Things have changed, Bea. We both need to roll with the punches and change with them."

He hadn't realized how much his voice had crept up until he heard the hard cough coming from the opposite end of the stable.

"Carter!"

Carter glanced meaningfully in Gray's direction before lowering his voice. "This discussion isn't over, but I need to go help Arthur. We *will* figure this out, Bea."

She laid a hand on his shoulder. "How can you be so sure about that?"

He reached up and laid a hand over hers, just as she was about to pull it away. "Because I love you."

He hadn't planned to say that. In fact, until those four words came out of his mouth, Carter hadn't even fully realized they were there to be said.

Only now that he'd said it, he knew he meant it.

Because he didn't just want Bea and their child in his life. He wanted them forever.

He was a bright man and he *would* figure this out.

He was a damn stubborn one, too.

And it was just his luck he'd found a woman who matched him toe-to-toe on that front, as well as in every other way that mattered.

"How DID I never know that your brother-in-law was Jackson Wayne, football god?"

Hadley smiled over at her editor, Jaycee, whose voice was unnaturally loud on account of the hair dryer over her head. Only as she caught sight of herself in the endless wall of mirrors that lined the salon, she had to admit that what she thought of as a smile was a barely held back grimace.

She had no problem talking about Jackson. It was something reporters loved to put in magazine articles when they talked about the Wayne family and it wasn't a secret. But she'd also always respected the fact that her own show and personal circumstances weren't about dragging other family members into her life. So she doled out information sparingly. And since there was no way in hell Jackson Wayne, football god, was ever going to come on an episode of *The Cowgirl Gourmet*, it had always seemed crass to her to talk about him at length within the confines of the show.

But there'd been no way not to tell the moose story—which had made for a diverting conversation as they primped and prepped for the Total Foods event—without mentioning Jackson.

"He is."

"Aren't you excited about that?"

"I've known Jackson since I was a kid. We grew up in the same small town. So it's hard to think of him as a football god instead of just Jackson."

Fliss, her publicist, leaned over from where she was sitting in a nearby chair, her hair in rollers. "There's nothing 'just' about that man."

Hadley hadn't missed the bright diamond sparkling on Fliss's left hand and leaped at the opportunity for a subject change. "My brother-in-law might be an attractive man, but I'd like to hear more about the one who put that ring on your finger."

The question did its job and the conversation quickly shifted to wedding planning, bridesmaids dresses and the stress of dealing with the mother of the bride. Hadley took it all in stride, smiling and nodding, oohing and aahing, all while trying to figure out why she'd panicked after he got the call from Carter.

And even though he'd had to deal with the problem with Arthur, they'd still managed to get a couple of hours in shopping.

All was well.

Better than well.

So why the freak-out this morning?

"What about you Hadley?" Jaycee asked. "When will we be publishing a cookbook where the Cowgirl Gourmet makes baby food?"

She should have been prepared for it. Hell, they were talking about weddings and that inevitably led to talk of babies. But the question had well and truly smacked her upside the head, catching her utterly unawares.

"Oh, nobody wants to read recipes about mushed-up carrots and strained peaches."

"They do when it's you," Jaycee assured her.

Hadley didn't miss the sharp-eyed stare Fliss's stylist shot Hadley's own, but she kept her smile bright. "When the time's right, we'll know."

"When isn't the time right for babies?" Fliss asked, still dreamy from the discussion of her wedding.

"It's a big decision. And I'm not sure I'd be as comfortable with people seeing into the lives of young children anyway. Recipes about my own growing up or Zack's is one thing. But to bring a child into the show who has no say in it feels a bit unprotective."

Jaycee didn't seem to register that her question

might have exploitative underpinnings and Hadley was grateful the subject faded when her own stylist squeezed her shoulder before speaking up. "I see you got the latest *People* magazine there." She pointed toward Jaycee's lap. "The photos of the baby royals always tug at my heartstrings. That issue has like four pages of them."

"They're so cute!" Fliss's stylist added in and the discussion of families far more famous than Hadley's own firmly shifted the conversation.

But it left her at loose ends.

This wasn't the first time her lack of a child had been brought up. It came up in person more often than she'd ever expected it to and she'd stopped reading the comments on the Cowgirl Gourmet's social media posts because someone often brought it up there, too, layering their comments with assumptions.

On some level she understood the reason for the narrative. It would be easy for others to assume her decision not to have children was tied to her career, but it wasn't. In her mind, the two things were separate. Deeply separate. *The Cowgirl Gourmet* might have expanded beyond every dream she could have imagined, but it wasn't a replacement for a child.

For Jessica.

It never would be.

But was that how the world saw her? Would Zack?

She'd learned a long time ago not to worry about what others thought. Their perceptions were rarely accurate and it expended poorly spent energy worrying about what someone else thought.

But if Zack thought that?

If he believed her unwillingness to get pregnant again was tied to all she'd built as the Cowgirl Gourmet, then they were further apart than she'd ever believed.

And it would only reinforce why she'd stayed silent on the subject for so very long.

ZACK STOOD IN the middle of frozen foods and marveled at what the Total Foods marketing team had created. Smack in the middle of their Bel Air grocery store.

If he hadn't walked through the front doors, he likely wouldn't have even believed he was in a grocery store. The aisles had been changed and shifted and moved around. Spaces made for tables and even a dance floor. And there in the middle of the vast space, in front of what he believed was the meat counter, currently hidden behind a step and repeat, sat Hadley behind a table, a long line snaking up to her.

She smiled and chatted, happily signing books for everybody who came up. He'd stood by her for quite a while, watching how quickly she put everyone at ease, and how easy she was with her fans. Some had been eager, some shy, some had barely let her get a word in edgewise. But no matter the person, she was the same with everyone.

He was so damn proud of her.

"She's quite a woman." Louis Edgar had taken

up the spot next to him, obviously pleased by what was happening in the middle of his store.

"Yes she is."

"You're a lucky man."

"After having spent the evening with you and Madelina, I can say the same to you."

"I know it, man. Every damn day."

Zack considered the man beaming beside him, the things he'd thought after their dinner once again coming back to him. Louis understood what it was to run a business, to be responsible for people in their livelihood, to work with vendors. Total Foods was on a different scale than what Zack did with Wayne and Sons, but the responsibilities were the same.

"You manage a lot. From staff to real estate to the product that you sell. Did you ever expect it to get this big?"

"To be honest, I don't know that I did. That vision belongs to Susan."

"She has a deep love for the work. That was really clear last night."

"She does and she's good at it. It's a shame she doesn't get a lot of credit for much else." Louis hesitated, seeming to weigh his words, before he continued on. "She never did from my parents and really doesn't even now."

Zack was struck by the man's words and the insightfulness underneath them. "Hadley said something recently about a woman she works with on the show. Surprisingly similar, actually."

"She thinks I don't see it, but it's not that. I can't

fight Susan's battles and I don't expect her to fight mine. I can only support her and lift her up when I have the opportunity. But I can tell you—" Louis nodded to the large room spread out before them. "This right here. This is all my sister. And I'm incredibly proud of what she's done."

"Do you tell her that?"

Louis Edgar's family relationships were hardly his business, but since the man had shared, Zack figured he would take a shot.

"Tell her what?"

"Tell her that you're proud of her. Tell her that her work matters." *That her life matters.*

"She knows that."

"Does she?"

He'd spent his life on the ranch, outdoors and working with animals. He'd known who he was— who he was meant to be—his entire life and hadn't ever really had need to question it.

Or have others ask questions of him that suggested they wondered if his life had value.

He was the heir to Wayne and Sons, but he was also his own man. And he'd been given the room and the space to be that. First by his family, then by his staff. And, once he met her, by his wife.

No one questioned if his days were well spent or fulfilled, or if he was providing value to the world by virtue of being married or having a family. Yet in the span of a week, he'd been told of two women—two highly accomplished women—who questioned the same about themselves.

And suddenly Hadley's tipsy rant the other night made more sense.

It's this idea that people are objects. Or worse! It's like they've taken people and put them into groupings like they're our cows.

As the snatches of that conversation raced through his thoughts, he remembered what he'd told her in return. And what he now saw, right here spread out before his own eyes.

That's why you're successful. Right there. That passion and excitement and belief in what you're doing. That's what people are responding to. That's why they want to watch your show or buy your book. It's you, Hadley. You make the difference. In your passion they see themselves.

Wasn't that what she'd done the night before, when she acknowledged Susan's contributions in the conversation? Madelina's, too. And all the support and ready defense she'd had for Bea.

She was a champion for others who pursued what made them happy and fulfilled, whatever that might be. He'd always had her support. She'd never once complained about his four o'clock wake-up calls. Nor had she ever really been bothered that they couldn't take long vacations away from the ranch.

She just supported him.

Believed in him and in what made him happy. What made him who he was.

It was a gift, to see others that way, and his wife had it in spades.

Which made the fact that she was hiding from him whatever it was that *she* truly wanted—no, what she truly *needed*—way down deep inside—the most frustrating part of the past few years.

He loved her and supported her. He always had. And despite all that, she still refused to tell him what was wrong.

HADLEY AND ZACK were seated at a table of honor at the front of a luxurious tent that had been set up adjacent to the store. It was a lovely gesture and they shared the ten-person round table with some of Total Foods's biggest investors. Louis and Madelina had been seated at the table on Hadley's left with another group of high-profile business partners, and Susan had been given the table on Zack's right, again with several of the partners the Edgars wanted to thank.

Or court, Hadley mused, as she introduced herself to everyone around the table.

She and Zack had already been briefed on what to expect by Bryce, and then Louis and Susan had regaled them the night before with stories of the people they'd be sharing their table with. But nothing, Hadley had to admit to herself, could have prepared her for Winston Foxglove the Third and his sixty-years-younger wife, Sasha.

Nothing.

Not a stack of soap opera scripts detailing the lives of the rich and famous. Not a tell-all biography. Not even a full-on rumor-fueled gossip session with the Edgars.

Nope. The Foxgloves simply had to be experienced live and up close.

Zack had lightly kicked her foot at least three times already and it was all Hadley could do not to poke him in the thigh to make him stop. Each tap made her want to burst out laughing and the last thing she wanted to do was hurt anyone's feelings.

But, at twenty-three and shockingly vapid, Sasha Foxglove simply dominated the table.

Every attempt Hadley made to engage others had fallen short so she and Zack had finally settled into some sort of shorthand whereby he took on conversation with everyone else and she embraced the crazy to her left.

"No, no, Pookie, let me tell the story."

"Of course, baby." Winston sat back, his smile indulgent.

"So here we were, shopping in Beverly Hills, when I was putting a picture of us on the 'gram. And that's when I saw the post you were going to be here and I said to Pookie we have to go."

"What did he say?" Hadley asked. She didn't mean the question to come out quite as facetiously as it did, but was happy that Sasha seemed too into her story to notice there might have been an overtone.

And damn, you need to work on your overtones, Hadley Allen Wayne. Sasha and Pookie might not recognize them, but six other people around the table were sure to notice.

"He said of course!" Sasha gushed. "And then, he said to me, he said, 'I've been a big investor in

Total Foods. So let me just call up Louis and let him know we're coming.'"

Hadley smiled as brightly as she could manage in the face of all that megawatt enthusiasm. "It's great that you saw a post on Instagram about this event. I know Susan Edgar and her team have worked really hard to get the word out and make the night a success. Do you like to cook?"

Sasha's big blue eyes grew even wider, if that were possible. "Oh no."

"Oh." Hadley looked at Winston to see if maybe he was the chef in the family but he was too busy staring indulgently at his wife. And possibly—oh, who the hell was she kidding?—most definitely down at her cleavage, too.

"I just like your kitchen. I told Winston we needed one of those."

"A kitchen?"

"Sure. We've redone the mansion twice now."

"Three times, baby."

Sasha nodded, smiling at her husband. "Three. That's right."

"That sounds like a lot of upheaval in your home."

Sasha waved a hand. "It's no big. We just go to the beach house while they're working. It lets us work on our real project."

"What's that?"

"A baby. I want one so bad." She leaned in, her voice dropping to conspiratorial. "Real bad. But it's not working yet."

"Well, these things take time, sometimes."

"Like you and Zack? You don't have kids yet."

It was basically a repeat of Jaycee's question at the salon that had caught her so off guard, but the direct hit from the Kewpie doll sitting next to her was like being run over by a train.

One that flattened everything in its path.

"It hasn't been the right time for us."

"You'd better get going," Sasha said knowingly. "Time's ticking."

"I'm sure we have plenty of time to make that decision." *Or not make it*, Hadley slashed a mental riposte.

Sasha scrunched up her nose. "Actually, not really. The best time to have babies is in your twenties and you're past that now."

Hadley considered how to play this, not sure how her reproductive life had become the center of conversation, but it was Zack who neatly stepped in. He kept his voice low and his smile kind, but his voice was laser sharp and just as direct. "Babies are a rather private matter, don't you think?"

The eager eyes and slightly strained postures leaning forward around the table suggested otherwise, but it was Sasha's tart response that stopped the conversation cold. "It's natural and wonderful. You must want children, don't you?"

Zack's eyes narrowed, all traces of warmth vanishing from his voice. "We don't discuss that part of our lives."

As if he'd finally keyed into his wife's overstep, Winston laid a hand on her arm. "You're always so enthusiastic, baby. Leave others to their privacy. They're entitled to it."

Sasha harrumphed as she sat back in her chair, like a child who'd been denied a cookie. "Then why's she famous if she doesn't want people poking in her life?"

It was Hadley's turn to press her foot to Zack's and she added a quick squeeze to his thigh under the table. Pasting on a bright smile, she shifted her gaze around the table, zeroing in on the woman with the warmest smile and kindest eyes. "Amanda, right?"

The woman smiled at the fact she'd been remembered and Hadley used the quick moment to her advantage. "You mentioned in the book signing line that you and your husband are big weekend grillers. What are some of your favorite recipes?"

Amanda and her husband launched into a story of their first Chateaubriand they'd attempted on the grill while vacationing and the curious bear who'd come to check out their leftovers, quickly pulling the entire table into the story.

Everyone except Sasha, that was.

The young woman continued to pout until finally standing and leaving before the dessert.

Hadley wanted to follow, but something held her back. She hadn't meant to embarrass anyone, but she deserved the same courtesy in return. And whether she and Zack wanted children or not, the woman had overstepped.

Seriously so.

Her self-righteous indignation kept her inside the ballroom, mingling with the people at her table and then, during the after-party, with other guests who made their way over to talk.

She'd nearly put the whole thing out of her mind, convinced she could worry about it later. After the party and book launch had wrapped up. After the holiday special. And after they'd all settled down from the rush of the holidays.

That had been her plan.

Until she and Zack stepped out of the tent at the end of the night and straight into a reporter, waiting to pounce.

"Hadley! Zack! Is it true America's favorite country sweetheart and her husband don't want to have a family?"

Chapter 15

Hadley dragged a complimentary bottle of water off the bar counter in their suite and tore off the cap. She was so dry. Parched, really. And her throat was scratchy and tight, like she'd cried for an hour, even though she hadn't shed a single tear.

Not one.

Zack hadn't said anything the entire ride home. He'd just continued to hold her hand, squeezing every so often before loosening his grip, only to return a few minutes later with another comforting squeeze.

Just like the day they lost Jessica.

God, what a difference twenty-four hours made, she thought bitterly as she stalked into the bedroom, dragging off the dress she'd so carefully selected for the evening. She snagged one of her heels on the circle of material where it lay in a pool but other than dancing forward a few steps to right herself, didn't even care if the material ripped.

She didn't care about anything.

Not one single thing except that her efforts to keep her life her own and her most private of thoughts *actually* private had blown wide open.

The publicity team had whisked her and Zack away quickly from the intrusion of the reporters, but the damage was done. She'd already texted Bea to let her know what was going on and had gotten the confirmation in return that the news was online. She and Zack had even been a text alert on three of the major entertainment news sites.

"Hadley!"

"I'm in here!" she hollered back. Zack had stayed down in the lobby to finish his phone call with Carter, checking in on the sick horse. He hadn't been more than five minutes behind her, but it had given her a bit of breathing room to think.

Space to handle the inevitable.

She picked up the dress from where it lay on the floor and balled it up, tossing it into her open suitcase. The strange-bordering-on-inane dinner conversation played over and over in her mind. How was it that the simple, clueless young woman had managed to strike so swiftly at the heart of all her problems?

It had to be pure dumb luck because she and Sasha Foxglove had nothing in common.

Nothing.

It wasn't that she begrudged Sasha her bright-eyed optimism or the woman's right to her own personal wants and needs. It was a snap judgment to look at the young woman and her considerably older husband and assume they weren't a match or that they didn't fit with one another.

But it was equally unfair for anyone to assume what Hadley should want or need.

Had that been what had bothered her? Moreover, wasn't that what she'd been so angry about for Bea? Why did others feel they had a right to intrude on her choices? And worse, why was the personal choice she wanted to make for herself always seen as coming up short?

You're not making the choice just for yourself. What about Zack?

On some level, she knew that judgment was the price she paid for being a public figure. She'd accepted that when she became the Cowgirl Gourmet; accepted that it would be a part of her life.

No, she amended, her and Zack's life.

Because if she were fair to him, he'd accepted it all right along with her.

And she no longer wanted to give him the one thing that would make them a family.

Zack came into the bedroom. "What are you doing?"

"Putting on my pajamas and going to bed."

"Did you want to talk a little bit? Now that it's just us."

This question was quiet, soft really, and in it she understood why he had said nothing in the car. The driver had been there, and the conversation wouldn't really have been private.

"Do you want to?"

"I think we should."

She nodded, already reaching for the tank top and pajama pants. She was about to grab them from her suitcase but reconsidered. This evening, she needed a bit more armor. Clothes that were a bit less flimsy. And something that didn't remind her of the night before, when her husband had stripped them off her.

She grabbed a T-shirt and a pair of yoga pants and quickly got dressed. "How's Arthur?"

Zack was making a similar change on the other side of the room, but she could still hear his muffled voice through his T-shirt. "Gray confirmed what Carter already thought. Laminitis."

The pain of the moment vanished as that news hit. Hard. Images of their pretty bay with the large freckles on his forelegs assailed her. "Are we going to lose Arthur?"

Zack's head popped out of his T-shirt. "Gray's pretty sure he got to it early enough we can treat it. Arthur's going to need to be babied through it and with his age I'm not sure he'll ever fully be a working horse again but he's ours and we'll see that he's happy."

"We will."

"Come on." He walked around and extended a hand to her. "Let's go sit down and we'll talk about our own happy."

She stared down at his hand. So solid and strong, the fingers callused and work roughened. Tough.

Zack Wayne was tough.

But as she took his hand she was quite sure this conversation was going to leave bruises neither of them were ever going to fully recover from.

ZACK HAD KNOWN this conversation was coming. It was the conversation they'd needed to have for some time now. He'd thought he was ready for it. But as he and Hadley walked into the outer room of their suite, he had to admit to himself that he was scared.

Bone-deep scared.

He loved Hadley. Deeply. Fully. He always had. But over the last couple of years something had happened to them. He knew he had a part in it and he knew he had a responsibility to them, but so did she.

He'd come on this trip with so much hope and over the last few days had come to realize they both had. They'd shared the unspoken belief that they could get it back. But it was increasingly obvious if they were ever going to get anything back, they had to work their way *through* this problem. He was willing.

He believed himself willing.

But was she?

"Want me to pour you a glass of wine?"

"Sure."

It gave him something to do, and he was willing to grasp at that small lifeline. That small delay in the inevitable. But even that task didn't take all that long and in what felt like milliseconds he was handing her a glass and settling down opposite her with his own.

"Thanks." She took a small sip before shifting to fully face him. "You said something to me. Several weeks ago, now. In the barn."

"The thing about us. I said that thing about us and making a decision."

"Yeah, you did. And you left me with the impression that you wanted out."

He remembered that night. The raw-boned tiredness after such a long day. The fear of losing the calf. And the hopeless anger that he couldn't seem to get his marriage back on track.

But he'd been a dick to say it and then leave it that way. So here, now, in this moment, he owed her complete honesty. Not some half threat hanging between them, just opaque enough to hide behind.

"I do want out. Out of what we've been living. I want things the way they used to be. If we could go back to what we used to have, if we could find a way, I don't want out. I love you. I always have. But I don't want what we've been living."

The words were out and they cut as deep and as hard as he'd expected them to. And at the same time, he felt air. For the first time in years, he felt sweet, clean, *honest* air coming into his lungs.

He wanted her. Wanted to be with her and wanted a life with her. He didn't want the secrets or the fights or the frustrations. He wanted the normal marital fights that meant they had something healthy and honest.

Not the ones they'd been having that meant they had secrets and ideas that didn't include the other one.

She took another sip of wine, before setting the glass down on a coffee table. "I think I know what you mean. I mean I think I understand. We've been dancing around our problems, or ignoring them, or trying to keep busy enough to pretend they don't exist. But they do."

"Yeah, they do."

Her lower lip trembled but no tears sheened her vivid green gaze. Instead, he saw earnestness and an honesty that had been missing for far too long. "I don't know how to go back to what we were, though. I've thought about it. Endlessly. I don't know how we get back to that place."

"Do you want to?"

He could have sworn he held his breath, desperate—no, desperately aching—for the answer to be yes.

"Yes, some parts of it." Her gaze was direct and he saw her struggling which was unto itself a surprise.

He *knew* her. Knew her innate kindness, and warmth and desire to do right by others. And she had always put him first on that list.

"What parts?"

"I know on the surface it's going to sound like it's about my job. Like it's about *The Cowgirl Gourmet* and all that goes with it. But it's not."

"Okay. Then tell me what it's like."

"The kitchen has always been a safe place for me. It was after my mom died. I learned how to cook the basics then and it gave me something to do that reminded me of her and frankly"—she laughed, even though it wasn't really funny—"it made sure that Dad and Harper and I were fed."

"Otherwise it would have been hot dogs for life, right?" He reached out and laid a hand over hers.

She turned her hand palm up and clasped his, nodding silently. "Yeah, it would have been."

She sighed, but kept her hand in his. "Only after a while, it stopped being a necessary chore and it became a sanctuary. The day I figured out how to make bread or the day I made cupcakes for Harper to take to school. Even the day I made my dad sticky buns and he smiled for the first time. Really smiled and laughed with us over dessert.

"It was my refuge, Zack."

They'd talked through the years about her mother. Small snippets of stories she'd share, around the holidays or at odd moments when she remembered something. But he'd also recognized that the making of those memories had been cut woefully short by the fact that she'd lost her mother so young.

So he hadn't pushed or, to be fair, when she didn't say anything, given it much consideration.

That reality hit him, a solid jab to the gut that he'd never really understood until this moment how deep that loss went.

He'd always had his own distant memories of her mother. Stopping in the grocery story as his mother visited with hers or quick hellos on the town square during holidays. He'd known Maria Allen in that vague way kids did. She was always

Mrs. Allen to him, a lady in town who his mom knew, but he'd never really *known* her.

And somehow he'd substituted that memory, along with Hadley's stories, for the truth.

For the picture Hadley carried in her own mind.

"I'm sorry I never fully understood that."

"How could you?"

"I could have been more understanding."

"It's not your story, Zack. She wasn't your mother and it's not your relationship to bear witness to or honestly, to think about."

"You're letting me off the hook way too easily on that."

Her brow knitted together, considering that, before she pushed back. "How am I letting you off easy? It's on me to talk about things. To talk about how I feel. I did deal with losing my mother. I dealt with it with my father and with Harper. I also dealt with it alone. And I found a way to accept it. Not to forget her or to stop wishing that she were here, but to accept the loss."

"As your husband, shouldn't I be here to help you? To help you with that."

"But it's not a path you can walk. You can't do it for me. Just like we can't fix what's happening with your parents. Or whatever this thing with Jackson is, you can't fix that, either."

Was that what he was trying to do?

Was he angry because he'd been shut out? Or was he really, way down deep angry, because he thought he needed to be the one to solve it? And he didn't have that power.

Couldn't have that power.

Because he couldn't walk someone else's path.

And that included his wife's.

"You said tonight wasn't about *The Cowgirl Gourmet*. What's it about, then?"

Something changed in the air at his question. It was subtle, but it was clear.

Clear in the way her hand slipped from his. Clear in the way she shifted her body slightly away from him when she reached for her glass. And it was clear in the way she lifted that glass, holding it to her lips with both hands, as if she was hiding behind it.

Or fortifying herself to tell him the truth.

"Do you ever think about Jessica?"

Jessica. Their daughter.

"Yeah, I do."

"A lot?"

"Not as much as at first. But yeah. It would probably still be classified as a lot. Every day, at least."

"I do too. And if I could go back, or things could be different, or if we could have her—" Hadley broke off, staring down at her wine before reaching over to set it back on the coffee table.

"What I'm about to tell you isn't about her. If I could have my baby back I would. If I could have *our* daughter back I would." She reached out for his hand, taking it and then laying her other overtop. "You have to understand that, Zack. Please, if you don't understand anything else I tell you, you have to understand that. And believe me."

He saw the urgency. Sensed it. Knew it. On a cellular level, he even *understood* it.

"We can't have her back, Had."

"I know."

Just like the loss of her mother, it was a grief she'd had to accept and live with. Something she'd had to absorb and keep on moving forward with.

Only unlike her grief over the loss of her mother, this was a path they walked together. Just the two of them, forever intertwined with each step.

"I know that. And I feel like I'm betraying her and you by saying this. But I don't want to try again."

"Because you're afraid to risk losing another baby?"

"Because I no longer want that life. I wanted to be Jessica's mother. And I know I always will be, yet at the same time I understand I will never be what the world sees as a mother. I'll never watch her grow, never watch her learn, never watch her have her own child. But I don't want that with anyone else. I don't want to get pregnant again and I don't want to have a child anymore."

Of all the things she could have told him—of all the secrets she could have kept—this was the most simple, explainable reason in the world.

The most understandable.

And the very last thing he'd ever expected to hear.

Chapter 16

The departure from the hotel and the flight home two days later was a nightmare. The Total Foods sales conference that Zack and Hadley had already committed to gave the press—a streaming take-no-prisoners horde of them—a full day to find them and stake them out at every entrance of the conference hotel. Even with the publicity teams for Total Foods, Hadley's publisher and the Cooking Network working overtime to stem the avalanche of press, the attention had been an endless problem.

Zack and Hadley had attended the conference as if nothing were wrong, smiling, holding hands and acting like the happiest couple in the world, but from the increasingly dire texts and emails from Bea, Hadley had begun to believe it wasn't working.

People had even stared at the airport and she'd

seen a small story come up late in the morning news running on the airport closed-circuit, revealing that "America's Sweetheart" was contemplating a childless life.

She'd nearly walked away from the monitors, but the chance to see what Sasha Foxglove was actually saying was too big a temptation, so she'd forced herself to watch, sneaking to a corner of the executive lounge where she could find a less crowded TV to watch the horror show.

And was treated to a shockingly self-confident performance from the young woman she'd sat beside at the Total Foods dinner. The woman had been nauseating, but what had really stuck with Hadley was the way the morning show shifted the story off the Foxgloves and onto the issue of career women having children.

The story dripped with the same judgmental overtones she'd heard in the PANK conversation with Bea. Overtones that extended into a barrage of stories on social media.

Bea had texted her several times before take-off and Hadley could tell by the careful, overbright tone that she'd spent some solid time on crafting her words. But the net-net of it was that they needed to connect when she got home and game plan the next few weeks because the press stories had shifted from discussions of a baby to bigger discussions that she and Zack's marriage was in trouble.

Those overbright tones never said the words, but Hadley heard them loud and clear, regardless: The network was concerned their family-friendly

Christmas special was going to bomb when there was no sign of a family as well as an equal lack of a happy couple who people could imprint their hopes of an impending family on.

She and Zack had spoken sporadically on the way home, the conversation stilted. Their discussion about children had ended quietly, both of them realizing there wasn't much else to say. He didn't have many questions after she told him the truth of her feelings, and when she had mentioned heading to bed he didn't stop her.

Nor had he come into bed that night, instead sleeping on the couch. A situation he'd repeated the next night.

She'd barely slept either night, but the lack of mussed covers or a dented pillow told her all she needed to know. Even when she had drifted off, Zack had remained on the couch.

The drive home from Billings had been even quieter, and it was only when they made the last turn to the ranch that Hadley realized things had gone well beyond her wildest expectations. Visitors were barred from entering ranch property, a reality they'd had to put in place a few seasons into her show, but that hadn't stopped reporters from staking out the area opposite the ranch entrance.

"What the hell is this?"

"It looks like the reporters weren't just waiting for us at the conference," she said.

"Why didn't anyone tell us it was this bad? When Mike from security called me a few hours ago he said there was a bit of commotion out front.

This"—Zack gestured to the line of SUVs that were parked on the brim of the road for what looked like at least a hundred yards—"is hardly a bit."

She shrugged. "I really don't know."

Zack shook his head as he made the left into their front entrance, the notes of disbelief clear in his voice. "This is all for us?"

"Seems like it."

"Because you sat next to a dumb blonde at a party with a big mouth?"

Again, all she could do was agree. "I guess so."

"Ridiculous," he muttered.

He opened the gates with his remote, ignoring the press of cameras and screaming reporters outside the window. Their security team was already standing sentinel behind the gates and stepped through the moment they were open, holding everyone back.

Zack pulled through, allowing the gates to swing closed behind them, before putting the truck in Park and jumping out to talk to Mike, their head of security. Hadley considered going out with him to get a handle on what was happening but decided the long telephoto lenses she'd seen held by several of the people they'd passed as they drove up told most of the story anyway.

Why was this happening? And why now?

Her hesitation to talk to Zack about having children—to tell him how she really felt—sat solely on her. But how was it that situation had collided so deeply and intimately with her professional life? As if the two were tightly intertwined.

She meant what she'd told Zack. Her career had nothing to do with her feelings on children. They were separate in her mind. Her work hadn't replaced Jessica—it never would—but it had created . . . something in her life.

And in that creation of a new life and a new dream and a new focus for her happiness Hadley had realized that she no longer carried the need inside of her to have children.

She'd come to accept that she couldn't go through that experience again. Even if she had a healthy child—and all suggestions from her doctor had always been that she could carry a healthy child to term—she still couldn't see her way to wanting that experience any longer.

Hadley had always known that wasn't a conversation that would go smoothly with others. The persistent questions of when she and Zack would start a family was the resounding clue to how others saw her life and her marriage. Add on the persistent cultural norms that suggested the only way to a fulfilling life was by having children and she'd accepted that very few would understand her decisions.

But what was happening outside these windows proved something else.

People didn't want to accept her decisions, either. In a matter of hours, she'd become a pariah, one who'd engendered discussion on morning talk shows and garnered pop psychology diagnoses of her choices on social media threads.

She'd scrolled through a few of those threads,

while waiting for her flight. A mistake, to be sure, but she'd done it in hopes of understanding what was being said. And despite her deepest conviction that her work was not at fault for her choices not to have a child, the world did not see it that way.

But how did she make that clear?

Headline-driven stories about "a childless life" on morning TV couldn't do it. Hashtags saying she was a "bad woman," a "bad mother," and "would be sorry later" certainly didn't make it clear.

But worst of all, she wasn't sure she'd made that entirely clear to Zack.

So why was it all cratering now?

Bea kept telling her that her career had gone to the next level. Was this scrutiny a consequence of that? Because more and more people were interested in her work, did that suddenly make her an object instead of a person?

As she glanced over to the side mirror on the truck, the reporters and photographers evident in the reflection, she knew the answer.

Yes.

Only what right did she have to be mad about it? She took this on. She had *chosen* this, fully. The show, the holiday special, the books. She'd chosen it all.

And now all that she'd tried to keep from her husband—whether to protect him and yeah, to protect herself, too—had exploded into a million pieces.

The genie was out of the bottle.

And her former life that bottle represented would never be put back together.

BEA CONSIDERED ALL the ways of how to play the current situation as she waited for Hadley to get home and, as of yet, hadn't come up with one damn answer that seemed to fit. So she'd taken a page out of her friend's book and had baked two pies, three batches of cookies and tried her hand at a tater tot casserole Hadley's father-in-law swore by.

What had been the bigger surprise was Carlene Wayne bustling into the Wayne kitchen around lunchtime, a few sacks of groceries in her arms and her mother-in-law in tow, confirming to Bea that she'd made a nice dent in their comfort food needs for the next few days but they still had a lot more to do.

The women seemed unphased that Bea was not only there, but had spread herself out in Hadley's kitchen like she belonged there. And then the three of them had promptly rolled up their sleeves, and worked through two more casseroles, a double batch of biscuits and a meatloaf Mamma Wayne had assured her would be the first thing to go.

Bea wasn't sure she'd ever seen so much cheese, sour cream or cream of mushroom soup outside of a food set, but she couldn't deny the sense that she was doing *something* instead of sending increasingly panicky texts. And she'd also taken heart that after three increasingly senior-level calls with the network that she excused herself to take, she'd convinced the Cooking Network brass to not only stand behind Hadley but to proudly broadcast the show.

All while marveling at how fast their loyalty had evaporated to "their favorite star," "the future of their network" and the woman who'd single-handedly helped make their streaming launch two years before a raging success.

"Sit down and get off your feet. You're pregnant and you need to eat a few of these biscuits." Mamma Wayne shoved a plate at her and the scent of biscuits and melting butter on top hit Bea so hard she actually salivated.

Before her eyes popped wide open. "How? I mean, why—" She broke off, dropping onto one of the bar stools that hugged the edge of the counter. "How do you know?"

"Aside from the fact I had four myself?" Mamma Wayne wagged a finger before tipping it under Bea's chin. Her dark brown eyes bored into Bea's, direct but innately kind. "A woman knows, sweetheart. And it's been no secret you and Carter have eyes for each other. How'd he take the news?"

Carlene smiled from behind her mother-in-law, but instead of providing her support in getting Mamma Wayne to quiet down and butt out, she shrugged, snagged her bottle of water off the counter and grabbed a seat next to Bea. "That man is fine. So come on. Spill."

Which was how Bea found herself doing just as she'd been told, spilling her guts to two women who listened, nodded, agreed, poked, prodded and, in the end, supported her. All while she managed to eat four biscuits.

"Oh my God." She clutched her stomach, suddenly panicked the biscuits were preparing for a return trip.

Only as she sat there, thinking about it, not only *wasn't* she sick, she could actually have another one if it wouldn't be so mortifyingly embarrassing to inhale more food.

Which was how Hadley found them, wheeling her suitcase through the garage door and on into the kitchen, her expression crumpling when she caught sight of the entourage assembled in her kitchen.

"You're here. You're all here." Big tears streamed down her face and it was Carlene who moved first, pulling her close in a tight embrace.

"Don't you worry about this. We've got you and we'll figure it out. We're all going to figure it out."

"It's a mess. The things they're saying. The stories. The—" Hadley broke off on a hiccupy sigh. "The reporters are everywhere."

"Sold out the Ramada downtown and the Hilton three towns over," Mamma Wayne piped up before wedging her way in between Carlene and Hadley to pull her granddaughter-in-law in for a tight hug. "So let's give 'em something to report on."

"I don't want them to report on anything. I want them to go away." Hadley's voice was emphatic but the tone held little hope for that outcome.

A sentiment Mamma Wayne obviously shared. "That won't be happening, baby girl."

Mamma Wayne was small and slender like Hadley, but when she stepped back, her arm still around Hadley's waist, Bea saw something rather remarkable.

Solidarity and a common front that was as tough as bedrock and twice as deep.

Hadley laid her head against Mamma Wayne's. "Thanks for the pep talk."

"I never was a cheerleader." Mamma Wayne waved a hand. "But I do know how to get shit done. And that's what we're going to do."

"I don't think it's quite that easy. Those reporters have sunk their teeth into this."

"That may be true," Carlene said as she handed Hadley a fresh glass of water. "But in here is a safe space and we're going to figure this out. Together."

"In the meantime, Bea and Carter are having a baby, so let's talk more about that."

Mamma Wayne's words were just what the doctor ordered, and Hadley's expression went from sad and miserable to absolutely elated in the span of a heartbeat.

"You are?" She ran around the bar, pulling Bea close in a tight hug. "I'm so happy for you. So happy for you both."

Bea clung back, the hidden fears she hadn't even fully realized she had spilling out. "You're not upset about it?"

How hadn't she realized telling Hadley was a factor in her feelings about her pregnancy? For all the people at the Cooking Network who worked on Hadley's behalf, Bea was the face.

The conduit, really, to the network.

She'd worked hard to keep a proper, professional distance, but the two women had become friends anyway. Good friends.

But even a strong friendship couldn't change the fact that they were in a high-stakes work relationship. Hadn't those calls to the network, her pressing to keep the holiday special while her boss's boss's boss prevaricated on what to do, been a prime example of that?

Whether she liked it or not, Bea had a responsibility to her job. And just as she'd worried that Hadley would think less of her for fraternizing with one of the Wayne and Sons staff, nothing could change the fact that Bea would be the one to deliver bad news about Hadley's career.

Any bad news that came from the network.

It slammed into Bea how real that suddenly felt, after two full days of bad press had descended on Hadley's empire. Two days of reporters broadcasting a reality Hadley's fans didn't want to believe. Two days of giving the world an understanding that the woman they'd built up in their mind had a mind of her own and thoughts of her own for how her life should look and feel and *be*.

They might have diverted disaster for the holiday show but it was only the start. No matter how the top brass had spun their decision to keep the special, Bea also knew canceling the show now, after selling out the advertising for the night, wouldn't be practical.

But what came after? If the press didn't leave this

subject alone it had the power to derail more than a holiday special. It could affect Hadley's book sales. Her holiday sales of cooking equipment. And the future of the show itself.

The public loved Hadley, but they loved what made up her life, too. And at the top of that list was the fantasy they'd made out of the romance between Hadley and Zack.

What would happen if that all went away?

THE MOMENT HE saw his mother's car in the driveway, Zack knew he wasn't quite ready to go into the house. So he'd left his bags at the entrance of the garage, and promptly turned and headed for the stables. He needed to talk to Carter anyway, and check on Arthur's progress, so it wasn't exactly an exercise in hiding out.

But it certainly had the overtones of it.

The stables had been empty when he walked in, but he had no sooner settled behind his desk and booted up his computer when his father knocked on the door as a perfunctory step before walking right on through. "What in the ever-loving hell is going on around here?"

"You watch the news don't you?"

"The news *I* watch doesn't usually run to celebrity gossip."

"Then I'll recap it for you in one. The world found out Hadley doesn't want kids about two hours before I did."

"Oh." His father sat down hard on the chair opposite Zack's desk. It struck him how oddly similar the moment felt to the one they'd had a few weeks ago, bonding over good Scotch.

He'd felt miserable that night, too, but for an entirely different reason. He'd blindsided his wife that night, in a way that betrayed what they were and what he'd vowed to her.

And now here he was, blindsided by her.

He'd been on a rollercoaster since that night. From the lowest depths to the highest heights and now even lower than when he'd started. If you'd asked him before that disastrous night in the kitchen, he'd have already said he was riding that out-of-control coaster. The increasing problems in his marriage. The fights. The endlessly swinging moods.

But since then?

Fuck, it had been a nasty ride.

One with endless twists and turns that refused to give him a break. Each time he thought he had his breath and his footing, the ground was pulled away and he was knocked flat, all that air whooshing up, up and away.

What was he supposed to do about it? How was he supposed to breathe around the goddamn pain of it all?

He loved his wife. Wild, crazy love that filled him up and made him who he was. Gave him a reason, damn it, to get up every day.

Which made the oily bitterness he couldn't shake that much worse.

How did you love someone and resent them all at once?

Was that love?

Because it sure as hell wasn't a definition he'd ever heard.

His father finally spoke up. "How do you feel about that? The kids part?"

Zack ran his hand through his hair, tugging on the ends. "Honestly? I don't know."

"Okay."

Zack laughed, the sound anything but gleeful. "Okay? What's okay about it?"

"She dropped a bomb on you, one that you have to deal with. Worse, you have to deal with it in a very public way. But you have a right to think on it. To really consider what *you* think about it. About what you want."

"What's there to think about? People get married and they have babies. Hell we tried to do that. And then—"

Charlie's gaze was direct, but Zack saw how his father's throat worked as he swallowed around his words, his voice thickening. "And then the world threw you a really nasty break. Threw you both one," Charlie said.

And wasn't that the bitch of it? Zack stared down at his hands and wondered why the bitterness he should be feeling—hell, the bitterness he was *entitled* to—never came.

Life had thrown them a bad break. The worst he'd ever experienced. But they'd survived. They'd grieved and cried and worked through it.

Together.

Only now he had to wonder if that had really happened. He'd believed they'd healed. Not in a way that suggested Jessica had never happened, but in the way that suggested they'd moved forward with the scar of losing their daughter on their hearts.

Only now, with the news that Hadley didn't want children . . .

How could he not know this was how she felt?

After a few minutes of silence, Charlie stood. "I'm going to leave you for a bit. I'm here if you need me, but I get the sense you need some time alone right now."

"Thanks, Dad."

Charlie waved it off, turning for the door. It was only as he got to the entryway that he stopped and turned.

"It's hard. Those moments in a marriage when we forget that it's two people. Two individuals who make up the whole." He tugged on his earlobe. "Who make up something better as a whole, but who are still individuals, too. I've forgotten that these past months. Put your mother and you and your brother and your sisters through hell for it, too."

Zack was touched by his father's words and despite the heaviness of their conversation, he couldn't resist teasing Charlie a little bit. "You can put the ranch hands on that list, too, you know."

A small gleam lit Charlie's brown eyes. "The terror of the bunkhouse."

Zack had heard some subtle whispers but didn't realize they'd made it back to his father. "You caught wind of that, did you?"

"Hell yeah. And once I heard it, I did my level best to earn the title."

"You old son of a bitch."

"That I am, and I come from a long line of 'em."

Zack did laugh at that, and the fact that his father had known what was being said about him by the ranch hands was vintage Charlie.

"The thing is, you really do need to take your time here. You're upset and you're feeling mislead and you have a right to it. I love Hadley more than I can say, but she owed you that conversation a lot sooner than now."

"I know."

"But what I also know is that woman isn't mean or manipulative or hurtful. And she loves you with a depth that people envy. So if she feels that way, you owe her that time to think on it, too. And maybe ponder on why she waited so long."

With that, his father turned, leaving Zack to his thoughts.

They were heavy and dark, but if he were honest with himself, there were small, broken pieces of honesty that kept trying to poke through that darkness. And as he let those shots of fairness swirl around, punching through what had felt like a betrayal from his wife, he realized a few things.

At the top of that list was the sense of betrayal that she hadn't told him. That all they'd been through for the past few years sat squarely on her unwillingness to talk to him. It hurt and it flew in the face of everything he believed about his marriage. About their relationship with each other, one that had been rock solid—and damn it, *communicative*—from the first.

As he let that sink in, he gave the hurt its proper space and room to breathe.

Even as more truths kept pressing in close.

Like Hadley, he missed Jessica—and what could have been—desperately. But if he were fair, he hadn't given much thought to having another child in the years since. He'd think about a family, but it was always something in the distance. A future life that was hazy at best and never fully dislodged his present with Hadley.

Just the two of them.

He could blame her for not wanting another child, but he hadn't exactly pressed the point, either. Nor had he ever taken the time to really think about what that said about what *he* wanted.

What if the reason that future had remained so hazy was because he felt the same?

Chapter 17

Hadley curled up in one of the over-stuffed chairs in the library, Bea sitting opposite her. It had been good to have Carlene and Mamma Wayne there. Their presence—and their voices of experience—had gone a long way toward calming her nerves. An even longer way toward seeing that the reporters camped out at the end of the driveway wasn't the end of the world and that they *would* get through it.

It hadn't hurt that Carlene had inadvertently lightened the mood when she lectured Mamma Wayne about all the hand gestures or screams out the car window she could *not* make as they departed the ranch.

But now that it was just her and Bea, it was time to be a bit more forthright. And a bit more honest about what was really going on.

While she was under no illusions her mother-in-law and grandmother-in-law hadn't seen through the cracks of her marriage, they'd all diligently avoided bringing it up. As it had for years now, the subject felt off-limits because they loved her, but they loved Zack, too. And telling them what was going on was akin to asking them to take sides and she couldn't do that.

No, she mentally shook her head, she wouldn't do that.

So she went for the easiest conversation starter because it gave her a few more minutes to get her own head on straight. And, hell, because it was *fun*.

"So you and Carter?"

"That makes us sound like a couple."

"Aren't you?" Hadley asked the question gently, but knew she'd landed a direct hit when Bea's eyes widened in a mix of happiness and terror.

"How can we be?" Bea stared down at the mug of decaf tea Carlene had made her before bustling out of the kitchen. "We don't live anywhere close to one another."

"You seem to have figured it out so far."

She wasn't immune to the challenges Bea and Carter were facing. Their distance was an issue and dismissing it wasn't helpful. But at the same time, as she kept thinking about the two of them together, Hadley could see how right it was.

How much they had in common.

Similar traits and attitudes that weren't tied to having a baby. Even if a child had become the lynchpin that brought them together, ensuring they could no longer remain apart.

Or use their differences as an excuse.

They were both devoted to their jobs, each with an astounding work ethic. They were both deeply kind, a trait that was shown off to perfection in their roles as natural leaders. She had always seen that with Carter and how he managed as their ranch foreman. He had a firm hand, but he understood that the people who worked for him were people. Individuals.

Bea faced no fewer challenges. She had a crew of people two thousand miles away from home that she was fully responsible for. She did it well and, like Carter, she also understood that all those people weren't carbon copies of one another, but human beings with individual needs and thoughts and personal situations. In the four years they'd worked together, Bea hadn't lost any team members to resignation, and that included the months on end they all spent in Montana.

That was exceedingly rare and something to be celebrated.

"What's that look for?" Bea asked.

"You. I was thinking about you and how freaking kick-ass you are."

"What?"

Bea was flustered, which was rare to see, but it further reinforced all Hadley already thought.

"You, my friend. You take on challenges that would fell most mortals and you're considerate of others while you do it."

"It's my job."

"No." Hadley shook her head, taking a sip of

her own tea. "It's more than that. You built a life for yourself, all on your own, and you should be damn proud of it."

"I am proud. Most days."

"And on the days you're not?"

Bea hesitated.

"What?" Hadley pressed. "What is it?"

"It's just that I don't want you to equate what I'm going to say with what's going on with these stupid headlines about you."

"Why not? Are they related?"

Bea shrugged. "No, but it's probably not too big a leap to make."

"Tell me anyway."

"Okay. But these are my experiences. And it really feels like bad timing since you're getting this heat all of a sudden because of that stupid woman's antics."

Hadley nodded, even more intrigued that her friend felt the need to qualify things so specifically.

And curious or not, it was a departure from Bea's normally direct nature. "Fair. But maybe you can also help me see this in a different light. Because one moment I'm having a random conversation with a stranger and the next my life is upside down. It's surreal and I'd like something new to think about other than how I could have had that conversation come out with a different ending."

Which was her most fervent wish and also a way-down-deep cop-out. Sasha Foxglove was the villain in this little byplay, but Sasha wasn't responsible for Hadley's not talking to Zack about this sooner. She could mentally shift blame all she wanted, but that one sat squarely on her.

Which was why she didn't want to let the subject drop. "I'd like to know what you think. Why are there days you're not proud of your accomplishments?"

"I hate that they have asterisks on them."

"What has asterisks?"

"My accomplishments. How I spend my time. My life." Bea sighed, curling her legs up under her on her chair. "You know, how they put an asterisk to denote something that has a caveat. Or needs to be called out."

"Yeah, sure."

"That's how my life feels sometimes."

"Why?"

"It's like this strangely repetitive talk track with everyone I meet. They hear what I do for a living and think it's neat and cool and wow, isn't that a big deal. Then as the conversation continues, they inevitably ask me if I'm dating anyone or if I'm married and if I have kids and when the answer is no, I get this knowing smile and sort of patronizing 'well, you've got this incredible job' response.

"And I call it an asterisk because it's like they suddenly need an excuse to both give me credit for the kick-ass job and a pat on the head that I don't have the societal norm they're asking about. Or like I'm outside the norms because of this great amazing job I have."

"It happened at that dinner we had. A few weeks ago, in New York." Hadley had forgotten about it, caught up in the flow of conversation, but now that Bea mentioned it, she had observed that very discussion. "And it happened in just the way you described."

"And it sounds so petty, you know? Like wah-wah, poor me. And I don't mean it that way. At all. But I don't see why anyone feels the need to console me. Or excuse me. Or fill in some sort of conversational hole I don't feel or even see."

"It's like they make the hole when all anyone needs to say is 'wow, what a great job' and leave it alone."

"Exactly! My job isn't a replacement for a husband or children. It's my job. I can keep those lines clear and clean in my mind." Bea took a sip of her tea, staring down into the mug, considering. "I'd always believed that, but then I'd convince myself I just *thought* that to try and feel better."

"And now?"

"Now I know I was right. I am pregnant and I'm so excited about this baby. And I'm scared and worried and trying to figure out these feelings for Carter which are a whole other matter." Bea waved a hand, even as a smile creased her cheeks as she spoke his name. "But never once did I think, 'Oh wow, now I'm having a baby so I can quit my great, kick-ass job and go work in accounting.'"

"You'd suck at accounting."

"I know! And not that there's anything at all wrong with accounting. But my entire professional life didn't suddenly stop because my uterus is finally getting some action."

"Then why are you trying to stop what's happening with Carter, too?"

"I'm no—" Bea stopped. "Okay. Maybe I am because I'm confused and still trying to figure out the whole where we live part and I'm not going to be here forever."

"A fact I've likely sped up with my public shaming." No sooner did she have it out than Hadley clamped a hand over her mouth. It was selfish and self-centered and she'd have snatched back each and every word if she could. "Oh, Bea. I'm sorry. That was so insensitive and horribly flippant. I don't want to lose the show. I don't want to put people out of work and tank this for the network. Or for you."

And as that reality swamped her, Hadley felt the tears that had been strangely absent well up and spill over.

Bea waved a hand before setting down her tea. "Pregnancy hormones. If you cry, I cry."

Hadley dashed at the tears, willing them back. For the first time, she felt like she was having a conversation that made sense—strange, alien sense—but sense all the same.

"I haven't put the show above my life. And if it all ended tomorrow, I'd still be me. I'd still have the people I love in my life. I've never lost that perspective."

"I get that."

"Sort of like your point about the job. I don't think this is just lip service I'm telling myself. I know it. I had a life before *The Cowgirl Gourmet* and I'd have one after."

"I think you would."

Hadley knew she would. She loved her job and knew she was privileged beyond measure for what her work had brought to her life. But she'd already walked through fire twice, first losing her mother so young and then losing Jessica. And now, if she didn't get things figured out, she'd face it a third time by losing Zack. Nothing about her job or her celebrity would ever mean the same to her.

Ever.

"But?" Bea's smile was gentle, urging her to keep going.

"I've thought a lot about that conversation we had at the Branded Mark. The whole demographic discussion and women without children and the assumptions that were made about them by that stupid marketing researcher."

"That bothered you?"

She smiled at that before admitting ruefully, "A lot more than it probably should have. But it sort of coalesced a point in my mind that I couldn't quite wrap my head around."

"Deep thoughts amidst the peanut shells and rousing games of pool."

"Deeper than you could have imagined."

Because in that conversation she'd gotten a better sense of how she felt about her own situation. Zack was owed a discussion about children—and he'd been owed one for quite a while now. But each time she considered how to approach it or what to say, she kept coming back to expectations.

From society.

And, even more importantly, from herself.

What did it say about her that she didn't want to be a mother? Especially because when she'd been pregnant, she'd wanted nothing more.

She felt the same for Bea. The excitement that her friend was going to have a baby was real. Deep. And from a place inside of her that was absolutely genuine and sincerely excited.

So why didn't she have that for herself? Where had it gone? And maybe a better question, *why* had it gone?

"What is this really about, Hadley?" Bea was still exceedingly gentle, but in the directness of her question, Hadley heard the truth.

She couldn't keep running from this.

And she might not know the "why" of it yet, but she'd damn well better figure it out. Because if she didn't, she had no hope of saving her marriage.

"I don't want children. And I'm afraid that by finally admitting it, Zack and I don't have a future together."

"Why are we doing this?" Zack's words hung heavy between them in the car as they headed determinedly south toward Jackson Hole.

"Because we bought a money pit which we've never seen, the paparazzi camped outside our home show no signs of leaving and we both need to get away. Besides," she added as an afterthought, "the sky looks gorgeous with the sun coming up."

She was right. The sky did look gorgeous. A small side benefit for waking up at one in the morning and leaving at two to avoid that mess of paparazzi who typically gave in around midnight each evening and crawled back to the hotels they were staying in. When he and Hadley had planned how to exit they'd agreed it was the only way.

And since no one knew about the Jackson Hole property, nor had Hadley ever mentioned it on air, it was a safe bet they'd be able to stay relatively hidden. His mother had helped by bringing over enough food to feed them for a month and he and his father had loaded up some repair tools as well, not knowing exactly what they'd find at the other end. Jackson's complaints had extended to moose issues and repeated claims the house was "a piece of shit," but nothing much more constructive than that.

So here they were.

Not that he minded getting away. He'd snapped at anything that moved for the past two weeks—fourteen endless days full of those paparazzi as well as the fallout from LA—and he was sick of himself and his own voice.

Not that he'd used it much with his wife.

The network brass had pulled out the big guns, going into overtime damage control. When he wasn't bitching or moaning at anyone, he was taking selfies with Hadley around the ranch, putting on a face of solidarity as well as eyes and smiles full of mutual love and affection.

It should have worked.

He felt like it should have worked.

But all their together time had only served to

push them further apart, despite the increasingly glowing remarks on social media and in a full page article in *People* magazine. The tide had definitely turned, with some blowback coming at Sasha Foxglove as an immature attention seeker.

Zack had been glad to hear it but Hadley had admonished him, reminding him that she was the liar in this scenario. And that while Sasha's intentions hadn't exactly been honorable or noble, she hadn't technically said anything that wasn't true.

Since he'd always operated from a place of keeping your damn mouth shut to and about other people, he wasn't ready to be quite so generous.

"Oh yeah, that's right." Zack pulled his conversational head out of his ass as the signs for their turnoff came up. "We have a vacation home that's got a moose infestation."

"The Realtor said nothing about an infestation."

"My brother did."

"Did you ever figure out why he was up here?" she asked, before quickly adding, "Not that he's not welcome. But none of us even knew he was heading this way."

"Mom's been quiet about it. I think she knows but isn't letting on."

"Knows what?"

"Whatever it is that has him all worked up."

Since that same ire that had dogged him for the past two weeks threatened, Zack took a deep breath. "He mentioned something the last time we talked about the pressure and the situation with a newcomer to the team. I think it's harder on him than we realized."

"Change is hard. And not being the superstar is even harder."

"Isn't that why we're on this little adventure ourselves? The Cowgirl Gourmet has a tarnished halo and we're escaping the endless dog and pony show."

Silence dropped into the car with all the finesse of a hurricane, his wife going completely still.

"Is that how you see this? Because I think someone's intruded into an area of our lives that's none of their business."

"I agree."

"Then why are you poking at me about this?"

"Why are we putting on a show about it? Why can't we just be honest."

"Our family is no one's business."

A hard laugh spilled out of his chest as the GPS gently barked orders to make an upcoming turn. "That's easy to say and harder to live. For nearly five years, we've invited everyone in. To our home. Our lives. Our family's lives. The world even knows the comings and goings of our ranch hands. It's a bad time to get cold feet, Hadley."

"We're entitled to our privacy."

He'd believed that. For a long time, he'd held tight to that very point. And while he hadn't fully worked through his own thoughts on the matter, deep down inside he didn't think their personal decisions were anyone's business.

No one had lived through losing Jessica except the two of them.

And a decision to start—or, as it increasingly appeared, not to start—a family belonged to no one but him and Hadley.

But now? After all that had happened he'd begun to question . . .

"Are we anymore?"

Hadley seemed ready to say something when a hard, strangled gasp left her throat. Alarm hit him before quickly morphing at the evidence of what upset her.

"This is ours?" Hadley whispered as he made the turn into a small dirt lane. Although the house wasn't yet in view, the stone driveway was barely visible for all the overgrown brush, weeds and brambles that nearly obscured it.

"Home sweet home." Zack gritted his teeth as he navigated the bumpy stones toward the center of the property. A mixture of embarrassment and curiosity—twin emotions he'd never realized could coexist—filled him as he considered this place from his brother's point of view. His successful, famous, too-cool-for-school-brother whose shit didn't stink and who had the admiration of all the world. Mr. *GQ* in the flesh.

And the stark proof, as that embarrassment heated his skin, that there were things in his life he regretted and hadn't ever really figured out how to deal with.

Things like his marriage. And his relationship with his brother.

When had his life become more about resentments than looking forward, excited for his own future?

It wasn't in his nature to feel this way. To be this way. Wasn't that one of the things that bothered him so badly about his relationship with Jackson? Of all the people in the world he should have a good relationship with, his brother should be at the top of that list.

Except he wasn't and he hadn't been for a very long time.

Now his wife was on that list, too?

He wasn't proud of himself, but even with more than two and a half weeks gone by, he couldn't wrap his head around Hadley's point of view. He knew he needed to focus on the root of what she'd shared. She didn't want children. But it was all bound up in his head with the fact that she hadn't told him.

Would she have ever told him if the whole situation with Sasha Foxglove hadn't happened? When he had just gone on believing it was a subject they agreed on, leaving him to assume there was something else causing problems in their marriage.

It was endless. This round and round of questions that only led to more frustrations. More resentment.

And a self-righteous, bubbling anger that needed somewhere to go.

Whispers of their happy night in LA filled his mind's eye, as it had done so many times over the past weeks. They'd found each other then. And all that resentment he'd struggled with hadn't been anywhere in evidence.

Why had he let it return?

Suddenly overcome, Zack pulled into the small space beside the house and jumped out. He needed air. A few minutes to collect himself in front of his disaster of a house while he wallowed in his disaster of a marriage.

And maybe, if he took some breaths deep enough, he could find his way back to those glorious moments in LA. The ones where he laughed with his wife, talked with her, too. And when they made love like there was no one else in the world but the two of them.

HADLEY CONSIDERED WAITING for Zack to go inside and see what their "sight unseen buying spree" had wrought, but when he headed for the side of the house with a waved hand and a "go ahead and go on in" for her, she figured it was time. She had a head of mad of her own but it was as much for her husband as it was for herself.

And if that car ride had given her one more task that she was going to handle, it was to pry open this seething, festering resentment toward Jackson.

She and Zack might be having their issues but it was damn time he addressed whatever it was that pissed him off so badly about his brother. Zack was already mad at her. She might as well take advantage of it and push him on all the things he didn't want to say or talk about when it came to the subject of his younger brother.

But first . . .

"Oh my God." She came to a standstill inside the front foyer, settling the cleaning supplies she'd retrieved from the back of their SUV on the floor. The house spread out before her, a mix of 1970s decor and an odor that spoke of deer musk and windows that hadn't been opened in roughly a decade.

Was something dead inside?

She briefly toyed with screaming for Zack—this was his mistake, too, after all—but pulled her shirt up over her nose and pressed forward. She'd take damn care of whatever it was that had settled itself in for the winter. And she'd handle it.

Alone.

Like an asterisk on the rest of her life.

That thought hit with swift punches, the smell in the house coupled with the image of handling the rest of her life without Zack nearly taking her down at the knees.

She was a strong woman and she could handle anything that life threw at her. Or so she'd always believed. But now faced with the threat of having to actually live that way, she felt small and lonely.

And fuck it, sad.

For all she felt in her heart. For all she hadn't been able to say. For all she hadn't been able to even put into words.

Hadley had always believed she was in control of her life, the constant whirl of work and decisions and commitments suggesting as much. But was that true? Because as she stood there, thinking about a life alone, she had to admit that Bea's reference to asterisks had felt real. That every accomplishment had an exception attached to it.

Had she done that with a baby? Somehow believed she couldn't voice what she really wanted without being judged? Or that her success with *The Cowgirl Gourmet* would be diminished or used as the excuse for something she felt so deeply inside?

Because maybe it was time to acknowledge she'd put the asterisks on her own life.

And she'd put her marriage in serious jeopardy because of it.

Resolved to add that to the discussion list with Zack, she pushed forward into the house. For now, she had a more pressing problem. One that she could tackle with some good old-fashioned elbow grease and sweat. An odd anticipation filled her and she took the supplies Carlene had given her and headed for the kitchen.

The house looked as desperate as she felt. But maybe with a little work she could get it back. Maybe she could . . .

The scream filled her lungs and flew out of her throat without warning. Because right there, in the middle of her kitchen floor, was a dead mouse and what looked to be about fifty fly carcasses. That same odor—the one she'd dubbed eau-de-dead-deer—filled the room and any hope she had of salvaging the house vanished. They should burn it. Clear down to the ground. Because if this was what she could see, who knew what she couldn't.

A sort of hazy misery stamped itself over her as

tears tightened her throat when Zack thundered in behind her.

"What's wrong? Are you okay?" He had her in his arms, the action pure instinct and, based on the pounding in his chest, adrenaline.

"I'm fine. I'm—"

"What happened that had you—" He broke off, his focus somewhere over her shoulder. "This made you scream?"

"I . . . I mean, yeah."

"A mouse?"

"A dead mouse and a science fiction movie full of fly bodies."

"That?" Zack pointed, a subtle rumble starting low in his chest.

She knew that sound. Knew when the very controlled, very solid Zachary Wayne found something absurdly funny. It didn't happen often, but when it did . . .

His head back, peals of laughter lit up the sorry excuse of a kitchen as he pointed to the floor. "Some wilderness woman you are. That's what made you scream?"

"It's gross. And this is our house!"

Her answer didn't do anything to stem his laugher. If anything, it might have made him laugh harder. "And it's been empty for four years. I'd say we're lucky that's all that's here."

"Oh God, you think there's more."

"I think you need to arm yourself for the very real possibility there's going to be more."

The expression on her face must have held the abject terror coursing through her body because Zack moved close once more, his arm going around her shoulders. "Want me to go with you?"

"Go where?"

"Around the house. Checking in every crease and crevice."

"I thought you could do that."

Zack stepped back, his expression wry. The humor hadn't faded from his eyes, but his words suggested an edge she'd never heard before. "You've been thinking a lot of things about what I want or don't want."

"I just thought you could—" Hadley stilled, realizing that he had a point. And maybe it was time she acquiesced to it instead of fighting him. "You're right. But maybe we can go on this little scavenger hunt together?"

He extended a hand, his fingers barely brushing hers. "Let's go hunt some wabbits."

"They're mice." Even as she corrected him, she took his hand in hers. "Small, sweet mice who are just lost and alone, trying to find their way to a more welcome home."

"Or there could be rats," he said amiably, as his fingers closed over hers. "Roaches, too."

"That's not funny."

He squeezed her hand before picking up the broom she'd carried into the kitchen with his free hand, then moving them toward the pantry on the far side of the room. "Yeah, Hads, it actually is."

Chapter 18

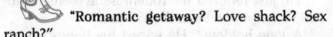 "Romantic getaway? Love shack? Sex ranch?"

Zack had muttered some variation on the same theme as they walked the house from top to bottom, looking for interlopers of the rodent and insect variety. They'd saved the master bedroom for last and Hadley let out a small sigh of relief when the sleeping quarters had turned up mercifully empty.

"Sex ranch?"

He wiggled his eyebrows as he turned away from cupboard in the master bathroom. "Not at the moment, but it could be."

"I go back to my original assessment. This place should be burned to the ground."

"Aww, I don't know. It's got good bones. And isn't it a health hazard to burn that late '70s pea green paint?"

Lead pain hazards aside, Zack did have a point. The place had been beautiful once. Very likely charming if the wedding ring quilt she'd found in the master bedroom closet was any indication. But it had long since fallen into disrepair and neglect.

Neglect most of all.

And to be fair, the '70s touches were limited to the kitchen and the bathroom plumbing. The rest of the house had beautiful hardwoods, albeit full of scratches. And once they got through the acres of dust and grime on the windows, she could tell there was incredibly crafted finish work waiting underneath on the framing and sills.

"I'm just relieved the rodent issue seemed limited to the poor fella in the kitchen."

"A lone holdout." He wiped his hands on his jeans. "But I'll go through and make sure there aren't any holes for his descendants to make a return visit."

"Thank you."

He stopped and turned to her, his smile wide. "You're welcome."

Despite their rocky drive to Jackson Hole and the frustrations they both arrived with, the past few hours looking at their cozy cottage from hell had been an odd bonding experience. One she would've braved a hundred mice for, now on reflection.

Zack's smile fell as he stepped out of the bathroom and glanced around the large rectangular room. "I think Jackson slept in here. I can see the divot in the master bed."

"After walking around this place, I'm surprised he stayed." Hadley shuddered. "And I'm giving him a hard time over the dead kitchen visitor next time I see him."

"That might be more recent than we realize. He probably shook up the place opening doors and moving around. That insect funeral pyre looked pretty recent."

"Maybe so but—" Hadley broke off, realizing she wasn't going to get a more perfect shot. Might as well take it. "You seemed pretty angry at him earlier. Well, most of the time you seem pretty angry at him."

Zack's expression shifted, a myriad of emotions flashing in a matter of seconds. She might know her husband and his emotions well, but it didn't take ten years of marriage to see the bigger problem. Or see the deep hurt beneath the hard set of Zack's jaw.

"You resent him, don't you?"

"I hunted mice for you and this is the thanks I get? A conversation I don't want to have about my brother."

"Yeah. I think it is."

"Resentment suggests an emotion beyond apathy."

Hadley waited a beat. Zack might be stubborn—to a fault at times—but he was honest with himself. But when he didn't add anything, she took the lead. "Then I'd say *resentment* is the perfect word. You're no more apathetic about your brother than you are about anything else in your life. When you feel something, Zack Wayne, you feel it."

"What do you want from me on this? Some deep, dark confession?"

"No. I want the truth. Why does Jackson bother you so much? Why do his actions bother you so much?"

"He has no responsibility. No weight to his actions. He wants something, he takes it." Zack waved a hand at the bed, that impression from Jackson's body still imprinted on the covers. "Even this. He's always welcome in my home, but he didn't even ask. He just came up here like the fucking king of the manor."

"But you just said he was welcome."

"But he could have asked! Could have given me the courtesy of a conversation. He said he needed to get away from Houston. Why?" Zack threw up his hands. "He won't say. Obviously he had some sense to run to family, yet even there he hid behind my mother, asking her for the damn key."

Zack dropped heavily on the bed, his own weight pressing the corner down. "I know we don't have a great relationship, but he doesn't talk to me. Doesn't take the time to ask me anything or actually talk to me. He didn't about the house. He doesn't about his career. And he sure as hell didn't when it came to Wayne and Sons."

And there it was.

The proof that the things in life that Zack valued, Jackson didn't.

"He didn't reject you, Zack. Not you or your father, not your family, either. He wanted a different life for himself."

"One he hid behind bravado and supreme asshole behavior. He did growing up and he's never grown out of it."

While she might be pressing him for the sake of the discussion, Hadley couldn't fully argue with Zack's points. Jackson had never been easy, a fact Carlene had lamented more than once. Where Zack understood responsibility to others, any sense of obligation or accountability Jackson had was more inwardly focused. His motivation and determination were always about what he got out of a situation. If his teammates benefitted from that, then fine. But it was still the Jackson show, first and foremost.

Zack didn't know much about what was bothering Jackson, but if Hadley had to guess, it was the very real, very distressing news that he wasn't the king of the football field any longer. There was always a younger, more fit player nipping at your heels. That would have been true from the start of his career, but would have only gotten more pronounced as he aged.

And there wasn't enough God-given talent in the world that could get someone past the equally God-given challenges of aging. Jackson had had his moment in the sun. Several of them, actually. Now the only person who could address his future was Jackson.

But that wasn't Zack's problem.

"You have to know that he didn't reject you." She moved closer, to where he sat on the edge of the bed hunched over, his forearms settled on his knees.

"Then why does it feel like a rejection?"

"Jackson wasn't mean to be a rancher. He never was. That's who he is."

While she refused to excuse Jackson's carelessness with his family—especially with Zack—she couldn't fault him for choosing the life that made him happy. Especially when that knowledge now rubbed up uncomfortably close to her own choices. The difference was that Jackson's choices—as a single, unattached adult—didn't infringe on anyone else.

The same couldn't be said for her.

Zack had as much right to become a father as she did for not wanting to be a mother. And there was no way around that immovable and immutable fact.

Not negotiation.

Not arguments.

Not even love.

"It might be who he is, but it doesn't change the fact that Jackson rejected the family."

Zack's words pulled her from her own dismal truth to the reality of his. His brother mattered to him and he'd taken Jackson's actions far more personally than Hadley had ever realized.

But how to help him see that those choices weren't about Zack. What felt personal was actually an act of self-preservation.

"No, sweetie. He rejected an opportunity that didn't suit him for one that did."

He finally looked up at that, that deep brown

gaze shifting from something only he could see to capture her face. "That's easy for you to say. Your name isn't on the ranch. On the business."

She tilted her head, the import of those words striking a chord she hadn't expected. "It has been for ten years." *I'd like it to be forever.* "It's a name I wear proudly."

"You do." He smiled at that. "You always have."

"The name Wayne means something. In Rustlers Creek. In Montana. And in the beef industry. But those aren't the reasons I wear it proudly."

"Oh no?" He cocked his head, a lone hand snaking up toward her hips, his fingertips barely brushing her hip bone before that hand fell back to his lap.

"I took your name all those years ago because I believed in you, Zachary Wayne. *You.* Not your family business or your ranching empire."

"And now?"

"I still believe in you. I never stopped believing in you."

"Why didn't you tell me then? Trust me with the truth?"

It was raw and real and in his searching gaze Hadley tried to find the words to make him understand. "I didn't know how."

"It's me, Hadley. The one you say you believe in. Did you stop?"

"No." She shook her head. "Never."

"Then why couldn't you tell me? After Jessica—" He broke off, something catching hard in his throat. "Why couldn't you talk to me about any of it?"

God, she wanted to find the words. The right way to explain all she felt and all she couldn't say. Thoughts and ideas she'd barely understood herself, only felt, deep down in her gut. In her heart. In her soul.

Wasn't that the worst part of all of it?

She loved Zack with a soul-deep love she'd never imagined experiencing in her entire life. Even the past two years hadn't been able to tarnish that feeling or diminish it. But it was with that same certainty that she knew she didn't want to try for another child.

"I don't know, Zack. Honest, I don't."

She stood there like that for several long moments, the winter sun shining in through the dust motes in the room, their gazes locked as each desperately sought something in the other. Some explanation to make it all make sense.

Maybe because there wasn't an explanation—or maybe because being together was explanation enough—she leaned down and laid her lips against his.

There might be so many things she couldn't explain, but wanting him and loving him had never been lacking.

And as Zack responded to the kiss, his lips opening beneath hers, Hadley wanted to steal a few more moments for the two of them.

Moments like they'd shared in LA.

New memories to keep close as they navigated the increasingly untenable waters between them.

SEX SOLVED NOTHING, yet as Zack's hands drifted up over his wife's hips, he had to admit it could go a hell of a long way toward smoothing over the resentment that never fully faded. That swirling bitterness that was as much for himself as for Hadley.

He hadn't stopped being angry, but here, with her, he found the internal contentment he'd had since the day they met.

It was odd how she could rile him and soothe him, all at the same time. Even discussion of his brother—a personal hot button wrapped up in more of that swirling bitterness he'd become quite good at—had a soft place to land when he was with her.

But it was those moments, the two of them together, braving the deepest corners of the house, that he'd really felt it. His partner in crime and his emotional equal in all things.

It was what made the past two years so frustratingly hard to understand or accept.

With a firm grip on her hips, Zack pulled her close, laying a cheek against her stomach. He wanted her. So badly he ached with it. And he had no idea how to reconcile the whirling emotions that never seemed to settle.

So he did what he knew how to do. What he knew with unerring assurance made sense to them both.

Lifting his head, he stared up at her as his fingers slipped to the waistband of her jeans. The button slipped free easily, followed by the zipper. Zack never took his eyes off her, using his hands and the familiarity of her body to keep his movements steady and sure. It was only when he had her naked, her beautiful body displayed for him, that he shifted her, laying her down on the comforter that spread across the bed.

The rest of the house might be a disaster, but the comforter still carried the fresh scent of being new. An addition Hadley had already speculated had come from the Realtor in an effort to upgrade the photos for the house listing. All Zack cared about was her comfort.

And her pleasure.

With that focus foremost in his mind, the thoughts of all that didn't work between them faded. Instead, the feel of his wife in his hands and beneath his lips took over with an urgency that bordered on madness.

His destination clear, Zack moved his lips over her neck and traced the soft line of her collarbone. That slim bone gave way to the flesh of her breasts and while he lingered for a moment, he already knew his destination.

What she needed.

What they both needed.

And as his lips covered the most sensitive part of her, Zack knew the truth. The physical might not solve anything, but pleasuring his wife wasn't meaningless. Or empty. Or a hollow gesture.

They might not have the words to say what the

other needed to hear, but they had this. Communication that was physical; a proxy for all they couldn't say.

"Zack!"

His name had never sounded sweeter as he pressed her harder, his tongue delving deeper as he drove her toward orgasm.

This might be for her, but it was as much for him. The proof that there was so much still between them. So much that they still needed from one another. A physical manifestation that all they felt for one another and all they shared—even the silliest moments hunting for furry house intruders—was more when it was done together.

And as her pleasure crested, a riot of sensation electrifying her body, she called his name once more, her hands dragging on his shoulders to pull him closer. He held out, determined to ride her through the storm, finally giving in when she tugged his still-clothed body to strip him as bare as she was.

When that urgency remained, refusing to fade even after the release of her body, Zack felt his own need rising. All he'd kept banked—all he'd willed aside in the goal of pleasuring her—flamed high and out of control. And as she pulled him close once more, opening for him with complete abandon, Zack finally gave in to the demands of his own body. Filling her, burying himself in the woman he loved, he allowed that blaze to consume them both.

CHARLIE UNLOCKED THE front door of his own home and walked in. He hadn't done that in a while—far too long. The thought snagged at him with guilty claws—and he breathed in deeply of the familiar scents of Murphy's Oil Soap and leather.

The Murphy's came from Carlene's ruthless polishing of every wood surface in their home.

And the leather was all him. Oh, how he did love his leather recliner. And his leather couch. And the leather jacket that had hung in the front closet for decades now. He'd worn it through in places, but he loved the way it fit.

Like Carlene.

He'd loved the woman from the first day he'd caught sight of her, out one night carousing at a bar in Bozeman with his friends. He'd believed himself both invincible as well as deeply in love with his bachelor life and his bachelor ways. To hell with anyone who said it would change. He was all of thirty, running his own ranch and full of piss and vinegar.

He knew his mind and he knew what he wanted out of his life.

And he'd taken one look at Carlene Butterfield, sitting all sexy and prim on a bar stool, and had fallen so hard he'd seen stars.

She hadn't made it easy, but she had accepted his courtship. And the same piss and vinegar that had made him so convinced he was destined to be a bachelor had been the same ingredients that had made him pursue the woman like his very life depended on it.

Because, somewhere in the courting, Charlie had realized it did.

Carlene was his match in every way. Where he was hard and salty, she was soft and, to his never-ending delight, equally salty. The woman could flay his skin off with the whip of her tongue and she could drive him to the heights of desire with the same speed.

She still could.

What had he been thinking? Hanging out and pouting in the bunkhouse for the past seven months?

He hadn't been thinking, that was the real problem. Zack had told him he didn't want him out on a horse any longer and that had been it. All he'd worked for—all he professionally cared about—felt like it was crashing down around him. In reality, the only thing that had crashed was his pride.

And all that piss and vinegar he'd believed he'd worked out of his system forty-two years ago had reared back up, suggesting it hadn't gone anywhere.

The worst part was that he'd sold his formal interest in the ranch to Zack years ago. He'd always believed the business of the ranch should be passed on and he'd had a plan from the start to ensure his children had the proper passing of assets.

But in that long-term vision he'd always seen himself riding the ranch and helping out.

Until the day his son said no more.

It had burned his pride and, damn it, it had burned the way he saw himself. He had no fucking desire to sit a horse for ten hours a day any longer. His bones couldn't take it, his ass couldn't take it and, if he were totally honest, he didn't really want to.

But he hadn't wanted to be dismissed, either.

It had only been the past few days, when he saw the issues between Zack and Hadley, that Charlie had begun to see things in a new light.

Zack hadn't ignored the situation of having his father working on the ranch. He hadn't avoided the tough conversation. And he hadn't left it fester, hoping it would somehow go away if he didn't talk about it.

He'd hit it head on and taken responsibility.

Wasn't that the hardest thing about Hadley's behavior? He loved his daughter-in-law and thought she hung the moon, but his son deserved to hear her perspective and point of view, her wants and needs, sooner than this.

Zack deserved to know how she felt.

"You going to stand there thinking about coming in or are you going to actually come in the house?" Carlene stood at the opposite end of the hallway, at the entrance to the kitchen, her arms folded where she leaned against the door frame.

"Do you want me to come in?"

She barely shrugged, but he felt her disdain from twenty feet away. "Up to you."

"Then I'm coming in."

Even after all these years, he'd never fully learned how to manage his wife, but he had learned how to manage himself. In the end, he supposed that was all you could ask of a marriage anyway. He didn't want to be managed by his family—hadn't that been the problem these past months?—and it wasn't his place to tell them how to behave in return.

But he wanted his wife.

God, how he wanted her.

Carlene turned away from him and moved back into the kitchen, leaving him to follow.

No, Charlie admitted to himself as he headed down the hall to the kitchen, she wasn't going to make this easy. Was he expecting anything less?

Since he wasn't, he headed to the kitchen and accepted his fate, fully prepared to apologize, beg and grovel.

And believed that forty-two years of marriage had to stand for something.

HADLEY KNEW BAKING was her personal therapy. It had seen her through the loss of her mother, the endless days after losing Jessica, and it had been a soothing balm for any other thing in her life that left her feeling out of sorts and at odds with the world. But, as she twirled around the decrepit, pea green kitchen, she realized something else.

Baking was her joy.

And when she felt happy, that joy was amplified.

Not even the lingering memories of what had been in the middle of that kitchen floor before her sexy cowboy had removed it had deterred her. Even if she *had* done a deep clean of the space before she'd set out her baking equipment.

She hadn't even had a clear baking destination in mind until the recipe sort of just came together, the ingredients seemingly mixing themselves step by measured step.

It was her complete focus on her work that had her jumping as Zack tickled her from behind. "You used to make these at the bakery."

He reached out, picking up one of the sugar cookies she had cooling on the counter, turning it over. Although this batch was still bare, they were a holiday staple in their home and she always piped different colors around each holiday shape.

"I did." She turned from the counter to smile at him, her breath catching hard and fast at the light scruff over his chin and the bare chest that spoke of a life spent in hard manual labor. "That first Christmas we were together you bought twelve dozen."

"I had to show off your work."

"You were trying to show off your pockets, as I recall."

Hadley still remembered the day he came in and made the order. The line had been four deep and while she'd seen him come in, she was busy filling orders and hadn't had a chance to acknowledge him. They'd only had one date up to that point and she also still had some odd notion of playing it cool around him persistently running through her mind.

But despite those attempts at cool, her heart still sped up when he came in each morning to flirt with her. It had been a few years later when

Zack had finally confessed that he'd moved back his wake-up each morning to three thirty so he could get his morning chores done and then get into town for breakfast at the bakery.

During that time there had been another guy from one of the neighboring ranches, Rob Lawson, who used to do the same thing. Each time he and Zack managed to hit the bakery at the same time, the subtle insults would fly and their testosterone-fueled peacock feathers would stand on end.

She hadn't had any interest in Rob from the start, their two-minute slow dance in ninth grade—and his roaming hands that she'd removed four times from her ass in those endless two minutes—had turned her off any future interest.

But Zack hadn't known that.

And when Rob, two spaces in front of Zack, had purchased a dozen decorated sugar cookies for the holidays, Zack had doubled down. Or times twelved down, as it were.

"Lawson's eyes were a bit too attentive."

Hadley considered Zack, forcing her attention off his chest and firmly on his face. She could have sworn she'd told him this, but at the same time couldn't remember actually having the conversation. "I never had a moment of interest in him, you know."

"I know that now. Then, all I could see was the competition and I didn't like it."

"So one hundred and forty-four cookies was the answer."

He shrugged but she didn't miss the familiar

hints of his cocky smile. "It seemed like the right move at the time."

"You nearly gave me finger cramps and piping elbow trying to get that many extra done over-night."

"That's a thing?"

"It felt like it at three in the morning."

He glanced down at the cookies before looking back up at her. "You should tell that story. On the holiday show."

"No. I mean—" She let her gaze roam over his face, those features she loved so much so earnest. Would they even have a marriage by the time the show aired? The thought depressed her, deflating those huge bubbles of joy with that dismal re-minder.

Only she didn't say any of those things. Instead, she just said, "That's a private story."

"It's a fun story at my expense. People will love it."

"I'll think about it."

"That sounds like a no."

Hadley was surprised to realize how quickly she braced for an argument before realizing that there wasn't any hint of ire in Zack's comment. In fact, there was a stillness there—a calm, really—she hadn't heard in a while.

A long while.

"It's just private, is all. People love those stories and it feels like I'm serving up bits of us that no one's entitled to know." She moved closer to him, laying a hand on his chest. "We've given an awful lot to the public these past few weeks. Maybe I just want to hang on to something for us."

Zack nodded, wrapping his arms around her and kissing her deeply. She sank into the kiss, wholly in the moment with him.

Or so she believed.

It was only as the sneaking thoughts wormed their way in between them that she knew the truth.

The stories of their life weren't just for the two of them.

If she gave them away, she might not have anything left just for herself.

Chapter 19

Carlene poured her and Charlie cups of coffee in the peacock blue mugs they'd used every day over breakfast for years. It was part habit and part defiance and part something to do to erase the nerves that refused to still.

He was here.

She'd wanted him to come home. In every hour since he'd left, she'd wanted him here. With her.

Oh, that wasn't what she'd told everyone else. To them she'd only shown the "I am woman hear me roar" attitude that suggested her husband was being an ass and she knew it and she knew she was in the right.

But in her private moments . . . oh, how she'd struggled not going to see him and attempting to work things out.

More than forty-two years ago she had stood before God and her family and made a vow to this man. It was one she'd intended to keep for the rest of her life. They'd had their ups and downs—a reality she'd expected from the start—but they'd managed every one of them.

Until this issue with Charlie and the ranch.

In some ways his reaction was expected. A surly attitude and some frustration that Zack had needed to talk to him was sure to put his balls in a sling. She'd been ready for that. Carlene had told herself she'd have to live through a week of moping, two tops.

Yes, her husband could be hardheaded, but he had never intended to run the ranch forever. He'd not only said as much to her through the years, but he'd made deliberate choices when he was still actively managing things to ensure their children took over to whatever extent interested them.

When it had become evident five of their six children didn't want the responsibilities or all the joy that came with the ranch, Charlie had worked to find an amicable solution for everyone. Jackson, Charlotte, Mackenzie, Keaton and Everly had gotten their shares of their inheritance and Zack had gotten his.

Along with it, Zack had gotten the opportunity to purchase the ranch and the broader enterprise and run it as he saw fit.

Charlie had managed that just fine. Better than fine, she recalled as he'd seemed to grow a few inches taller the way he strutted around the house, happy to have that heavy weight off his shoulders.

"Why are you here?"

"I'd like to come back. If you'll have me."

"If I'll have you?"

Charlie stared down into his coffee before lifting his head, his gaze direct. She'd seen a lot of stubborn in those eyes through the years, but in that moment all traces of it had vanished. Instead, she saw a sincerity that cracked her heart wide open.

"I haven't given you much to say in this, Carlene. I've been a bastard of the first water and I have been unfair. Unkind. And cruel, which I'm not, as a general rule."

"I'm not sure I'd use that word to describe your behavior."

"I would. Especially when it came to matters about the Trading Post." He took a sip of his coffee. "You're not a shopgirl. And you're not wasting your time, nor is Hadley freeloading off you for cheap labor."

"So why did you say it?" Carlene asked.

"Because I was angry. Stupid. And lashing out because it seemed like the easiest way to make myself feel better." Charlie reached out and laid a hand over hers. "Only it didn't make me feel better. Not at all. It only made us both feel bad. And I'm sorry."

"It's not the first stupid thing you've said to me in forty-two years."

A small smile edged the corner of his lips. "It won't be the last, either."

"I'm counting on it you stubborn son of a bitch."

"I want to come home, Carlene. And I want to quit being a stupid old man who lives in the bunkhouse." He shook his head. "Damn, some of those kids are young. And what the hell is a TikTok? And the music." He rubbed a hand over his forehead. "Woman, please deliver me from that awful music they play nonstop."

"You mean you don't want to be the terror of the bunkhouse anymore?"

"Not for one more minute."

"Then I think you should come home."

"That's it? You don't want me to grovel?"

"Not really. I'd like you to come upstairs and make it all up to me."

She'd watched the man's eyes grow sexy and hazy with need for more than four decades. And for more than half of the past year, she'd missed seeing the same.

Anger and stubborn pride had a place, but as far as Carlene was concerned, that place wasn't her kitchen. Or her bedroom. Or her home.

They'd spent far too long apart.

It was time to move forward.

IF BAKING WAS her joy, Hadley had opted to revel in it over the next few days. Her life had narrowed down to three things: making love with Zack, baking and cleaning their money pit. Because while she was determined most of it would be ripped out and refreshed, she'd be damned if it was going to look like a neglected pigsty when it went.

And if it was all an effort to stave off the inevitable well . . . it didn't feel like it. They actually seemed to be making progress. Discussing the house. Talking about the holiday show. Laughing and talking easily about anything and everything.

Well, not anything, Hadley admitted to herself as she rolled out dough for dinner rolls.

They still hadn't discussed children.

She might be grateful for the reprieve but *not* talking about having kids was what got them into this situation. Continuing down that path was only going to produce the same result. Which was why she'd tried to bring it up. Only to find Zack anticipate her and execute a rapid subject change.

No matter how much it bothered her—that desire to have it out and talk about it now consuming her thoughts—she couldn't deny that Zack was entitled to some space and time. She'd certainly taken enough of it.

On a sigh, she covered up the dough to rise one more time. After washing up, she loaded up her arms with a few garbage bags, some wood oil and few soft cloths and headed for the attic. It was the last inch of the house she hadn't touched and while Zack had already done a rodent check for her, she'd spared him the deep dive into what looked to be about five dressers waiting for a good going through. One of the garbage bags was for any clothes that would make it to donation and the other for anything that just needed to be tossed.

Once the clothes were dealt with they'd wrestle the dressers down out of the attic and consider stripping and refinishing what they could. She'd already earmarked one of them for the back office of the Trading Post and another that Mackenzie might want to refinish for the new apartment she was moving into in February.

It was all straightforward and Hadley estimated she'd be through the dressers in less time than it took the dough to rise a second time. A feat she was well on her way to achieving until she hit the fourth dresser.

And opened up a drawer full of baby clothes.

Dresses and onesies, footed pajamas and even some frilly panties that would go on over a diaper filled each drawer. They made as much sense there as the rest of the clothes she'd pulled out of the other dressers. Vestiges of a life that had been stored and set aside, forgotten as it was trapped in time.

She should have been able to look past it. Realistically, Hadley knew those small clothes were nothing more or less than the other three dressers she'd emptied. But sitting there, looking at the memories of what another family had used to clothe their child, she felt a soul-deep bitterness that she couldn't find the same for her and her husband.

What had changed so much inside of her?

And why had she given up the dream that she and Zack both shared? Or maybe the better question, why couldn't she find it again?

She'd loved Jessica. She still loved her, those few months when their lives were intertwined were some of the most precious she'd ever had.

But there was no way she could think herself out of the bone-deep certainty that she didn't want to try again.

It was in that certainty that the tears began to

fall. Great, heaping sobs, welling up inside of her with the gale force of a winter squall that whited out the world around it. Because wasn't that what this decision had done to her life?

Whited out everything so she couldn't see a hand in front of her face. Her future was in jeopardy and her way wasn't just unclear, but invisible.

For herself. For Zack. And for their marriage.

She'd never been more certain about how much she loved him and never more unsure about staying married to him.

ZACK STOMPED INTO the house, surprised when he didn't see Hadley in the kitchen. There was a bowl on the counter, covered with a towel, and he could smell the yeasty scent of the dough inside of it the moment he moved fully into the room. But she wasn't anywhere to be seen.

He'd been outside inspecting the property and making a few small repairs before chopping wood. He'd have seen her if she'd left to go into town and, besides, the car was still in the driveway. Only after calling for her a few times, he heard no answering response.

Increasingly alarmed, he searched the first floor before heading up to the second, taking the stairs two at a time and calling her name more urgently.

Still nothing.

"Hadley!" he hollered once more, before something caught his attention. A muffled sound, coming from the far end of the hallway and the open door to the attic stairs.

Was she hurt?

He double-timed it to the end of the hall and up the stairs, bursting through at the top only to find her in a seated position on the floor in front of one of the dressers, her face covered in tears, sobs shaking her shoulders.

"Hadley?" He moved to her side, pulling her close. "Talk to me. Tell me what's—"

The rest of the words died in his throat as his gaze roamed over the stack of baby clothes on the floor, more spilling out of the open drawers.

As if struck, he moved back, dropping to the floor beside her. "Are you alright?"

"No." The word came out on a half sob.

"Come on, Hads. Talk to me."

"I can't."

Zack wasn't sure if it was the adrenaline rush of worrying she was hurt or his own shock at seeing the stacks of baby clothes, but in that moment, something broke. Hard and fast, like a bone snapping in two, he felt something close fast inside of him. "Can't? Or won't?"

In the ensuing silence, he felt the air change around him. It was a second sense he'd honed from a lifetime spent working with the unpredictability of nature. From a spring storm that came up on you unawares, to an animal that suddenly changed course with a head of mad on, he knew how to read that swift and immediate shift.

He and his wife had done their own shifting and dancing around this problem for far too long and it was long past time to do something about it.

Tears stained her face, but despite the watery look in her eyes, her voice was surprisingly clear. "I don't want to fight with you, Zack. But I can't keep on like this."

"Like what?"

"Like we can push the inevitable off any longer. The only way out is through and we have to get through this."

In the firm set of her shoulders and sharp tilt of her chin, Zack knew she was right. And before he could hold his thoughts to give her room to speak, the words were spilling out of him. "I'm so mad at you, Had. I can't see through it, and the weight of it eats at me. These last three days. They've been goddamn nearly perfect, and I'm still so mad. I don't know what to do with it all."

"What do you want? For me to apologize. To take responsibility for it? Because I do. I know this is on me. All of it's on me."

"Right there. That." Zack jabbed a finger at her, into the air between them. "That pisses me off. It's the two of us here. Two of us in this marriage. When did you forget that?"

"I didn't forget anything."

"Could have fooled me. Here I was, thinking we had some problem and racking my brain trying to figure out what it was. For two damn years I've spent days on end trying to understand or dissect what happened between us. But all along the fucking problem was that you wouldn't talk to me."

"And you wanted to hear I didn't want to try for another baby?"

"I wanted to hear the truth! From you!"

The words tore from the depths of his chest, from the very foundation of his soul. "I love you! And I believed in us. And all along, you didn't believe enough in us to tell me how you feel. To talk to me. To give me an opportunity to understand what you were going through and how you felt and what you wanted."

She stood then, slim and still and strong. She looked like a goddess, he realized, her stance unwavering under the barrage of his anger and his words.

"I didn't want you to think it was because of the show."

He stood, too, unwilling to stare up at her as they got this out. "Why would I think that?"

"Doesn't everyone think that?" She threw a hand in the air. "Haven't we been in freaking *People* magazine because the world doesn't know or understand why we don't have a child?"

"Fuck the world! The world isn't here. You and I are here."

"Yeah. You and I are here." A laugh escaped her, broken and brittle. "I've been here for two years. Right here with you all along. And what did I get? My husband in one bedroom and me in the other. Cold glances in the hallway, and fake smiles that never reached your eyes around other people. I own all the things I haven't said. All the things I haven't told you. But I'm not owning the way you treated me. I'm not the one who checked out."

And she wasn't.

Hadn't he seen that?

Over and over, each time they had a fight. He'd latch on to the littlest things, using them as a proxy for all the big things he couldn't say or put into words.

And where had it gotten him?

To the exact same place he'd have gone if he'd just said those things in the first place.

"Maybe I did. But Hadley, why couldn't you trust me with the truth?"

HADLEY FELT THE verbal daggers spear through her skin, one after the other, a running litany of her sins. And she'd earned them. Every one.

But damn it, she didn't earn them alone.

"Tell me the truth, Zack. What would you have done if I'd told you two years ago I didn't want to try for kids any longer."

"I'd have—" He broke off, going silent.

"You'd have what?"

His silence continued, a strained, humming thrum between them, noisier than both their raised voices in unison.

"I'd have said you were focused on the show." He took a long, hard breath. "And I'd have said you weren't ready to try again yet, after losing Jessica. And I'd have said—"

He stopped again, before pushing on with the thought. "And I'd have said that you'd change your mind."

"That's what the world thinks. What people say to others when they don't understand the decision.

I never thought you'd understand, Zack. I know I wasn't ready to tell you, but I also didn't think you'd understand."

She blew out a hard breath. "I'm not changing my mind. I can't go back to that place. I've moved on from it. I can't have my child and I don't want any other one."

"Then what do you want?"

"I want the life we have. The one we've always had. Together. The one where it's just us, day in, day out. Every day." She took a deep breath, the pain roiling and rolling through her system with all the undulation of a snake over flat ground. "And if I can't have that, then I will be alone. Because having a child isn't the path to my happiness. And it's not going to fulfill me.

"Can you live with that?"

He stared at her, that all-consuming way of his that drew her in and lifted her up.

"I don't know."

"I can't be someone else for you. Not anymore." She nearly held back the next words, weighing them in the moment before letting them go. "Just like your brother can't be someone else. Your father, too."

"What the hell does this have to do with either of them?"

"You've been quick to judge both of them, too. Quick to take out your anger and your frustration on all the things they weren't doing to agree with you."

"That's got nothing to do with us having a child."

"It has everything to do with it. You can't control others' lives. You can't solve their problems for them and you can't make it better because you're Zachary Fucking Wayne. They have to take that journey on their own, whether it's convenient for you or not."

He stood there, unmoving, and stared at her for the longest time. She saw in his gaze that he recognized the precipice, the one where they stood at the edge.

With a fall that looked endless.

"I can't be someone else, either."

"I'm not asking you to. Really, I'm not. I want you to be happy. And I don't want to do anything to take that away."

"I don't know if I can be happy without you."

Hadley's gaze was unwavering as she stared into those dark brown eyes she loved so much. "And I don't know if you can be happy with me."

ZACK DIDN'T KNOW what to make of her words, even as they still hovered in the air above them like a thought bubble in a cartoon.

And I don't know if you can be happy with me.

Zack had the oddest sensation that he could reach up and touch them. But if he were able to do that, he'd rearrange them. Reorder several. And throw away the ones that had no place in a happy marriage.

With me I know you can be happy.

Those were the words he wanted. The words he'd believed since the day they'd met.

"You don't think it's possible?" he finally asked her.

"I don't think we can make this right or whole any longer."

Zack loved his father but he'd never envisaged Charlie Wayne as the sagest of men. Smart, with a business savvy that often surprised his opponents, yes. But a wise man with wisdom to spare? Not so much.

Which made it odd, then, that his father's comments the day he and Hadley had come home from Los Angeles were such a complement to Hadley's now.

It's hard. Those moments in a marriage when we forget that it's two people. Two individuals who make up the whole. Who make up something better as a whole . . .

He and Hadley were better together. Nothing would ever convince him otherwise.

But they hadn't been whole for a very long time.

"We can't go back, Zack. No matter how badly we want to."

"Why can't we have it again?"

"Because we're not the same people we used to be. We've had immeasurable loss. We've had equally immeasurable joy. And we've grown up in the past ten years. All of it combined together is the proof that we're not the same."

"I refuse to believe we're that different."

"How can you say that?"

Zack didn't know if it was desperation or desire, need or a necessary recklessness, but he couldn't let her walk away.

More to the point, he couldn't walk away from her.

"Because we still have this."

Without stopping to check himself, he moved into her. She was still the only woman he wanted to share his life with, no matter how impossible that seemed. And in closing that gap between them, the most amazing thing happened.

She took the last few feet to reach him.

As their lips met, that recklessness exploded in an aching dance.

One he was quite sure, even as he struggled to admit it to himself, was one of goodbye.

He was desperate for her. Desperate to get back what they had. And even more desperate to imprint himself on her senses, in a way that she would never forget when that goodbye they didn't want to utter inevitably forced its way between them.

It wasn't like that night in their kitchen. He didn't want to take over. He wanted something totally, completely mutual. As their bodies crashed up against one another, soft caresses morphing into urgent touches, clothing dragged off in haste, Zack took what he wanted.

And knew that Hadley took fully in return.

Chapter 20
ᗄᎧ

Hadley lay draped over Zack on the couch. She wasn't entirely sure it was healthy to lay two naked bodies over the couch that had probably been minted during the Carter administration and likely never cleaned since, but couldn't muster up the will to care.

Because when they finally got off this couch and left this home, the world would intrude again.

One she'd have to face without Zack.

They hadn't said it, but the sex had been a goodbye. She knew it and so did he.

But in some sort of mutual agreement she had no idea how to define, yet was completely real, she knew neither of them was going to mention it.

"There's one topic we'd better hash out before—" She'd nearly said "before we're no longer together," but caught herself in time. "—we get home."

"What's that?" His voice was as lazy as the circles he was drawing over the skin of her upper right shoulder.

"Bea and Carter are a thing."

"A pregnant thing."

"We need to support them. And I'd like to minimize the issues we're having when we're around them."

"It's not like Bea doesn't know what's going on, Hadley. She's been running the PR campaign to make the world think we're happy and whole."

Although he wasn't casual, the words were frighteningly honest and Hadley couldn't help but chafe a bit under them. "I know, but that's for her job. In her personal life, I don't want to upset her. She's very hormonal right now."

"And she's got a man who's crazy about her. They'll figure it out."

Hadley scrambled up, aware she wasn't making a lot of sense wrapped up in Zack on the couch. "But they live two thousand miles apart."

"Again, they're adults. They'll figure it out."

Zack was right on every count, but as much as she wanted to, something in the reality of Bea and Carter's situation had dug deep in Hadley's heart. She wanted good things for her friend and she wanted her to find happiness. All that ridiculous PANK stuff had only solidified her feelings on the subject and she wanted Bea to have every bit of joy and happiness she could squeeze out of life.

And what about yourself? What about your happiness?

Was she channeling this energy into Carter and

Bea because they were her friends? Was she just determined not to feel like the whole world had turned good relationships on their ear?

Or worse, Hadley admitted to herself. If she focused on someone else, she could ignore the impending reality of her own life.

THE DRIVE BACK to Rustlers Creek from Jackson Hole was quiet. Contemplative.

And a hell of a lot sadder than Zack had anticipated.

He and Hadley had lain together on the couch until dawn, both quiet. Other than the short reprieve when they discussed Carter and Bea, they'd said little else. It was as if all the words had been said. All the anger and bitterness had finally spewed out.

And all that was left was the formality of finally saying it was over.

Zack made the last turn for their home, envisioning the life that stretched out before him. Without Hadley by his side.

The street in front of their turn-in for the ranch was blessedly quiet, the reporters having left for greener story pasture. Their presence had given the Rustlers Creek economy, small as it was, a sizeable boost and he nearly laughed at that thought.

Even as he recognized how terribly sad it was.

Mike waved at him from the security booth as they passed through the gates, his smile wide, obviously oblivious to the quiet gloom inside the car. And in minutes, Zack was pulling into the wide space in front of the garage, the door lifting for them.

Hadley turned in her seat to face him as he put the car into Park. How many times had he done this in their marriage? Come home from somewhere away, pulling into this very spot.

Together.

"I know we didn't figure everything out with this trip," he started in, "but we do have a better handle on the house. And now at least it's clean and not in imminent danger of falling down, despite Jackson's early report."

"No, it's not." Hadley's smile was small and a little lopsided, proof his aim at lightheartedness hadn't quite hit its mark.

But it was her next words that spoke of the real truth they'd avoided discussing on the drive home. "We might not have solved much, but I think we did come to a sort of silent agreement."

"I think we did. About us."

"It's no one's business, but it's everyone's business and I think we need to tell our families before the holidays. I'm going to spend Thanksgiving at my dad's. I think it will be easier."

He'd nearly forgotten about the holiday in all that had gone on, but now that she said it he realized it was in a few days. Which meant the holiday season would follow on its heels.

"And Christmas?"

"I think it'll be better apart. We'll make the clean break and not have to live through that torture of putting on a bright smile." Hers hadn't widened, and one lopsided edge began to quiver. "We can start fresh and neither of us will have to pretend anymore."

No more pressure to show the world something that wasn't.

No more anger or frustration over what they'd lost.

No more Hadley.

"Okay."

She nodded back, that quivering taking over her whole mouth as she held back tears, before she slipped from the car and ran into the garage and on into the kitchen.

Zack shut off the engine and sat for a long time, staring at that closed inside door to the house, willing himself to go inside.

And he would go inside.

As soon as he'd rid himself of the bitter tears that wouldn't stop falling.

ZACK STARED AT the TV, the blur of movement on the screen barely registering as he took a sip of his beer. Although Jackson wasn't playing today, they'd all gathered around the living room of his parents' house to watch him be interviewed on the pregame show about his game coming up on Sunday.

His brother had done well, his movie star good looks, ready charm and light flirtation with the female reporter making for a smooth, easy-to-watch conversation.

Nowhere in evidence was the man who'd

screamed at him in terror a few weeks ago because of an eager moose.

One who Zack had seen from afar and who didn't have any interest in him, Hadley or the cabin.

When Zack had also found one of the moose's shed paddles up against the back corner of the house, he'd finally surmised that all the pressure and worry Jackson had over the moose was likely just the animal trying to shake off his antlers for the season and using the house as his own personal scratching post.

It would have been funny if he weren't so miserable.

"You're quiet."

Charlie took the seat next to him, handing over a fresh beer as he popped open his own. Zack's mother and sisters had already scattered to the kitchen after the interview had wrapped. They'd each showed their concern for him in their own way, with hugs and quiet attention since he'd arrived.

But everyone had diligently avoided discussion of Hadley.

Neither Hadley nor Zack had filed papers yet and she hadn't even fully moved out. The prep for the holiday special needed to happen at the ranch and he knew there were still a million details to work out about where she'd make the show once she no longer lived on the ranch.

Yet one more necessary conversation that still had to happen, even though thinking about it and all the other decisions made his head spin.

So he'd spent every waking minute in the stables or out in the increasingly cold weather riding the property. And she'd kept to the kitchen and her bedroom. Other than an accidental sighting in the hallway on Tuesday night, they hadn't seen each other or spoken since getting home from Jackson Hole.

"I moved out of the bunkhouse while you were away."

Zack turned toward his father, glad they had something to discuss that didn't revolve around him. "Carter said."

"I imagine the hands were doing a dance of joy, too."

"Gar might have done a small jig," Zack said. "Though that also might have been because he finally snagged a date with Chantal."

Charlie's smile widened. "That makeup artist he's crazy about?"

"Yep. He's been texting her since the crew left a few weeks ago. Finally wore her down."

"Or gave her the space to come back."

Zack heard the entirely unsubtle point in Charlie's words and nearly let it go.

Nearly.

"What's that supposed to mean and why do I feel it's directed at me?"

"It means you don't have to make this permanent. You can go back to her."

"I thought the whole purpose of a separation was that it was the waiting room for a divorce."

"Or it can just be a temporary holding pen while working through things."

Zack shook his head. "We said what we had to say."

"You want children so bad you're willing to walk away?"

There wasn't any censure in his father's tone. Instead, he heard a deep solidarity, layered amidst the sadness. "I want her honesty with me about it."

Charlie's gaze sharpened. "That wasn't my question."

"Yeah. Sure." Zack took a pull on his beer. "I guess I do."

"That's awful noncommittal for a man who's about to let his marriage fall apart over it."

"What if I want them someday? She doesn't want children ever."

"But do you want them now?"

Although he should have realized it sooner, in his father's question Zack had to admit that he'd spent precious little time thinking about the actual *having* of children over the past few weeks. Sure, he'd spent time being angry that Hadley hadn't told him she didn't want children. But the actual reality of holding a baby or raising a young child into adulthood hadn't really crossed his mind.

A strong counterpoint to the discussion he'd had with Carter the other day. The man hadn't stopped talking about being a father, and in his words Zack could already picture the small girl or boy who had captured his foreman's heart in every way.

Yet he didn't have that for himself.

Despite the near-constant talk of children and

the implications on his own future of Hadley's decision, he still couldn't see them.

Couldn't picture his life as a father.

All he could see was the void left with Hadley gone.

THE SHARP, SHRILL piercing of the fire alarm had Bea up and running from her small living room in bare feet. She'd passed the morning sickness stage and, when the thought of preparing raw turkey for cooking hadn't turned her stomach over, had decided to take on creating a feast for her and Carter for Thanksgiving.

One that hadn't involved the potential for a kitchen fire or, she cursed a blue streak as she opened the oven door, a blackened dish of turkey breasts.

He wasn't here yet and they still had a lot of things to say, but she'd looked forward to a quiet day. Together. Assuming she didn't manage to starve them in the process.

"Bea!"

Carter's shout echoed through the small apartment and she heard the heavy footsteps as he raced into the kitchen.

And came up short as he stalled in the doorway. "What's going on?"

"I suck ass as a cook." She unceremoniously dumped the small pan of burnt turkey into the sink before whirling on him. "We make shows about this, you know. Hour-long episodes about how to make the perfect Thanksgiving dinner and how to avoid disasters like burnt food and over-cooked side dishes and savory leftovers."

Carter moved to the sink, eyeing what she'd dumped there, before stepping back. "How long did you cook it?"

"The recipe I had said you put the turkey in around 6:00 a.m. for an early afternoon meal."

"For a whole bird. What did it say about just cooking a few of the breasts?"

Bea set the now-empty pan down with a hard clank on top of the stove as the determined heat of embarrassment flushed through her chest. "I'm not answering that."

"Because you thought they cooked the same?"

"It said to put the turkey in at six."

He tugged the potholders off her hands, one by one. Peeled them off, really—and who knew potholders could suddenly be sexy?—before pulling her close. "We'll eat pie for dinner."

"We can't do that."

"We can when we go to the diner and order it. I think we should eat it first."

"You can't eat Thanksgiving dinner at a diner."

"Sure you can. Lots of people do it." He stepped back and stared down at her. "I've done it most of the past two decades, actually. They do a great job and they actually know how to cook turkey."

"I'm a failure."

"At this? Yeah, you are."

She wanted to be angry but something in the simplicity of his quick reply stopped her.

When had life become about being perfect in all things?

Her job certainly supported that point of view. The lifestyle networks were all about achieving a sort of Zen through stylistic living. How the right throw pillows could bring order and calm into your space. How the right do-it-yourself home project could create a haven. And, in her case, how the right mix of food could entertain the masses all while holding you up as the hostess divine.

Had she ever found that?

She had plenty of throw pillows in her apartment in New York and not once had she felt some sort of overarching calm looking at them beyond the delight she'd had in the colors the day she bought them. And that time she attempted to create an herb garden in her kitchen window she'd ended up with a very pretty, very decorative installation that had become overgrown in a matter of weeks.

And her cooking?

Well, it had always sucked. That was why she had a deep and lasting love affair with her microwave.

Despite those things, Carter loved her.

And she loved him.

Entirely and completely.

"What am I doing with you?" It wasn't the first time she'd asked the question, but up to now she'd only asked it to herself.

"Having a baby." Carter pulled her close. "And making a life."

Making a life.

She had that. For thirty-nine years she'd been Bea Malone. And for the two decades of her adult life, she'd been busy doing that very thing.

Alone.

"I'm scared."

"Me too."

"I've never lived with anyone. I've never made a life with anyone." It was an admittance—difficult to make and a little embarrassing, too.

Only in his response, she saw all the reasons why she had nothing to be embarrassed about.

"Me too. I've spent most of my adult life living in a bunkhouse with a bunch of other cowboys. It wasn't until I got the foreman job that I got a place of my own. That's a long time, Bea, to have to live with ribald jokes and short fuses and farts." He shook his head, his expression dark. "So much farting."

It should have been wrong or even absurd to talk about the rest of her life amidst a discussion of flatulence. But it was actually an odd sort of perfect.

Her sister Stephanie had always told her: *When you find the right person, Bea, it will all make sense.*

For all the things about her and Carter that made no sense at all, what she felt for him made every kind of sense. Because it was every kind of right.

"You're scared, too?"

"Quaking in my boots."

"You've got very well-made boots. I'm sure they can handle it."

"It's us, Bea. *We* can handle it. Whatever life throws at us. We can handle it together."

"Even the distance?"

"Sure." He shrugged. "New York works for the Naked Cowboy. I'm sure I can figure something out."

"You want to live in New York?"

"I want to live with you. Wherever that is. However it is we decide to make a life."

"But your job. Your life—"

She stopped when his lips captured hers. "*Us*, Bea. I want you and me and our baby. Our family. Wherever we can get it."

"I want us, too." She stopped, an image of the Naked Cowboy as he strolled around Times Square filling her mind's eye. "You don't actually want to *be* the Naked Cowboy?"

He wiggled his eyebrows. "You think I could give him a run for his money?"

"I think perhaps there are other avenues we can explore."

"Good. I'd hate to be ogled by anyone but you."

She smacked him on the shoulder. "I don't ogle you."

"Yes, you do. And I'm shallow enough to admit that I both love it and have been doing stomach curls in the bunkhouse weight room."

"You basically exercise twelve hours a day. What do you need extra time in the weight room for?" At that a mental image hit her, of all the ranch hands and all the physical labor she'd observed over the years. "Why is there even a weight room in the bunkhouse?"

"Some guys like it."

"More like gluttons for punishment."

"We're men concerned for our long-term health." The smile that rode his features faded, his gaze so direct, so earnest, she could have cried for how sweet it was. "Please say yes, Bea."

And in Carter's ask, Bea heard it. That vulnerable underpinning that suggested he was still holding his breath, waiting for her answer.

They were having a baby. And they had a whole life in front of them that didn't entirely make sense in New York, even if he was more than willing to take it on. And they had each other.

Maybe that was the real trick.

It wasn't about being afraid. It was about moving forward anyway and figuring it out as you went. After all, throw pillows and DIY projects weren't the answer to a perfect life. Maybe the only way you got perfect was to embrace the flaws that were never going to go away anyway.

"I love you, Carter. And I want to make a life with you."

As he pulled her close, his lips firm and strong on hers, Bea thought about all that waited for her. And realized that she was about to have the best Thanksgiving of her life. She was carrying a healthy, growing child. Carter was here with her. And she'd likely be getting sex.

Oh, who was she kidding, she *would* be getting sex. And they'd already planned dessert with their impending diner pie.

As her mouth moved over his and her arms wrapped tight around his waist, Bea figured sex and pie was a rather terrific way to start your forever.

Chapter 21

    Snow piled up outside the kitchen window as Hadley put the finishing touches on all of her preprepped items the night before the show taping. The past three weeks since the trip to Jackson Hole and then Thanksgiving had moved at warp speed.

Even if it felt like her heart was stuck on Pause.

She had so much to do and as she fell into bed each night, she considered all she'd accomplished that day.

And then proceeded to lie there, tossing and turning, tortured by the fact that Zack was still down the hall.

They had so much to figure out. So much that it was exhausting to think about what was coming. Formal separation. Finding a new home.

Divorce.

At least they'd have some space in the coming weeks after Christmas to talk about it.

The new season of *The Cowgirl Gourmet* was done, which also gave her the time she needed to figure out a new kitchen space for future seasons. She'd toyed with the idea of using the Trading Post. It was her space and it had been designed as the next evolution of her own kitchen. Large and open, it fit the needs of a TV shoot.

And it was still intimate enough that she could feel like she was cooking in a personal space. Could make it feel like a kitchen.

Even if shooting a TV program there flew in the face of what she was trying to build with a business in downtown Rustlers Creek.

Of course, who knew what the network would say. They might hate the idea.

She was under contract for two more seasons and even with the change in her personal situation, her lawyer was confident nothing in her contract language would change the network's commitments. Getting divorced over irreconcilable differences wasn't a moral failing and would never hold up against the morality clause in her contract.

If the network just wanted to pay her out quietly for those two seasons, however, was another story.

Somehow, she thought she should be more worried about that outcome. More concerned that her country lifestyle empire was crumbling. But it all paled in comparison to the loss of her marriage.

Hell, it didn't even hit the concern-o-meter Top

10 she was currently carrying around. She'd simply worry about it when the time came. Even if the things she'd told Bea that night over tea in the library continued to haunt her.

I haven't put the show above my life. And if it all ended tomorrow, I'd still be me. I'd still have the people I love in my life. I've never lost that perspective.

No, she hadn't lost her perspective, but she had lost her family. Her husband. And, inevitably, his family, too.

She wasn't leaving Rustlers Creek and the Wayne family wasn't, either. And she'd see Carlene every day at the Trading Post, assuming Carlene wanted to stay on. Their collective lives would stay intertwined.

Even if they were now separate lives. Separate interests. Separate families.

She'd realized that truth on Thanksgiving, sitting at the old familiar dining room table in her father's house. The one she'd sat at for countless dinners, both before and after her mother had died. Her father, Harper and her had survived that terrible after.

Which meant she could do it again.

She *would* do it again.

But the thought of moving on broke her heart.

"That's quite a spread." Zack's voice was low, those familiar tones washing over her as he came into the kitchen. She had all her items spread across the large bar counter and he stood over them, his hands tucked behind his back, taking in her work. "And everything looks amazing."

"Thanks."

"You did the sugar cookies."

He pointed to the row of decorated cookies, all painted in various colors and matched piping. "The flour advertiser who is one of the show sponsors saw them in the cookbook and requested them special."

It had been a particularly painful discussion when Bea had gone over that ask with her, but Hadley hadn't been able to say no. Nor was she willing to explain why she didn't want to support the request. She'd suggested several other cookie options but the marketing lead had remained firm. They wanted the sugar cookies.

"Are you going to tell the story of the dozen dozen?" Zack asked.

"I figured I'd keep our marriage stories to a minimum. The news about us separating isn't out, but it'll seem really disingenuous if I talk about our courtship and then a few days after Christmas the news breaks."

He was quiet for a long time, but his gaze kept drifting to the cookies. She sensed he wanted to say something, so she waited, her breath catching before she realized it.

"I never meant for us to get here. Not in my lack of understanding of what you were going through or in creating a space between us that you couldn't tell me."

"I never meant to make you feel that way, Zack. And I'm sorry it took such public intrusion into our lives before I finally did tell you how I felt."

He nodded and shoved his hands in his pockets, seemingly stuck in place, even as she sensed he wanted to move.

Nay, needed to move.

"If there's anything I could change, it's that. And I just thought you should know."

"I guess I'll leave you to it, then."

Finally in motion, he headed out of the kitchen to disappear somewhere on the ranch for the day.

Heart empty, Hadley shifted her attention back to the list of items she wanted to finish before the crew set up that afternoon to take establishing shots of the food.

And couldn't stop thinking about that morning, so many years ago, when she'd piped out twelve dozen cookies for a smitten cowboy.

ZACK KNEW IT was a long shot. Hell, he'd likely be putting Bea's job in jeopardy with the ask. But he needed her help and the clock was ticking and he really couldn't figure out any other way.

The world needed to know that he and Hadley were going to be okay. And the only way to do that was in front of an audience. Social media influencers and staged photos in magazines weren't going to convince the people who really needed convincing.

And if it was only about what the public thought, Zack wouldn't give a shit, but he needed Hadley to understand.

And that required something big and important and as grand a gesture as he could make it.

"How much time do you need?" Bea stood opposite his desk, her gaze running down a list on her clipboard.

"How much time can you give me?"

"We've got a three-minute block at the end. But if I'm going to pull this off I'm going to need something else."

"Anything."

"You're going to need to do press about it."

"Done."

Her gaze was skeptical but marred slightly by the well of tears sheening her eyes.

"Are you okay?" He rushed around the desk, taking her elbow and settling her in the chair opposite his desk.

"I'm fine. And you're sort of a jerk to make a woman with raging hormones cry like this." Her words were harsh but he didn't miss the sly smile that tilted the edges of her lips.

"Your hormones need to cut me some slack. I love my wife and I'm desperate."

"Oh! Oh!" The tears started in earnest then and Zack stood by helplessly as Bea cried. It was only the shout from outside the door that had Zack turning in a mix of terror and relief.

"What the hell, Wayne!" Carter rushed in and dropped to a crouch beside Bea. "What'd you say to her?"

"I said I loved my wife."

Carter glanced up then, his gaze dark. "Damn it, what is *wrong* with you!"

What was wrong with *him*? Before he could ask the question, Hadley's sage words came back to him.

I know, but that's for her job. In her personal life, I don't want to upset her. She's very hormonal right now.

Who knew asking for professional help was going to do this to the calm, cool, collected Bea Malone?

Since he wasn't really interested in sticking around to find out, Zack lifted his hands and waved at both of them. "Please. Take as long as you need. I'll just step out here and give you some privacy."

As he closed the door to his office behind him, Zack considered his next move. And realized that he might have made a pregnant woman cry, but that well of panic as he'd seated her was a small price to pay for her help.

"THIS IS AMAZING." Susan Edgar marveled for about the fifth time since arriving as Hadley showed her around the kitchen. "It's exactly what we see each week on the show. And I'm standing here!"

Gone was the terse, unpleasant frown of a few weeks ago. In its place was a woman who had a bright smile, an interested gaze and a kind comment for everyone she'd met.

For all her sadness about her current situation, Hadley couldn't help being happy she'd extended the invitation.

The crew was buzzing around her and Hadley had already been through pre-prep, makeup and an hour of show notes review with Bea.

She was ready.

All that prep gave her a few extra minutes to spend with Susan.

They found a quiet spot in the dining room, away from the busy hum, where the network's caterers had set up a food spread for the crew and guests. She and Susan each took a water before moving to sit down at the end of the dining room table.

"I hope I can say something that won't upset you for the evening. But I'm not sure what's going to happen after and I owe you this apology." Susan wiped the condensation off her bottled water before looking back up. "My brother and I both do."

"Okay."

"I'm beyond sorry for what happened at our sales dinner. With the Foxgloves."

"You're hardly responsible for someone else's behavior."

"Maybe, but we are responsible for putting that ridiculous woman at your table. Louis and I have known Winston for years. He was a friend of our parents. He's always been eccentric, but since he's met Sasha that trait has come out in spades."

"He seems happy."

"He'd better. It's the only thing that would make looking so ridiculous worth it."

"They've obviously found something with each other."

Susan's lifted eyebrows suggested her skepticism, which made her next comment a bit more dissonant than Hadley expected. "I do think they love each other. For as strange as it seems to outsiders,

I've known Winston my whole life and I've never seen him happier since the day he met Sasha."

Susan shrugged. "Maybe when you find love later in life you savor it more. And you're more focused on taking the gift because you spent so much longer without it."

Unbidden, memories of the night she and Zack made love in LA came back to her. Hadley had thought about that night, over and over, but her memories had been steeped in the connection. The familiarity. And yes, the pleasure.

But as she considered Susan's description of Winston, Hadley was reminded of the thoughts she'd had with Zack.

Marriage was about saying yes to the promises you'd made, every day.

And as she heard Bea call for her, interrupting those last few minutes with Susan, Hadley recognized the truth of what she'd done to their marriage.

She wasn't at fault for saying no to children.

But she was completely at fault for taking that personal no and turning it into a secret from her husband. By avoiding the subject with Zack, allowing it to build and grow into something too big for either of them to hold back, she'd stopped saying yes.

And that no would haunt her for the rest of her life.

THE FIRST YEAR the Cooking Network set up on their property, Zack had been amazed by how the set decorators had transformed everything they touched. Whether it was a vast outside shot or the smallest, most intimate capture of one of Hadley's dishes on the counter, they left nothing to chance.

Ignored nothing visible in the shot.

But standing here, staring at his kitchen, Zack was awed by the transformation.

And even more awed by the idea that by the time he got up tomorrow morning it would all be put back to rights and would look like it did every other day they didn't have more than one hundred people roaming through their home.

He thought about the item he'd stowed in the bottom drawer of the kitchen island. It had been a late-breaking decision, made around two that morning, long after their conversation the night before in the kitchen, but he'd known exactly where to find what he needed.

What he needed to tell her how he felt. More, to *show* her how he felt.

He knew what he was about to do. What it all meant. As a gesture and as a decision about the rest of his life.

And he knew it was the right one.

Because as he'd turned his discussion with his father over and over in his mind, Zack had finally been forced to admit the truth.

He didn't want children, either.

He wanted her. And he wanted their life together. From the very first, across that expanse of counter in the bakery, he'd seen her. Hadley Allen. And he'd fallen, so hard and so fast he'd never recovered.

There had been a time when he believed they would have a family. That the love they felt for each other would expand and grow, building on itself. And as they'd waited and prepared for Jessica's arrival, they'd both reveled in that truth.

But in the after of losing her, that rushing urgency to have a family had faded.

Until, as he'd finally understood, it had subsided.

It was a humbling realization and one he'd likely never have come to if circumstances hadn't forced them to it. But now that he did understand it, he had a decision to make. Move through that crossroads with his wife.

Or find a way down a different path alone, with a distant promise that his future might be different.

He didn't want a future if it didn't include her.

HADLEY SMILED THROUGH the end of her segment, waiting the requisite time until the director called "cut!". She'd never done a live taping and despite the rehearsals, it had been a whirlwind to get through. The timing. The stage marks. And the absolute lack of room for any deviation from the script.

On some level, it was the perfect way to end the year. She had no time to think or worry about the foods she'd selected or the memories they engendered because she had to hit her cue, give the overview and move on.

No do-overs and no stopping.

It was an oddly helpful stress that had made the first four live segments move at a swift clip.

All that was left were the desserts.

Even without the time to dwell on it, Zack's request the night before played over and over in her mind. To tell the story of the sugar cookies and his obnoxious order of so many of them.

But she couldn't share it. Just like the details on the chocolate silk pie in her cookbook, she wasn't holding it back for some fear that the public would be angry with her for what could come later.

She held it back because she didn't dare share something so special and private with the masses. She had a lifetime of memories with Zack, but she was facing a future where they wouldn't make any more. And like a miser hoarding his gold, she found she didn't want to give any of them up to the public.

To anyone.

Bea caught her eye, hovering on the edge of the kitchen, out of sight of the camera lens. Zack stood beside her, waiting for his cue to come on scene. He was part of the last segment and she could already envision how it would go. He'd come in, do his standard sweet cowboy routine as he tasted the fruit cake she'd prepared, and they'd wave everyone off to a happy holiday.

Quick. Easy. And no more than three minutes in length that she already knew would be endless.

Quiet was called at the one-minute mark and Hadley stood on her mark behind her counter. The set dressers had already laid out the last arrangement of items and Bea smiled and gave her a thumbs-up from across the kitchen.

It was go time.

Hadley heard the countdown as her gaze roamed over the assembled desserts on the counter. Unbidden, her gaze stilled on those sugar cookies and she felt her throat working, swallowing hard against the sudden tightness.

Now wasn't the time. She couldn't do this *here*. She could *not* break down.

There'd be more than enough time to do it later. A lifetime, in fact.

With a surreptitious swig from her water glass stowed under the counter, she took a deep breath just as the light on top of the camera winked red, shocked when her voice sounded normal and she began talking about the variety of desserts available to make, at varying levels of difficulty, for the holidays.

The words came out of their own accord, and she let them flow, pleased to see Bea's bright smile and nodding head. Even more pleased to see Bea's network head smiling right beside her.

She just had to make it through. A few more minutes of inane conversation about fruit cake density and the perfect parchment paper to bake cookies on and she'd be done.

The camera followed her as she walked to the fruit cake, welcoming Zack as he came on scene.

"Hey there, cowboy. You come to thieve some of my Christmas goodies?"

"Maybe." He leaned in and pressed a kiss to her cheek, pulling her close.

"Only maybe? Did one of the bulls hit you coming out of the paddock?"

The joke felt stilted and weird, but the hum of laughter from the audience in the kitchen ensured she'd hit the mark.

"My head's intact. But I'm not really interested in fruit cake this year. I'm more interested in those sugar cookies you've got over there."

She nearly fumbled, their remembered conversation the night before spiking her irritation. She'd said she didn't want to tell that story.

Why was he pushing it?

"Come on, Hadley." He took her hand, pulling her around the counter. "Tell them all what I did."

She'd already seen the shot setups and knew how close the third camera was on close-ups, so she kept her smile deliberately wide as she pointed to the sugar cookies.

"You mean these cookies? Just like the ones you decided to buy all those years ago?"

"Those are the ones." He nodded.

Hadley glanced at the show clock perched high on the opposite wall and knew she had about thirty seconds to tell the story. She also saw Bea's broad smile and nodding head, bobbing along with the network brass, so she went for it. With a sort of short-handed list of the high points, she told the audience how they'd only had a single date, but another cowboy was sniffing around and Zack had foolishly purchased twelve dozen cookies to spite him.

But it was Zack's answer and Bea's move closer to the counter, just out of camera range, that had her convinced the show was going off the rails.

Even if Bea was smiling.

It was only as Zack bent over to the drawer below that real panic set it. It was a production no-no to go off camera like that and she nearly made a joke about where his head went when she saw what he came back up with.

An old bakery box, yellowed with age, that had the name of her first bakery printed on the front.

"I've kept this box, all these years. It held the dozen cookies I kept for myself. After I gave all the other ones away to every person I knew."

The tears that had threatened welled up again, her throat working around the fervent need to hold them back.

"They were sweet, but nothing has ever before or ever since been as sweet as you."

"Zack. I—" She broke off, unable to say anything else as he pulled her close.

"I made a vow to you, Hadley Allen Wayne, all those years ago. I said yes to a lifetime with you and I meant it."

Laughter and clapping started around the kitchen, but it was Zack's words that echoed the loudest in Hadley's ears. Words that spoke of how much of marriage was about saying yes.

And here.

Now.

Staring up at Zack, with a hundred people watching her and hundreds of thousands more at home, she realized there was something else to that yes. More than something else, actually.

The real magic was in accepting that yes in return.

And that was everything.

"I love you, Zack Wayne. Forever and ever."

"I love you, too."

And as he bent his head, giving her an appropriately chaste kiss for live television, she knew what she had.

What she'd always had.

And how good it was to hear her cowboy say yes once more.

Gray McClain has never managed to forget the girl he loved so long ago.

Harper Allen left town and tried not to look back.

When she returns, will these lovers have a second chance at happiness?

Addison Fox will return to Rustlers Creek

Fall 2022